THE GUARDIANS OF THE FINISHER'S FURY

THE GUARDIANS OF THE FINISHER'S FURY

FRANK L. COLE

Bonneville Books
An Imprint of Cedar Fort, Inc.
Springville, Utah

ISBN 13: 978-1-4621-1221-0

Published by Bonneville Books, an imprint of Cedar Fort, Inc.
2373 W. 700 S., Springville, UT 84663
Distributed by Cedar Fort, Inc., www.cedarfort.com

Library of Congress Cataloging-in-Publication Data on file.

Front cover design by Shawnda T. Craig
Back cover design by Rebecca J. Greenwood
Cover design © 2013 by Lyle Mortimer
Typeset and edited by Melissa J. Caldwell

Printed in the United States of America

10 9 8 7 6 5 4 3 2 1

For Great-Grandpa Rolph,
who ran from the devil all those years ago.
Stories are meant to be shared.
Even the scary ones.

Praise for

THE GUARDIANS OF THE FINISHER'S FURY

"Frank Cole is a master storyteller. No one is better at combining history, lore, and adventure. *The Finisher's Fury* is furious fun!"

—B. K. BOSTICK, author of the Huber Hill series

1

Amber, honey, wake up." My mom's muffled voice cut through my dream and roused me from sleep. "Someone's here to see you."

I squinted at my alarm clock resting on my bedside table. The neon red lights blurred until I blinked my eyes into focus. "Is it really 5:30?" I asked.

My mom nodded.

"In the evening?" I clarified.

"That's right."

"What day is it?" My pillow felt damp from perspiration. Wiggling my fingers through my hair, I grimaced as the tangles pulled at my scalp.

"Tuesday. Yes, Tuesday, dear." She folded her arms at her chest. "You've been asleep, more or less, for the past twenty-four hours."

Tuesday? That couldn't be right.

"There was plenty of codeine in that final dose they gave you yesterday at Dr. Walters's office, but we were worried we'd have to throw cold water on you to finally wake you up. How are you feeling?"

My arms and legs felt unnaturally heavy as I sat up and swung my feet over the side of the bed. Did I really sleep for twenty-four hours? A whole day! That was the most I had ever slept in my life.

"Okay, I think." Pressing my hand against my chest, I inhaled to test my lungs' ability. Though I could feel a slight rasp in my throat, I no longer felt pain. A week ago, I came down with a bad chest cold. Then, after a couple days of a fever and almost non-stop coughing, my mom finally broke down and took me to our family doctor.

Pneumonia.

Not a bad case and we caught it early, but still. Old people and infants contracted pneumonia, not fifteen-year-olds enjoying the second week of summer break. My two and a half months of relaxation started off on my sick bed.

Dr. Walters used a new aggressive form of medication on me. Three shots. Each one more powerful than the previous. I could faintly remember the drive home from his office yesterday evening.

"Drink this." My mom handed me a fizzing glass of yellow liquid, and I immediately pushed it away.

"Yuck! I'm not drinking that." Her weird concoction of flu medicine, citrus, and herbs smelled like a mixture of cold chicken soup and menthol cough drops. "I'll throw up! I promise."

"You can keep a little down."

Reluctantly, I sniffed the glass. Out of the corner of my eye, I noticed a torn envelope and an acceptance letter poking out beneath my lamp.

"I know you haven't had a clear head as of late, but have you given any more thought to that?" She gestured to the letter.

Summer school. I enjoyed learning, but taking a month out of my vacation to attend a summer term wasn't my idea of fun. "I don't know, Mom."

"It could be really helpful with your courses," she coaxed.

Last Friday, while I wheezed in bed, the principal of Roland & Tesh called my parents to inform them of my acceptance into the program. Summer school at Roland & Tesh wasn't a punishment. On the contrary, it was a very prestigious accomplishment offered to only a few students each year.

"You'll need to decide soon. Principal Calhoun will be calling and we'll have to let him know." She flipped her hand indifferently. "Either way is fine with me and your father. It's totally your decision."

My decision—but their disappointment if I turned down the offer. I managed two meager sips of the nauseating drink before I plopped back on the pillow and hugged my comforter.

"Nope. Don't go back to sleep. Someone's here, remember?" Her annoying fingers pried the floral fabric from my tight grip.

"To see me?" The thought of descending the stairs seemed daunting. My bed felt all the more cozier now that I had sufficiently worn in the sheets and a warm Arizona breeze drifting past the blinds carried the smell of charcoal briquettes from the neighbor's grill. I could easily lie there for another twenty-four hours. "Mom, I'm sick. Can't you tell them to come back tomorrow? Or they could text me later, I guess."

My mattress sunk from her weight as she sat down near my feet, placing her hand on my knee. "Well, he says it's important and that you'd want to talk to him."

Instantly, my eyes snapped open and I propped my body up on my elbows. "*He* says it's important?"

"Yes, it's a boy. He's cute, but I didn't think you were seeing anyone right now." Her light blue eyes glinted with amusement and a hint of an obnoxious grin tugged at her lips.

"Mom, shut up! Who is it?" I looked past her into my dresser mirror, suddenly appalled at my appearance. Yep. I was more or less a zombie returned from the grave. Why would a boy be downstairs waiting to see me? It was summer break, and I had spent the past four months and most of my teenage years living two thousand miles away at the Roland & Tesh Private School for the Advanced in Parkersburg, West Virginia. I hardly knew any kids my own age, let alone boys in my hometown of Gelding.

She stood and tossed me a brush from my bedside table. Sliding a stack of books aside with her foot, she plucked my bathrobe from the floor. "I don't think he said his name, but he did say it was about an artifact of some sort. I think he attends Roland with you. I didn't know you had a class-mate here in town."

Fully awake, I sprang from the bed and tugged the sleeves of my robe over my arms. Artifact? A boy from Roland? Was it Trendon? He was my best friend, and the only boy I knew who would visit me about an artifact, but he lived in Washburn Lake, New Jersey. That was quite a commute, and he wouldn't just fly to Arizona. My mom also said the boy was cute. Would she consider Trendon cute? I suppose he was in his own way, but . . . I caught my breath in my throat.

It was Joseph! It had to be.

I hadn't seen Joseph in almost a year. What did he want to talk about? Did he have important news from Dorothy and the others? I could sense my lips moving as I formed multiple questions in my mind, but once again I stepped in view of the mirror and released an audible gasp.

"I can't go down there like this! I need to shower first!"

"You look fine. Don't worry." My mom took the brush in hand and pulled it through my tangled hair. "Just stop in the bathroom and brush your teeth."

I nodded vigorously, too excited to keep Joseph waiting and too curious to hear what he had to say.

The short trip from my bedroom down two flights of stairs to the foyer neglected to give me enough time to prepare for Joseph. When I saw him last, he was leaving Dorothy's compound in Jordan to go somewhere on his own. His Uncle Jasher's death had left him without any family, but that hadn't mattered to him. He chose a different life. One of traveling and solitude. I missed him, but my feelings for him had definitely dimmed. I no longer spent hours worrying about him. Maybe this reunion would help change things.

I padded across the marble floor, my bare feet hardly making a sound. A cool burst of air conditioning chilled my neck and arms. From beyond the large bay window of the foyer, I caught a glimpse of a dingy and battered turquoise convertible parked in our driveway as I followed my mom into the living room.

Seated in one of the wingback chairs, a dark-skinned boy

with sleek black hair stared at a large brown envelope in his lap. He wore faded khakis, tennis shoes, a pair of sunglasses perched above his forehead, and a collared striped shirt. And unless he somehow changed himself completely and aged a year or two, he was not Joseph. Upon our entering, the boy glanced up from his hands and smiled awkwardly.

"Amber?" Standing, he dropped the envelope on the seat behind him.

"Um . . . hello," I stammered, uncertain of how to respond.

"I'll let you two catch up." My mom winked and left the room.

Catch up? That wouldn't take too long since I had never met this boy in my life.

"Wow! It's great to finally meet. I've heard all about you." He shifted his weight but kept his eyes trained on mine.

"Ooo . . . kay. Who told you about me?" Instinctively, I hugged my arms and self-consciously pulled the robe tighter around my neck. The initial worry I felt about how I looked facing Joseph compounded upon seeing the unusual stranger in my house.

"Oh, I apologize. Duh! How rude of me." The boy wiped his hand on his khakis and offered me a handshake. "My name's Paulo."

I couldn't place his accent, which sounded almost Hispanic and oddly familiar. Squeezing his hand lightly, I noticed his sweaty palm.

"I'm Amber," I said.

"Of course you are! *The* Amber Rawson. Keeper of the Tebah Stick. Controller of the Shomehr! I know all about you." He shook his index finger in the air. "I've heard all your stories—many times. My favorite is when you faced the man of fire and . . ."

"Who are you?" I suddenly exploded. "How do you know who I am and about those . . . *stories?*" I whispered the latter part and shot a quick lock into the foyer for my mother. I never told my parents about my adventures abroad in the Philippines and Syria, and I wasn't about to let some strange, enthusiastic boy divulge my secrets.

Paulo fretted, pressing his finger against his lips. "Aye! I apologize once more. I'm just nervous and . . . and you are a bit of a celebrity for me."

Why wasn't he making any sense? How did he know me? Who told him those stories? Calming myself, I squeezed my arms tighter and, when I spoke, had better control over my emotions. "Paulo, I don't know you at all, and you're talking about things only a few people should know about. So I'm a little weirded out. Would you please explain yourself?"

His mouth quivered. "Yes, yes. My, uh . . . I mean, I work for Temel Ridio. I have for as long as I can remember. And I think you know of him? Yes?"

Temel Ridio was one of Dorothy Holcomb's closest companions. He and Dorothy, my archaeology teacher, had been there with me, Trendon, and Lisa in Hama City, Syria, last fall when we found an artifact capable of calling fire from the sky. Although Temel exhibited odd and dangerous behavior, and liked to blow things up, I trusted him with my life.

"Yes, I know Temel! Is he here?" Unable to contain my excitement, I rushed to the window and searched for the camouflage- and flip-flops wearing man out on the lawn.

It would be wonderful to throw my arms around his neck and squeeze him.

"He's not here," Paulo explained.

My shoulders dipped dejectedly. "Why not? Where is he?"

"Well, he's in . . ." Shaking his fist, Paulo closed his eyes in frustration. "I cannot tell you. I want to, but not here. It's not safe. At least that's what Dorothy told me."

"Right." I lowered my voice and abandoned my search through the window. "You don't have to tell me. I totally understand." Temel's line of work required stealth and it would be dangerous for Paulo to reveal his location. "So you also know Dorothy and she's with Temel right now."

Paulo offered a curt nod.

"And they're looking for some sort of artifact, aren't they?"

He exhaled in relief.

Since Syria, I had no contact with Dorothy or Temel, but I knew they had begun their search for the final piece of a terrifying puzzle. We defeated Baeloc, a descendant of the original Architect of the Tower of Babel, in his quest to bring about the destruction of mankind. Dorothy's society, the Seraphic Scroll, imprisoned Baeloc, and now the Tebah Stick and Elijah's Fire—two of the three Weapons of Might—were already in her possession. All she needed was the final piece.

Even with Dorothy gone from Roland & Tesh and not having my extracurricular archaeology class as a distraction, spring semester had been my most difficult one to ace. I had trouble staying focused and suffered many sleepless nights reliving the nightmare of Syria. My best friend, Trendon, had an easier time of coping by burying his nose in his video games. Lisa, on the other hand, suffered too much and, after the fall semester, transferred back to a private school in New York City. Though we still spoke on the phone from time to time, our friendship had been put on hold.

With the summer vacation I hoped to finally catch up on some rest and almost succeeded, but the arrival of Paulo in my living room sent me surging back.

"How are they? Dorothy and Temel? Are they safe?"

"They're doing just fine. At least they were when I saw them last back in . . . you know." He flicked his chin toward the window.

Relaxing somewhat, I released my hold on my arms and walked closer to Paulo. "Why are you here?"

His eyes wide, he spun around and picked up the envelope from off the chair cushion. "I'm here to give you this. It's from Dorothy."

The padded envelope felt slightly heavy but was blank of any writing on the outside. After gently shifting the contents in my fingers, I pulled the tab at one end and opened it. Musty, crinkled packing material toppled from the opening as I reached inside and removed a smaller rubber-banded stack of what looked like several airline tickets. Folded within the stack, I found a handwritten note in Dorothy's handwriting.

> *Dearest Amber,*
>
> *Well done on your finals! Straight A's as usual. Most impressive. I trust your summer's treated you well so far. Staying out of trouble? I should hope not. But if you are, how about a little jaunt for an adventure? We could use your help. I know you'll understand why and will be*

gracious to offer your assistance. Your first flight leaves on the 7th at 4:30 a.m. (sorry so early!) I've planned a quick layover for you in Washburn Lake. It wouldn't be the same without Trendon around here. Good luck twisting his arm. I'll meet the two of you when you arrive. Oh, and this time, I'll leave the explaining to your parents up to you. My suggestion would be summer school. They'd buy that, wouldn't they?

    All the best,

    Dorothy

I swallowed and thumbed through the packet of tickets. The first was a single nonstop flight to Atlantic City International Airport in New Jersey. Then two commuter tickets to JFK in New York and a transatlantic flight to Dakar Léopold Sédar Senghor International airport in Senegal. The final airline destination was the St. Catherine International airport in Egypt. From there we would travel via public transportation to the St. Catherine Monastery in the Sinai Peninsula.

"I can't go to Egypt," I muttered, organizing the tickets into a neat stack. Dorothy wanted me to leave in three days. That was impossible! "There's no way my parents would let me."

"True, but your parents might let you attend summer school. The program at your academy is for the really advanced," Paulo said. "I have a hunch you've already been accepted."

My eyes narrowed as I remembered the acceptance letter on my bedside table. "Wait a minute. That was a fake? I didn't really get accepted?"

Paulo averted his eyes. "Well, not exactly."

"But Principal Calhoun called my parents on Friday telling them about it." I repressed a sigh as I realized Dorothy duped my whole family. "That wasn't really him, was it?"

Paulo shook his head. "I'm sure someone with your credentials would've received a call had there been more spaces. I'm afraid Dorothy has many contacts, some of which can sound very convincing."

"But there was also a plane ticket to Parkersburg, West Virginia. It was included in the letter from the school."

Reaching over, Paulo gently pulled the tickets from my hand and pointed to the first one in the packet. "This flight to New Jersey leaves out of Parkersburg, not from here. It will be best for you to create the illusion you're heading off to school. That way your parents can be kept in the dark of your activities."

I laughed, but it had no joy in it. Dorothy may have an easy time whisking me off on her escapades while keeping my parents oblivious to the danger, but I couldn't continue to lie to them. I gazed beyond Paulo's head at the wall, my mouth slightly ajar. This didn't feel like before when I left the school to follow Dorothy. This was my home. Though they had yet to talk about it, I knew my parents had plans with me for the summer. Vacations. Bonding. All of that would have to be put on hold. How could I do that?

"When would I tell them I'd be back?" I asked, more to myself than to Paulo.

"The first summer term is four weeks. Look! Did you not see the return ticket in the envelope?"

I found the ticket with a return date of June 4. Dorothy had taken care of everything. All I had to do was pack. If

I flat out refused, she would use more desperate measures. Though Dorothy would never force me to get involved (at least I didn't think she would), she would find a way to convince my parents to make me come. When I touched the Tebah Stick a year ago in the Philippines, the artifact gave me power to control the Shomehr. The guardian creatures could be used to locate things. Artifacts. If Dorothy needed my help it was because she needed the assistance of the Shomehr to find the last Weapon of Might and only I could control them. Normally that wouldn't be a problem, but the Shomehr were horrifying monsters capable of violence if they felt the need to resort to that. Because of the bond I created with them being the first to hold the Tebah Stick in more than four thousand years, I was the only voice they would listen to. Dorothy considered it a gift, but I didn't share that belief. I had seen what the Shomehr were capable of doing firsthand, and having that much power over them was anything but a gift.

"Will it be dangerous?" I never learned about St. Catherine's Monastery in any of my studies, but traveling to Egypt put me right back into a hornets' nest. Even with their leader, Baeloc, imprisoned, the remaining Architects were still deadly.

"Honestly, it will be a bit treacherous, but I assure you, it will be nothing like what you faced in Syria at the grave site of the prophet."

"You've heard about Syria, huh?"

His eyes twinkled. "Yes! And I know all about that too!" Struggling to hide his excitement, he pointed at my neck to where the blue locator stone necklace still swung from a silver chain.

I rubbed the stone between my thumb and forefinger. "Who told you all these things?"

"Temel, of course! He's crazy about you!"

I laughed and an image of Temel wearing sunglasses and chewing on a toothpick registered in my thoughts. I desperately wanted to see him again. It would also be great to spend more time with Trendon, if only I could convince him to come with me. Since Dorothy's departure from the campus, Roland & Tesh no longer offered any extracurricular archaeology courses. Trendon and I shared no other classes, and over the semester we kind of grew apart, hanging out occasionally on the weekend. I was so passionate about archaeology, but Trendon no longer liked to talk about Syria or the Philippines or anything involving Dorothy. If it were up to him, we would break all ties with our former archaeology professor and have our memories magically erased of that fateful evening when the two of us, along with our friends, Joseph and Lisa, were lured in by Dorothy's coded message to help find the Tebah Stick two years ago.

"How old are you?" I asked curiously.

"Me?" Paulo looked around the room as if someone else could've been the recipient of my question. "I'm seventeen."

"Seventeen? You're not that much older than me. What do you do in Dorothy's society?"

"Oh, I'm not in the society." He shock his head rapidly. "I work in ballistics with Temel."

"You mean you make explosions and cause destruction?"

Paulo grinned sheepishly. "More or less."

Silence settled in the room as I thought through my options. Who was I kidding? Maybe I could try to convince others how I needed to forget all that had happened, but within my heart it wouldn't stick. I needed to be back in the hunt to be truly happy. I could rest once we found the final artifact and destroyed the weapons. For that to happen, I had to be there with Dorothy and Temel.

"Okay." I tucked the tickets back into the envelope. "I'll do it."

"You'll go to Egypt?" Paulo asked, clapping his hands together.

"I'll go to Egypt."

"That's great news. Do you need help packing? I could provide you with a list of essentials."

"No, I'll be fine." Having survived two stints in foreign countries without any preparations at all, it would be nice to finally have my own suitcase and some of my own personal changes of clothing.

"Okay, I have many things to do to get ready, so I'll go now, but I'll meet you in New Jersey in three days." Marching forward, Paulo wrenched the front door open with a flourish. "I cannot believe I'll be sharing in this adventure with you."

"Relax, Paulo. I'm just a normal girl."

"No." He clasped his hands together and pressed his fingers to his lips. "You are so much more. You are Amber Rawson!" He stepped out and quietly closed the door behind him.

2

Three days later, Paulo greeted me at the baggage claim in the Atlantic City International Airport. At first glance, I mistook him as someone else. Though he dressed differently, he wore dark sunglasses and chewed on a toothpick.

"You act just like him," I said, heaving my suitcase off the conveyer.

"Who?" Paulo took my bag from my hands, refusing to let me carry it.

"Temel. You must spend a lot of time with him."

"Unfortunately, yes." Paulo winked. 'He doesn't trust me much. Even though this is a simple mission, he's already texted me twenty times to make sure I don't mess it up."

"He texts? May I see?"

Paulo handed me his phone and I read the most recent message.

Don't mess this up, P.

"See? Told you. P. That's what he calls me." Paulo flicked the toothpick into a trash can and wove his way toward the exits.

"How much do you know about the—"

Paulo held his finger up apologetically. "Sorry, Amber. I've been given strict instructions not to discuss any matters out in the open. Temel would be very upset if I didn't follow through with that."

"Okay, that makes sense. I'm just excited and I don't want to be caught off guard."

Paulo stopped walking and leaned closer to me. "I want to tell you so much. The mountain is so . . . unusual."

"The mountain's unusual?" I raised an eyebrow.

"Well, not the mountain as much as the monks."

I jumped when Paulo smacked his own forehead. The blow left a bright red mark. Hissing something foreign under his breath, he shot watchful looks over each shoulder.

"Maybe we should wait until later to talk," I suggested.

"Yes, thank you."

We hailed a cab and thirty minutes later the taxi drove into a luxurious neighborhood surrounded by a thick forest of blue-green pine trees just after 2:00 p.m. New Jersey time.

"So this is where he lives?" I asked as the taxi lurched up the long driveway.

"According to this address," Paulo said.

Flower beds overflowing with an assortment of color sat on either side of a cobbled sidewalk leading from the driveway to the north side of the red brick home. I could see several garden gnome statues poking their heads out from behind the shrubs. Wind chimes hanging from various lengths of chain from the wraparound porch awning bobbled in the breeze. On either side of the steps leading up to the wraparound were massive, perfectly hedged bushes with red berries. To the rear of the drive, a rusted basketball standard minus the net teetered as if a gust could send it toppling.

"Is there something wrong?" Paulo asked, noticing my dazed expression.

"No. It's just nothing what I thought Trendon's house would look like." I expected to see metal walls held together by massive rivets and a yard completely devoid of any grass. There would be a giant satellite dish, like the ones from another decade, rotating on the roof from where Trendon could hack into the nation's most secure computer programs. In all truthfulness, his home was quite lovely, but I seriously doubted Trendon ever dribbled a basketball before.

Paulo spoke with the driver as he paid and then joined me on the front porch. "I've bought us about a half hour. He's going to park out on the road. Will that be enough time?"

"Enough time to convince Trendon?" I snorted. "Ha! You might as well send the taxi on its way. We could be here all night."

Paulo gnawed on his lip, his confidence shrinking. "But Dorothy mailed him the same letter for summer school you received, and our contact called his parents. They sounded pleased with his acceptance."

"First of all, if I was having a difficult time deciding on going to summer school, the thought has never crossed Trendon's mind. Second, we're about to ask him to put his life in jeopardy . . . again. This is going to be hilarious."

"Should I wait in the taxi then?" Paulo clinched his teeth together.

"You know, that's not a bad idea."

"You're right. I'm a new face, and I wouldn't want to make things uncomfortable for him."

"He's not the one I'm worried about."

The doorbell released a melodious chime of Beethoven's Fifth Symphony, and after several minutes of waiting, the thud of heavy footfalls sounded beyond the door. The knob twisted, and Trendon's squinting face appeared in the opening. Half of his curly brown hair stood on end in a disheveled mess. He wore mismatched socks, gray sweatpants, and a bright yellow T-shirt tucked into his waistband. He blinked sleepily at me, his eyelids refusing to open completely, and he wore a faint look of bewilderment.

He turned and yelled at the top of his lungs.

"Marcy! Olivia's here. Get your butt out of bed!" He pulled the door open wide enough to let me enter. "She'll be down in a second."

"Trendon, it's me," I said, unable to keep from laughing.

"I know," he grumbled. "She's probably got her buds jammed in her ears listening to her awful music. I'll go get her." As he started to walk away, I squeezed his arm.

"Trendon," I said expectantly. "Look at me."

With one eye cinched shut, Trendon opened the other and scratched his ear. We stared at each other in silence until his eyes slowly widened. Confusion then set in as he peered past me out into the yard.

"Amber?" His voice cracked.

"Hey, pal. Nice outfit."

"What the . . . ? How the . . . ? Why are you here? Did I miss something?"

Unable to resist, I grabbed him in my arms. A few tears

actually welled up in my eyes as he hugged me back. It felt so good to be with him again.

"What's going on?" he asked once I finally released my hold.

"Can we sit down?"

We sat on bar stools around an island beneath a Viking hood; the kitchen was exactly what I expected it to be. Two stainless steel refrigerators stood next to the opened door of an overflowing pantry where boxes of Little Debbie cakes, bags of potato chips, and fruit snacks sat on shelves.

"You hungry?" He removed a glass dome of a half-eaten chocolate cake on the marble counter and cut a mammoth slice. When I declined the offer, he crammed half the piece into his mouth. "Stho wahnsup?" he asked through a mouthful, frosted crumbs dribbling on his shirt.

Taking a deep breath, I brought him up to speed and told him everything I knew about Dorothy's recent request. I didn't know much since I hadn't been alone with Paulo long enough for him to grace me with the details, but I knew the basics. Dorothy and Temel were in Egypt searching for the final artifact and they needed our help.

Trendon kept quiet as I spoke, but he finished off the cake without coming up for air. Wiping his hands on his sweatpants, he pushed away from the counter, and I watched him fill and refill a glass of milk from the refrigerator three times before he finally made a disgusting belch that rattled the windowpanes.

"What are you thinking?" I knew his silence wasn't a good sign.

"I'm thinking you're . . . a robot. Yep. A robot." He plunked the glass on the counter.

"What do you mean by that?"

"No, wait. Not a robot. You're a"—he snapped his fingers—"you're a stuffed animal."

I laughed. "Trendon?"

"Yeah, cause some robots can think for themselves, which wouldn't work. But a stuffed animal is just fabric and stuffing. It doesn't need to think. Have you finally checked out completely? Has your brain gone to pudding? You want me to fly with you to Egypt? By choice?" Trendon yelled the last sentence. "This is summer vacation! I'm not going to do anything at all for nine weeks. Scratch that, I've got about seven video games I need to beat and at least a million cupcakes I need to eat."

"Calm down." I held up my hands in surrender. "I take it you don't want to go."

"Uh, no, I don't want to go. Wow! Maybe you're not a stuffed animal after all."

"Look, you don't always have to throw a fit every single time I suggest something," I snapped, unable to ignore the sting of his rudeness.

"Well, *you* don't have to always suggest something insane every single time we talk."

"Good point." I expected the conversation to end up like this and I didn't want to make Trendon hate me for the summer. Arguing with him could be exhausting. "I didn't think you'd want to go, but Dorothy thought I should try. It was good to see you though and I hope you have a nice vacation." Hopping off the stool, I headed for the door. I could feel his eyes boring a hole in the back of my head as I left, but I didn't turn around. "Good-bye, Trendon."

Outside, the taxi idled by the curb. The driver had his

face buried in a newspaper with all four windows rolled down and the random chatter of a talk show blaring on the radio. I looked for Paulo but couldn't see him in the backseat of the cab. Maybe he was lying down. The door swung open with a loud bang and Trendon stormed out, his socked feet thudding against the wooden boards of the wraparound porch.

"That's it? You're just gonna go?" His eyes were wild and angry.

I clutched my chest in surprise. "Yes, Trendon. I'm just gonna go. I made my decision. My flight leaves later this evening."

"But what about your . . . your . . . um . . ."

"My what?"

"What about your summer? Don't you have things to do that don't involve monsters and fire?" He stared at the taxi and then returned his glare at me.

"I did, but things changed. I want to help Dorothy. I want to be involved. And I feel a little responsible to help."

"That's bull! She's just making you feel guilty. She's a horrible, horrible person, and you know it." He fidgeted with a few of the berries on one of the bushes next to the porch, smashing them with his fingers before tossing them out in the yard.

"I don't want to fight with you. It's obvious we both feel differently about Dorothy. I think she's trying to do the right thing . . . and, yes, sometimes she makes poor choices."

"Poor choices that involve us nearly dying over and over again. Aren't you worried about what could happen there in Egypt?"

I puffed out my cheeks. "Yeah, but Paulo said it won't be anything like Syria."

The driver honked his horn twice, and I waved in acknowledgment. The meter was running, and our time was almost up. Either we had to pay him more money for him to wait, or we needed to get going back to the airport.

"Who's Paulo?" Trendon found a smudge of chocolate frosting on his shirt and promptly licked it off.

"He works with Temel and Dorothy. I'd introduce you to him, but I don't think we have much time. He's really nice."

"Oh good grief. We can't do this! What did you tell your parents?"

"Summer school. They're excited for me actually."

"Are they just a couple of morons that will buy any ridiculous story they hear?"

I rolled my eyes and was about to argue with him, but he grumbled on, cutting me off before I could speak.

"See, my parents know better. If I tried to tell them I was excited about summer school they'd think I was living a life of crime or something bizarre like that." He pulled the front door shut behind him and once more fidgeted with the bushes. "What are you bringing? What did you pack?"

"What do you care?" I fired back. I didn't have time to play a game of twenty questions.

"I don't care. I just—"

Suddenly, two arms shot out from behind the bush where Trendon had been plucking and yanked him off the porch. I yelped, as did Trendon, but his voice immediately muffled. Then Paulo's face appeared, and he beckoned me from the gap between the house and the bush. I could see he hadn't harmed Trendon, but he had his hand clamped tightly over his mouth.

"Get down here! Now!" Paulo whispered urgently. I didn't argue and leaped into the bush joining the two of them. Trendon, his chest heaving, stared in desperation. "I'm going to let you go, but you cannot scream, okay?" Paulo said. Trendon's head bobbed rapidly and Paulo released his hold over his mouth.

"Who the heck are you?" Trendon gasped, scrambling away from Paulo and kicking up mulch and rocks. "What the heck are you doing?"

"This is Paulo," I whispered. "He's the guy I was telling you about."

"Great! That's an awesome way to introduce yourself, skinning up my knees and causing me to wet myself!" Trendon pressed his hands against the porch to climb out, but Paulo grabbed the waistband of his sweatpants and pulled him back down. "Geez! Get off me!"

Paulo promptly clamped his hand once again over Trendon's mouth. "You promised you wouldn't scream. Why are you screaming? There's a reason I pulled you down here." After another tense moment, Paulo let go and scooted back to give Trendon space. "It's not safe up there."

"Up where?" Trendon barked. "Up by the bushes? Am I going to get stung by a wasp or something?"

"Trendon, stop talking and listen to him!" I picked a couple of stray twigs and berries from his hair and straightened his shirtsleeve.

"I'm afraid we've put you in great danger. A member of the Qedet has followed us here."

Instantly a chill ran up my spine. "Are you serious?"

"The who?" Trendon rolled up his pants to examine his wounds.

"Don't you remember? The Qedet. The Architects!"

His head snapped to attention, no longer interested in his scraped knee. "Here? In Washburn Lake? You brought them here?"

"I'm sorry. I didn't think we'd be followed," I said, feeling horrible. We brought evil into Trendon's neighborhood. Now his family was in danger. "Where did you see him, Paulo?"

"Three houses down. By now he's realized he's been spotted and will have to make a move."

"Are you sure it's one of those creepy Architects?" Trendon asked.

"Positive. There's no mistaking their look."

"I don't know. Some of my neighbors are pretty pasty and weird looking. You may have just seen Mr. Barnes. He's like eighty. White as a ghost. Hobbles along with a stick."

I shushed Trendon, who had allowed his voice to return to normal volume.

The horn from the taxi blared again, but this time the driver laid on it for several seconds announcing the end of our thirty minutes worth of cab fare. I heard the car door slam, then the trunk opening. From a gap in the bush, I watched as the driver carried our bags over to the curb and dropped them.

"He's leaving!" I said anxiously. "Do we stop him?"

"It's too risky. If the Architect has a gun, then . . . No. I think we should hide out here and wait." Panic marred

Paulo's features and his chest heaved as he scanned the yard through the bushes.

"Oh, that's brilliant." Trendon said with a sarcastic smirk. "Instead of trying to escape in a getaway car, we're going to wait around until there's no way of escape and no witnesses. I like your way of thinking, Pablo."

"It's Paulo," Paulo corrected. "And you're right. It's a dumb idea, but I don't know what else to do. I'm sorry!"

I felt my pulse quickening as the taxi sped away from the curb and I tried to think of another way out. If the Architect knew we spotted him, he would have called for backup. The whole place could be swarming with the pale-skinned creeps in no time. We had to get out of the bushes and to a safer more open location. I didn't want to cause any more trouble for Trendon's family.

"Who's here at your house?" I asked.

"My sister, Marcy."

"What about your parents?"

"I don't know. I just woke up."

"Why are you just now waking up? It's two o'clock in the afternoon!"

Trendon threw his hands up in frustration. "Are we really going to have this conversation right now? In front of Pablo? Sorry. I mean in front of *Pau*-lc?"

The cadence of footsteps along the cobbled walk silenced us. They sounded quick and light, but the owner was not trying to cover them.

"I'm going to take a quick look just to make sure," I said. Maybe Paulo actually did see one of Trendon's neighbors walking around their yard. With the two of them gathered behind me for support, I quietly inched a few of the branches apart and poked my head up to peer through.

A pale-skinned face stared back at me, no more than a foot away from the bush. His green eyes sparkled in the afternoon sun, and I choked back a scream as he began to chatter in his awful language.

3

Seated across from us at the dining room table, the Architect undid the buttons of his shirtsleeves and rolled them up above his elbows. Most of his face bore an unnatural white color, but a portion of his forehead and the tops of his ears had burned pink in the sun. A pad of thick parchment paper rested on the table in front of him as well as a black fountain pen like the kind used in calligraphy. Beside the chair at his feet, a burgundy leather briefcase stood with the combination locks unlatched. He wasted no time beginning, his fingers dancing with each pen stroke across the parchment.

"Tell me again why we let this guy in my house?" Trendon whispered next to my ear. "I've seen the movies. Now he'll always be able to come in and eat us whenever he wants."

"He's not a vampire, remember? He's on our side."

The "he" was Sherez, a once loyal member of Baeloc's Architects who turned against them and joined forces with Dorothy. Sherez and Joseph formed a friendship last year and joined in the attack on Baeloc's fortress. Despite this knowledge, I understood Trendon's apprehension. Sherez looked and acted just like Baeloc, and though he seemed to be legitimately on our side, no one truly knew what motivated him to abandon Baeloc. Ignoring our conversation, Sherez continued with his message.

Paulo stood in the entryway of the dining room, making no attempt to hide his distrust as he held a handgun at his side; a long silencer was screwed into the muzzle.

"How do you get on board an airplane with that gun?" Trendon asked Paulo.

The toothpick switched sides in Paulo's mouth as he shrugged. "I have a permit."

"A permit? For a silenced weapon? Yeah right."

Sherez passed the paper across the table, and I noticed for the first time his fingertips. The skin beneath the nails looked yellow. Sickly. I wondered if he and the other Architects were indeed diseased. They had no ability to speak and any attempt to use their voices caused them immense pain. Their skin had little pigment, yet their eyes radiated with an emerald glow.

The Architects know about Egypt. We have all known for quite some time. The artifact is buried within the belly of Mount Catherine. And unlike the other two Weapons, this one should be relatively easy to discover. Dorothy has asked for your assistance, but her request will place you in grave danger.

"You're not going to convince me not to help. What are you trying to do?" I slid the page back to Sherez for his answer.

Sherez's smile widened as he responded.

Nothing in anyone's power could keep you from making the journey to Mount Catherine. I'm not here to stop you, just to warn you.

"Warn me about what?"

Sherez opened the briefcase and pulled out a laptop, which he placed on the table with the screen facing us. After maneuvering through a few programs, he clicked on a video link and an unusual scene began to play. The footage appeared to have been shot with a security camera. A black and white image with hazy numbers on the bottom left corner of the screen indicated the date the video took place; it was less than a week ago. There was no sound.

With eyes closed and a rigid posture, a bald man sitting cross-legged on the floor of some sort of prison cell appeared to be meditating. An unpleasant tingling struck my neck as I recognized the man.

Baeloc.

The greasy mop of hair he once owned had been shaved clean, and other than a ratted piece of fabric around his waist, he was naked. There were marks all over his body. Dirt? I couldn't tell. A bowl of clear liquid sat on the floor a few feet away from him. No furniture. No carpet. Just stone floor. I then noticed strange black markings covering most of the walls as if someone smeared them with paint.

"Who is that supposed to be? Gandhi?" Trendon asked.

"It's Baeloc," I said. "Where is this? What's he doing?"

Sherez motioned to the screen to keep us watching.

"It looks like a torture chamber," Trendon muttered.

I shared no kind feelings for Baeloc, but even with my hatred for him, I didn't feel torture was the answer. Why did they shave his head? Why was he almost naked?

Wavy lines distorted the image as I noticed something

change with Baeloc. His muscles tensed and his mouth dropped open. I could see his chest rising and falling with quick breaths. The unpleasant tingling I felt before transformed into something much worse. I could feel bile urging its way up. I wanted to turn away and block the image from my mind, but I couldn't stop watching.

Suddenly, Baeloc's upper body—head, shoulders, and chest—disappeared in a wall of white flames. It happened so quickly, like when a match lights a gas stove. I heard Trendon gasp and felt Paulo's hand grip my shoulder as he leaned in closer to see. The bright flames rose higher, thicker. All that was left of Baeloc's body were his legs, which still sat cross-legged on the floor.

A door in the rear of the cell burst open and two other men rushed in with fire extinguishers. But they were too late. No one could survive being burned like that. White clouds of vapor dispensed from the extinguishers and filled the screen, blocking everything.

"Why did you do that to him? You killed him!" I shoved away from the table and faced the wall, my hands shaking violently. Last year, when we defeated the Architects in Syria, some of Dorothy's people, along with several of the Architects who rebelled against their twisted leader, captured Baeloc and imprisoned him. He was an evil man and was supposed to be locked away forever. Even though I felt safer knowing he was gone, that didn't mean I wanted him tortured and then murdered.

"Amber," Trendon said. "You need to see this."

"It's disgusting. I don't want to see anymore." I couldn't bear looking at Baeloc's remains.

"No, Amber, you have to see this!"

The mist of extinguisher vapors still distorted the screen, but the two men exited the room. The fire had not killed Baeloc. On the contrary, the Architect's face bore a look of triumph and his shoulders quivered as he threw his head back and laughed. The markings on the walls darkened. It wasn't paint. They were scorch marks. Baeloc then knelt over the bowl next to him as the video ended. The final image remained paused on the screen as Baeloc looked to be praying with his face buried in the liquid.

We did not do that to him. He does it to himself. He burns himself but the fire does not harm him.

Sherez returned the laptop to his briefcase and latched the locks shut as I read his message. The words "he burns himself" seemed to shine on the page, and I began to think seeing Baeloc dead on the video would've been better.

"How's that even possible? The dude should've been crispy," Trendon said. I heard the distinct sound of a wrapper being opened as a few colorful gummy snacks fell on the table. Trendon promptly gobbled them up.

"I don't like this." Paulo finally holstered his gun, but he stood in the doorway with one foot out of the kitchen. "Not one bit. That's evil."

"Agreed, Pablo. Agreed." Trendon smacked his lips as he chewed. "Although he'd be handy on a campout with s'mores."

Baeloc is now linked with Elijah's artifact. He has spent his imprisonment practicing. In time, he will discover a way to harness and control this ability. And this will be done without the use of the artifact. You, Amber, share a similar connection.

I looked up from reading and shook my head. "Not like that. All I had were nightmares, but I still needed the artifact to control the Guardians."

Perhaps if you focused, you could control them whenever you needed.

"How come you keep writing everything down? You have a dumb laptop. Wouldn't this be a lot quicker if you typed what you wanted to say?" Trendon asked. Sherez merely blinked, unfazed by Trendon's brash suggestion. "Anyway. What good would focusing on the Tebah Stick do? Those monsters aren't friendly." Trendon patted his chest indicating the nasty scar he received from one of the Shomehr when it attacked him in the Philippines a year ago. "And let's not forget what happened to most of those . . . whatever they're called."

"Shomehr," I said.

"Yeah. Those. Remember when they went up against Baeloc and Elijah's Fire? Stir fried."

Sherez wrote another message.

Regardless, once Baeloc has mastered this power, he will escape and come for the weapons. And for you.

"Escape? Don't you have, like, a water prison you could put him in? Like a bubble in the ocean?" Trendon took over the conversation. He seemed determined to bully the Architect for the answers. "Or, I hate to say it, but why not do everyone a favor and put that chump out of his misery?" Trendon smacked the table for emphasis.

"Yeah. That sounds smart," Paulo said. "Why keep him alive?"

Killing Baeloc cannot be simply done anymore. We have tried and failed.

"You tried to kill him? Who authorized that?" My chin quivered as I glared at Sherez.

"Authorized? Why are you trying to sound so smart?" Trendon asked.

"Answer the question, Sherez. Why did you try to kill him?"

We were unsuccessful. Just as it is with powerful artifacts, he exerted a force capable of destroying anyone who tried.

"But you still tried?"

"Let it go. So what? So they tried to kill Baeloc. We should've done that when we caught him last year. Saved ourselves all the misery." Trendon had his arm draped over the back of the chair as he watched me. "Why do you care so much about him?"

"That's not the point," I said, unsure of how to explain my point. I knew I didn't want to be involved in an organization that found it easy to kill another life. I cared for Dorothy and for Temel, but I lost so much respect for them once I realized how they solved their issues. Rubbing my eyes, I turned and stared out the window. "You said you came to warn me, but that you weren't going to stop me from going to Mount Catherine. Why not?"

Sherez opened his mouth as if to speak but then focused his concentration on the pen.

The Weapons of Might are set in motion. Thousands of years lying dormant make no difference. The pieces want to be united together and the key players will be drawn to help Both you and Baeloc will meet once more before this has ended.

"Still want to go to Egypt?" Trendon leaned across the table.

My mouth felt dry, but I turned to look at Paulo. "Do you think Dorothy knows about Baeloc?"

"If she does, she's not told anyone. Temel would've said something to me. He typically does."

So she didn't know—or it didn't matter. With Dorothy, either one could be the truth. Whatever the case, she would have a difficult time finding the artifact without my help.

"How long do you think I have until Baeloc finds a way out?"

Sherez's lower lip curled and he shrugged.

"What's going to happen at the mountain? Won't the other Architects attack once I get there?"

You will be allowed to enter the mountain unharmed. The Architects cannot control the Shomehr, who must be used to locate the artifact. Only you can do this.

"Yeah, but once we do find it, you can bet they'll go nuts trying to get it." Trendon stood from the table and moved toward the door.

"Thank you for warning me, Sherez. It's nice to know I can trust you," I said.

Sherez's expression stayed constant as he too stood from the table.

"Wait a minute." I spun to face Trendon. "Did you just say 'once we find it'? Does that mean you're coming with me?" I reached for his hand and squeezed it in my fingers.

Trendon closed his eyes. "Don't get mushy. I better go pack and figure out a good explanation for my folks. Can I borrow your gun?" he asked Paulo. Paulo looked confused and promptly shook his head. "Worth a shot. Okay, Sherez,

I think your two minutes are up. Don't let the door hit you on your way out."

"Trendon! He just did us a favor."

"What? I'm doing him one. That door's been known to leave marks if you're not careful." He chuckled and he wasn't the only one who found it humorous. Paulo stifled a laugh, but only after he noticed I was looking at him disapprovingly.

Sherez's eyes narrowed, but he didn't protest. Before leaving, he grasped my hand with his and his eyes gave me a knowing look. Though he didn't communicate in any way I was used to, I understood what the look meant. Sherez feared for my safety. He had come to warn me, which meant he believed I could be in more danger than I had yet to experience.

4

Temel's going to kill me." Wrapped in thin blankets, Paulo grimaced in pain, shivering from fever. He mumbled incoherently as our plane pitched through a small pocket of turbulence.

The first flight out of Atlantic City went smoothly, though it lasted less than thirty minutes. The plane's landing gear no more than rose up before the pilot gave instructions for arrival into NYC. It seemed odd not to take public transportation the hundred and fifty miles from Trendon's home to JFK International, but Paulo had our airline tickets and insisted Dorothy's instructions were to avoid any unnecessary deviations from our travel plans. I slept through half the flight to Senegal, an eight-hour trip on a Boeing 747 across the Atlantic.

Paulo became sick somewhere over Africa less than two hours into our flight to Egypt. It started with stomach cramps, but then the fever kicked in and no matter how many blankets we wrapped him in, he couldn't keep warm. Trendon held out as long as he could, but the moment the cold sweats struck Paulo's forehead, my hypochondriac friend promptly asked to switch seats. Sleeping with his mouth open, Trendon lay with his head propped against the window three rows down the aisle.

"Is he comfortable?" a flight attendant asked, when Paulo couldn't keep his suffering quiet. She had dark skin and light brown eyes, and spoke with a thick British accent. She handed me another small pillow and a couple more blankets.

"Um, no. I don't think so. Do you have anything else you could give him?" A wide selection of various antacids and painkillers from the airplane first-aid kit had failed to make a dent in Paulo's pain.

The flight attendant tapped her tight lips with a long, sparkly fingernail. "That's all we're allowed to give him. If he could just move around a bit, perhaps he'd feel better." She knelt in the aisle and pressed the back of her hand against Paulo's forehead. "He is quite warm. Sir, the seat belt light has been turned off. Would you like to take a walk with me to the back of the cabin? It might help."

Paulo's eyes fluttered open, but they immediately closed as he once more squirmed in his seat.

"Do you think he has food poisoning?" I remembered the last time I saw someone writhing in that much pain. Abraham Kilroy, Dorothy's teacher's aide, had acted similarly to Paulo right before he died from poison.

"Maybe. Do you know what he's eaten?"

I rubbed Paulo's arm as I retraced our path from Trendon's home. We stopped for tacos at a fast food restaurant in Atlantic City, but that was almost twelve hours ago and all I could remember Paulo eating were a few hot sauce packets. Come to think of it, I hadn't seen him eat hardly anything at all. No plane food. No snacks. Could that be the problem? Starvation?

"Wait a sec," Trendon said, joining her in the aisle. "I think I know what it is." He finally woke up after spending the past hour listening to some podcast on his phone of an underground computer hacker organization called PZP. He wouldn't tell me what it stood for, but I knew they were probably illegal and wanted by the FBI. Rubbing his hands together in preparation, Trendon pressed his fingertips firmly into Paulo's side, just above his right hip.

Paulo's eyelids shot open. "What's the matter with you?" he shouted, but then buckled in even more pain once Trendon removed his hand.

"Yep. It's what I thought. Appendicitis." Trendon discreetly wiped his hand clean on the flight attendant's shoulder.

"Are you sure?" I asked.

"Positive. That's McBurney's Point, and he's showing signs of rebound tenderness." He sounded so official, like a professor reading through a student's file.

"What are you talking about? What's McBurney's Point?"

Trendon smirked arrogantly. "Come on. You dare question me when it comes to medical conditions? McBurney's Point is the area in the middle between your belly button and your right hip. During appendicitis, that spot will hurt something awful when you push it, but it's even worse when you pull away."

"Have you had appendicitis before?" the flight attendant asked, a look of amazement on her face.

"No," Trendon answered flatly.

"Are you some kind of doctor then?" She stood with arms folded.

"I'm not, miss, but I'm going to need some more biscotti wafers and peanuts at my seat, *stat!*" He snickered and smacked his lips hungrily.

"Okay, what do we do for appendicitis? Can he take medicine?" I had a cousin whose appendix almost burst and I could remember her passing out from the pain. Poor Paulo. We had to do something for him.

Trendon looked awkwardly at the attendant. "Um . . . peanuts, please. And another coke, but with no ice and let me have the can this time. Those dumb plastic cups aren't fit for hobbits! And when are you bringing out our meal?"

Clearly offended, the woman's eyes widened with surprise. "I'm sorry, sir, I distinctly remember bringing you a dinner."

"You call that dinner?" His mouth dropped open in shock. "I paid good money for this ticket and my dad's gonna throw a fit when I tell him how you starved me for seven hours!"

Remaining cool, she politely turned toward the front of the plane. "Of course, I'll see if I can take care of your request."

"Thought she would never leave. Honestly!" he said emphatically, once she was out of earshot.

"You didn't have to be so rude. And you didn't pay for anything. Dorothy did. Plus, she has been really nice and you could've just asked her for a moment of privacy!" I glared at Trendon appalled by how unexpectedly he could be disrespectful.

"Yeah, well, I guess I could've done that, but now I

think she's gonna bring me another plate of chicken. Did you eat all yours? I was impressed! I've never had anything good on an airplane before, but that wasn't entirely dog food. And those mashed potatoes actually had—"

"Can you please stay focused?" I interrupted. "What do we do about Paulo?"

Trendon leaned forward nodding. "Yeah, yeah, that's why I was trying to get rid of the nuisance. I didn't want her to hear me. I've got some pretty strong Dramamine in my bag. It's a prescription. Works like a charm. I figure it'll either knock Pablo out or . . . make his stomach explode. But either way, we can't do much for him until we can get him to a hospital to operate."

"Operate?" I almost shouted but kept control. "Really?" I whispered.

"What did you think? His appendix is popping like a balloon, or maybe not a regular balloon, but like one of those balloons a clown transforms into bunnies."

"We've got three more hours on this plane. Do you think he'll make it?"

On cue, Paulo moaned and his left eye opened to a thin slit. "I'll be okay. I have to be strong for you, Amber. I can't let you do everything on your own. Although, from what Temel tells me, you could easily take on all the Architects at—" He folded in pain.

"Take it easy, Paulo. Stop talking like that. I'm not this amazing person Temel has told you about."

"And I'm not chopped liver either," Trendon added. "I was on all of those adventures with Amber. If it wasn't for me, she would've been in big, big trouble."

"I doubt that." Paulo bit his lip. "I just need soda water,

I think, and maybe I will take one of your special pills, Trendon."

"It'll cost you. Those pills aren't cheap, and . . . okay, okay, relax, Amber, I'm only joking." Trendon scooted into the aisle, narrowly avoiding my fist. "I'll be back in a second with your meds."

"I can't believe this is happening," Paulo muttered after Trendon left. "Temel's going to be so mad at me."

"You keep saying that. It's not your fault you're sick."

"Yes, but he doesn't understand that. I wasn't supposed to mess this up. How can I keep an eye on you and help protect you if I'm in a hospital?"

"Do you really think I need protection right now? We're almost there. I think we're safe." Hoping to get his mind off the pain, I tried to change the subject. "Now, when we land in Egypt, are Dorothy and Temel going to meet us at the airport?"

"Oh my, yes!" Paulo shifted in his seat and a soft whine escaped his mouth as he tried his best to get comfortable. "He will yell so much. I can't let him see me like this."

I found Paulo's worry of letting Temel down both strange and humorous. From my experiences, Temel never acted overly strict. Maybe he had a different relationship with Paulo. "You need to relax. Don't get all worked up."

Trendon returned and tossed a brown pill bottle into Paulo's lap. When I glared at him expectantly, he shrugged. "Oh fine, here." After opening the bottle, he held one of the pills in his fingers. "Open wide, Pablo. Here comes the choo-choo!"

When Dorothy met us in the lobby of the Sekham Hospital in St. Catherine, Egypt, the first change I noticed was her hair. Almost entirely gray. The creases around her eyes seemed deeper and she looked like she hadn't slept in weeks. How old was she? Forty? Forty-five? I didn't know her exact age.

"There's my girl!" Dorothy said as she hugged me. "What a trip, huh?" She was dirty and smelled of sweat and unwashed laundry. Her khakis were ripped and covered in white powdery dust as though she just came from an archaeological dig.

I managed a slight smile, but it was after two in the morning and I hadn't slept. Paulo survived the operation, but it had been a close one. His appendix actually burst right before we landed in Senegal and the ambulance met the airplane on the tarmac. I felt so helpless watching him lie there unconscious as the EMTs hooked him up to an IV and oxygen. Had it burst any sooner, he might have died.

"I spoke with the doctors, and they think he'll recover soon. Good thing you guys were so close to this hospital. It's one of the best in Africa." Dorothy walked over and tussled Trendon's hair.

"Well, if it isn't the Wicked Witch of the West. But I guess we're in the East right now. So which one does that make you?" Trendon batted away her hand and momentarily looked up from his magazine. "Come on. You trying to mess up my do?" He casually slurped soda from one of the many cans stacked on the table next to his chair.

"I'm honestly surprised to see you here, Trendon. I didn't think you'd really agree to accompany Amber on this trip."

"Then why did you buy my airplane ticket?" He made no attempt to hide his sarcasm.

"I was still hopeful," she added.

"Ah, shucks. I feel all gooey inside."

I glared at Trendon, baffled by how disrespectful he could be at times towards Dorothy, but he just winked at me and returned to reading.

Dorothy sat down in the empty seat next to mine. "So I'm guessing Paulo hasn't had time to fill you in on what's going on. What with the appendicitis and all."

"I'd like to know," I said. Trendon groaned boisterously but closed his magazine and joined the conversation.

"What do you know of Mount Catherine?" she asked.

"Nothing," I answered. "At least I don't think I do."

"It doesn't ring any sorts of bells? No flashes of recollection in that photographic memory of yours?"

Dorothy loved playing games. Prying. Using clues to draw the information out into the open. I typically enjoyed it as well, but despite digging deep in my mind for something useful, I came up with blanks about Mount Catherine.

"How about you, Tren? Want to look it up on your iPhone and dissect it a bit?" Dorothy asked.

"Not really. I'd rather you just tell us and we find it and then I go home with straight A's in my summer school program to show my mom and dad. Oh yeah, I'm gonna hold you to that, Ms. H. Believe me."

"Very well. Mount Catherine—home of the infamous Catherine monks, the world's second largest religious library, next to the Vatican, of course, and, hmm . . . oh yes, and since Mount Catherine is really Mount Sinai, it is also the home of the burning bush." Dorothy's eyes twinkled as she stared between Trendon and me.

Several moments passed as the information sank in. "*The burning bush? As in Moses and the burning bush?*" Scenes from *The Ten Commandments* movie flooded my thoughts.

"Uh-huh. That's right."

"Not the real one, though. It's probably just a replica," Trendon said. "A ficus with fiber-optic branches. People gobble that stuff up."

"Oh, it's real all right. And powerful. We've known about it and watched it for years. It is truly one of the more remarkable artifacts in existence."

"How's that possible?" he asked. "I know the story, and that happened thousands of years ago. And it's just been growing in some mountain all this time. Why doesn't the world know about it?"

"The world does know about it. At least, some of it does. Which surprises me how you were oblivious to this fact. Mount Catherine is visited by hundreds of thousands of people every year. The monks that guard the bush are legendary. Now, this part makes the story so delicious. These monks have known all along about the burning bush's whereabouts. They have protected it, yet frequently allowed outsiders to visit their sanctuary. And though they come and tour the mountain and take pictures of the artifact and tell all their friends, no one has ever believed it to be true. They, like you, Trendon, just assume it's nothing more than a replica. A symbolic replica. One that gives them hope and increases their faith, but just a replica."

I imagined the Bible story where Moses followed a stray

lamb from his flock into a mountain and came across a bush that burned but never withered from the flame.

Put off thy shoes from off thy feet, for the place whereon thou standest is holy ground.

The plagues, the parting of the Red Sea, the Ten Commandments. All of that stemmed from Moses's first climb of Mount Sinai.

"So that's it. The burning bush is the final weapon?" I looked at Trendon and giggled at his skeptical look.

"Psh. burning bush," Trendon scoffed. "Sounds like a heavy metal band."

"No, actually that's not correct. The burning bush is not a piece of the Weapons of Might. It is a valuable artifact. One that we guard and protect, but it's not what we're looking for."

"It's not?" Trendon worked his magic on his iPhone and showed me a picture of the monastery. A walled fortress with rounded columns at each corner surrounded weathered stone buildings. Built at the seat of several towering mountains, the monastery blended with the beige, desert landscape. Another photo showed two tourists, cameras dangling from their necks, smiling beneath an enormous green bush. Its branches, like that of a willow tree, draped over the edge of a small stone structure.

"That's it?" I asked Trendon.

"According to Google," he replied.

"It is perhaps one of the best safeguards to the actual Weapon of Might. Because of its proximity to the burning bush, the artifact we need has gone unnoticed until now."

"So where's the artifact?" I handed Trendon back his phone.

"There's a false floor in the monastery library, beneath the southernmost wall. I have a contact that works with the monks who has gained us access to the secret passage. We have a small group, just eight of us, and we've worked on the excavation for several months. Our digging has led us beneath Mount Catherine and we've found a room."

"Obviously, you had some sort of lead, or why would you dig in that direction?" Trendon asked. "How did you know about it?"

"An excellent question, Trendon. I'm impressed. One of my team is well-versed in hieroglyphic translation." Dorothy pulled a folded piece of paper from her pocket and handed it to me. "This is not valuable so don't worry about ruining it," she said when she saw me carefully handling the paper. "It's the translation of the scroll we found in an area north of Jerusalem."

And Moses hid up the final device in the mountain wherein he first found the Lord. Thus allowing the final protector time to make certain no unsanctified hand unleashed the Fury of Har Megiddo.

After reading it, I passed it to Trendon. "Har Megiddo," I muttered.

"Yeah, so?" Trendon sniffed.

"That's Hebrew for Mountain of Megiddo or where Armageddon will begin." I could remember that from a class a few years ago.

Dorothy practically glowed. "Correct! About fifty miles north of Jerusalem is believed to be the Valley of Megiddo and that's where we discovered that scroll."

"What final protector is it talking about?" I asked.

"We're hoping we'll discover that inside the tomb."

Trendon gulped, but he wasn't being serious. It sounded like a poor imitation of Scooby Doo. "A tomb, eh? Awesome."

"Inside the room under Mount Catherine is a stone sarcophagus. And there are significant reasons to believe the final piece of the Weapons of Might is held within it."

"Problem solved then. Looks like you wasted your money flying us out here." Trendon pocketed his phone.

"Well, not exactly. We've hit a bit of a bump in our search. Believe me, there should be a feasible way to do it, but we are lacking in the necessary resources and tools to open the tomb. And we don't have much time at our disposal. There's a power keeping it out of our hands."

"A power that's gonna melt our faces off the moment we touch it," Trendon said.

"You watch too much television," Dorothy said.

"You don't watch enough," Trendon fired back.

"Well, the best solution is just to show you. Once you see it for yourself, you can help us decide how to proceed." Dorothy patted my knee. "Oh, I'm so happy you're here. And we are close, Amber. So very close to the greatest discovery of all time. And we have you. The both of you!" she immediately added, gleaming at Trendon.

I should've been thrilled by Dorothy's excitement. She needed my help, which I loved to offer, but something felt different. She didn't need me for my archaeological skill or my photographic memory. She didn't need me to crack codes or help her research. She needed to use the Tebah Stick, and only I could do that.

"It's just like what Sherez said. The artifact wouldn't be hard to find," I said.

"Sherez? You spoke with him?" Dorothy's eyes dimmed slightly. "What about?"

I explained his appearance at Trendon's home and about Baeloc, but the news made little effect on her demeanor.

"I was afraid of that, but don't worry, Amber. This won't be anything like Syria or Arayat, and if it makes you feel safer, I'll immediately place Temel on watch."

"Where is Temel?" He was always a constant on these adventures, and I couldn't wait to see the mysterious and unpredictable Temel.

"Oh, he'll be along soon. He's just visiting with his son," Dorothy answered.

"Shut up!" Trendon blurted. "He has a kid? I don't believe it."

I laughed. Temel. A father? I couldn't think of him changing diapers or playing ball with his child. He definitely didn't fit into the mold of a typical father figure. "Are you serious?"

"Of course I'm serious. He didn't tell you?" she asked when I gave her a confused look.

"Who?" Trendon and I both asked at once.

"Paulo."

"Why would Paulo tell us that? We just met him a couple of days ago," Trendon asked.

"Paulo is Temel's son."

5

It made perfect sense. The toothpicks. The hot sauce packets. Paulo's unusual accent and his constant worry about what Temel would do.

Temel had a son! Wrapping my mind around that concept was almost as difficult as when I first learned about the existence of magical artifacts.

"There's the proud papa!" Trendon pushed in the door to Paulo's recovery room and shook his fingers like pistols at Temel.

Temel stood by the window looking down upon the dark, poorly lit streets beside the hospital. He wore his dusty camouflage jacket and his usual white-and-blue flip-flops. His right hand rested on his holster while his other dug a toothpick between his teeth. Paulo slept peacefully in the hospital bed next to him.

"Ah, Fatki! Long time, no?" Temel tipped his beret toward us. His smile widened when I practically tackled him. "Easy, easy. Good to see you too. You ready to work?"

"I guess so. Dorothy said we would be leaving soon." I pulled back from hugging him. Waiting around wasn't an option. Dorothy wanted to have me beneath the mountain before the sun rose in the morning.

"Yep. Easy peasy. The monastery is not far from here. Twenty minutes, tops. Nothing to worry about."

"How easy?" Trendon gave Paulo's bed a wide berth, cautiously avoiding touching any equipment and sank into a chair in the far corner.

"We've already found Dorothy's artifact. It's just a matter of opening the casket. She says your furry friends will know a way to do that and all you have to do is ask them."

Furry friends? The Shomehr were indeed furry, but it was more like wet, matted hair. And I would hardly call them friends. Creatures of death didn't make great companions. Paulo, Dorothy, and now Temel had all told me how easy this would be. It was starting to get on my nerves. Had they forgotten how difficult it had been to control the Shomehr? They didn't exactly do as they were told. They used more mysterious methods. I shuddered as an image of the creatures popped into my thoughts. Gangly and wolf-like, walking around on their hind legs and completely covered in hair, yet faceless due to an unnatural mist that hovered around their heads. I remembered the time the creatures led me to Elijah's Fire and forced me to swim under a riverbed to find it. I almost drowned. Easy never factored into the equation.

"What if they don't listen to me this time? What if my control over them has run out?" The questions troubled me since reading Dorothy's letter in my living room. Everyone just assumed the Shomehr considered me their leader, but I knew different. I could feel their animosity toward me. They hated me controlling them and if given the chance, they would kill me just as quickly as anyone else.

"Don't ask me. If they help, great. If they don't, I don't care. My job is just to keep you safe," Temel said The toothpick barely clung to Temel's lower lip as he talked in his thickly accented voice. I kept waiting for the toothpick to fall, but Temel expertly kept it stuck. From that statement alone, I did feel safer. Temel never truly cared about the artifacts and he didn't share Dorothy's passion for protecting them. He was her hired help and her friend, but he was also mine. Temel constantly placed his life in jeopardy to protect me and it felt good to have him on my side.

"What about me, dude?" Trendon leaned forward in the chair.

"What about you? *Dude.*" Temel raised his sunglasses with his finger, staring hard at Trendon. "You can't take care of yourself?"

Our focus turned to Paulo as he slept in the bed, softly breathing. He regained some color in his face, but dark circles still surrounded his eyes.

"You never told us you had a son," I said, keeping my voice softer.

"You never asked. But I'm sorry you had to see him like this. It's embarrassing. He's a bit of a baby."

Paulo stirred. "I'm not a baby."

"Ah, he lives!" Temel cheered. "Tummy ache all better?"

Paulo grimaced as he felt along his side with his hand. "It's fine. I can get ready quickly if we need to go."

Temel raised an eyebrow and shook his head in disappointment.

"You're not going anywhere," I insisted. "You have

to stay overnight in the hospital. You've just had major surgery!"

Paulo opened his mouth in evident pain, but bit his lip instead. "It's nothing I can't walk away from. You need my help right? Don't you, Temel?" He raised his eyebrows at his father.

Temel stroked his mustache for a moment, contemplating what to say, but then turned to look out the window. "Nah. You'd just slow us down. We don't have time to change bandages and apply ointment."

"I can handle myself." Paulo swung his feet to the side of the bed, realized he wasn't covered too well from the waist down, and shied away under the sheets. "You won't have to worry about me."

"Take the night off," Temel grunted. "But just one night. We'll need you tomorrow and you better be ready to work."

Paulo studied his father, waiting for him to retract his offer, but then he relaxed and collapsed back on the pillow. "Okay, but only because I am pretty worn out."

The door opened and Dorothy urgently motioned for us to join her in the hallway. "I just got word from Darius," she said, once we closed Paulo's door behind us, allowing him some peace and quiet. "Chenzira died late last night and the brethren have already appointed a new Head of Restoration over the monastery library."

"Yeah?" Temel removed his sunglasses, spat on the lenses, and rubbed them clean with his thumb. "Is that bad?"

"It could mean trouble for us. The monk chosen is relatively new to the monastery. Darius has never met him personally. And to make matters worst, this new Head of Restoration's first inquiry was about the Codex Sinaiticus."

"Eh-hem." Trendon cleared his throat. "It would be easier to eavesdrop on you guys if you both spoke English."

Acknowledging Trendon with a tilt of her head, Dorothy's eyes softened, but only faintly. "Darius is our contact within the monastery and he's part of our team. He's the one who helps us keep a low profile. If the monks ever discovered what we were doing beneath their monastery, our search would be terminated."

"You said someone died," I chimed in. "Was he also part of your team?"

She shook her head. "No, Chenzira was Head of Restoration at the monastery. The St. Catherine Monks are world renowned for their restorative abilities with ancient texts. They spend their days restoring and preserving manuscripts. Chenzira was very old, and his death comes as no surprise. It's just inconvenient, that's all. A new Head being assigned so quickly and already he's snooping about our business."

"How so?" I asked.

"The Codex Sinaiticus is the oldest preserved manuscript of the Bible, and it sits in a glass case on the southernmost wall. I'm not worried about the codex, but the key to the secret passage beneath the mountain is hidden under its box."

"Do you think this new monk is trouble?" I leaned closer, trying my best to keep my voice from carrying down the hall. "That he could be working with the Architects?"

"Yes. I think the Architects know you have arrived and their curiosity is growing. We need to move now." All business with her tone, she checked the time on her watch. "Gather your things and meet me in the garage in fifteen minutes."

"Hold up, Ms. H!" Trendon stood and snapped his fingers to get Dorothy's attention. "How is this safe? Those creepy Architects are already storming the castle? This is false advertisement! I'm not going to some monastery and neither are you." He pointed his finger at me. Trendon could be an immovable force when he wanted to be. "It's okay. I knew this wasn't going to be a walk in the park," I said, patting the air to calm Trendon. "Temel's not going to let anything happen to us, are you?"

Temel crossed his chest with his toothpick.

"Oh, I feel better now," Trendon said.

"It will be fine. I'm just anxious." Dorothy took a step toward Trendon, but he put his hands out to stop her from getting any closer. "Like I said before, I know the Architects are there, somewhere, observing us, but they have made no attempt to disrupt us. They can't do anymore than we can, and they see no point risking a war until the time is right."

"You mean the time when Amber arrives with her magic wand."

Dorothy narrowed her eyes. "Yes, precisely. So we'll act fast, keep a careful watch, and get the two of you out of there before they realize what has happened. Amber, are you still okay to come along?"

I looked at her and then back at Trendon. "We didn't fly across the ocean for nothing, Trendon. Let's get this over with."

"That's not good enough." He sank down in one of the chairs in the hallway. "You're going to have to guarantee our safety. In writing."

Dorothy crossed her arms behind her back. "Look, we

don't have time for this. As much as it gladdens me to see you again, I don't need you here. We don't need your help. I'm not going to force you to do anything. So if you want to stay here while we go, be my guest. I'll have someone come to the hospital later to take you to a hotel, and then I'll book you on the next flight back. Is that what you want?" Her agitated words snapped through the hall, and Trendon recoiled in surprise. When he made a goofy face in an attempt to lighten the mood, Dorothy just stared on with cold eyes.

"Good night, Ms. H! That was harsh," he said, once the tension finally got to him.

"I apologize." She never let on by her expression that she was truly sorry. I too found it shocking to hear her talk like that. Trendon had a knack for getting under people's skin and Dorothy often fell victim to his antics. I could remember at least a dozen times when she actually shouted at him during an intense discussion in our archaeology class. But she always did so with a genuine apology afterwards.

Not knowing what to say, Trendon opened and closed his mouth like a goldfish out of water.

"So decide!" She once again checked her watch. "Are you coming or not?"

"Yeah, I'm coming." He slowly rose out of his chair but looked unsure of where to stand.

Dorothy turned and left, and the feeling in the room eased a bit with her departure. I could understand her wanting not to delay, but this was Trendon. Sure he said everything in a cynical tone, and at times his obnoxiousness could literally suck the life out of everyone in the room. Despite all that, he was still a good guy looking out for my best interest. I couldn't wait until we finished this and Dorothy could once again be at ease.

"What about Paulo? Should someone stay here with him and make sure he's taken care of?" I whispered to Temel as we exited through the door.

"He's a big boy." Temel sounded agitated as he pushed along. "He knows where to meet us once he's done napping."

6

Gravel grabbed at the tires as Dorothy's jeep pulled off-road. She drove another hundred yards before coming to a stop in a thicket of lush trees. A wall of stones stood next to the trees and beyond that I could the see the rooftops of a number of buildings. It wasn't the monastery, just the small city next to it. Dorothy spoke briefly during the ride about what you could find beyond that wall and what I learned surprised me. A number of hotels. Swimming pools. A variety of souvenir shops. All sorts of basic touristy essentials for the hundreds of thousands of people traveling there to see the burning bush every year. Beyond the buildings, about three miles east, we would find another wall protecting the actual monastery, our eventual destination. Dorothy explained if anyone recognized her jeep, they could easily follow us, so she opted to hide her vehicle west of the city. She planned to lead us on a hike back where we would enter through an opening in the southern wall.

Darkness enveloped every window, but the cold desert carried a hint of gray as the night neared its ending. The monastery and the neighboring city were built near an oasis, and the forested area felt entirely out of place next to so much sand.

Dorothy switched off the headlights and the ignition and armed herself with a handgun. A beam from a flashlight appeared on the hood and Temel lowered his sunglasses just enough to peer over the lenses and through the windshield.

"Darius," he whispered.

Egyptian with jet-black hair and scruff on his chin, Darius looked almost angry as he approached the vehicle. Sweat drenched his white tank top and I could see the distinct markings of a bluish tattoo on his chest. *The mark of a Sentry.* Dorothy taught me the placement meanings of all three tattoos in her society. The tattoo on the ankle or wrist, like the one on Dorothy's, meant the individual acted as a Collector, someone who hunted locations of lost or missing artifacts. The tattoo on the chest indicated a Sentry or someone placed in a position to guard the location of known artifacts. Then, of course, was the mark on the neck or throat, like the one on Dorothy's partner, Abelish. A Destroyer. One of very few left in the world capable of destroying dangerous artifacts.

Darius immediately began whispering to Dorothy in Arabic, but occasionally would look at me and his eyes would narrow. The Egyptian pointed to various spots around the city, his voice anxious. Dorothy's expression took on a look of concern, but because of the language barrier, I had no idea as to the reason.

Something tapped me on my shoulder and I jumped.

"Hello, friend. A joy as always." Cabarles had crept

noiselessly from the shadows. Had he been an enemy, he could've easily captured us. The last time I saw him, he had all but shrunk to the size of a scarecrow after suffering torture at the hand of Baeloc for information. Now, despite being just as dirty as Dorothy and Temel, Cabarles's body looked strong and healthy.

We hugged, and Cabarles shook hands with Trendon. The Filipino then held his finger to his lips while Dorothy and Darius spoke.

"Do you know what they're talking about?" Cabarles whispered close to my ear.

My shoulders shivered. "I'm guessing it's about the new Head of Restoration in the monastery."

"Yes. We don't even know his name. All we do know is that he's one of the newest members of St. Catherine. Very peculiar to be suddenly named Head of Restoration. A title generally extended to senior brothers of the monastery."

"What does he look like? Is he pale like the Architects?" Trendon asked.

"None of us have seen him yet, not even Darius."

"Well, how did Darius know the new Head of Restoration was snooping around then?" Trendon asked. Immediately, Darius fell silent and glowered at Trendon fiercely. "Sorry," Trendon apologized. After several painful seconds, Darius continued his discussion with Dorothy.

"Darius has spent over ten years building relationships with the St. Catherine monks. They trust him and tell him many things," Cabarles explained. "That kind of information is critical for our cause. Without Darius, we would've never made it into the monastery." Cabarles leaned closer to where only Trendon and I could hear him. "But he's a bit cranky and at times unpredictable. So I'd recommend not angering him in any way." He shot a quick look at Darius to make sure the Egyptian hadn't heard. Darius jabbered away in Dorothy's ear, showing no signs of offense. "Anyway, this new monk keeps a low profile, and other than inquiring about the Codex Sinaiticus, which I'm assuming Dorothy told you about, he has not left his living quarters in the western wing of the monastery." Cabarles cleared his throat. "There's more to it though. And it's slightly more troubling. Look."

I followed the direction of his finger to a spot in the distance where a strange light glowed, no bigger than my fingertip and less than a couple of miles away.

"What is that?" Trendon asked.

"That's a campfire. The first of many, I fear. Apparently . . ." His voice trailed off and I noticed him staring at Dorothy. Her unblinking glare spoke volumes. Falling silent, Cabarles ran his fingers across his lips like a zipper. "Later," he muttered.

"Keep the monks occupied while we enter through the library and then join us after. Understood?" Dorothy told Darius once he finished speaking. He bowed and then trotted away, vanishing beyond the grove of trees.

"You know what to do." Dorothy raised her eyebrows at Temel. "No one unauthorized gets close. Use whatever means necessary to ensure that. Stay on the radio. Understood?" She patted her pants to where the antenna of a walkie-talkie stuck out from the pocket. Temel flicked his toothpick into the darkness and, like Darius, he too vanished.

"Great. You just gave him permission to blow up half the city," Trendon grumbled.

"You haven't changed a bit. That's really sad." Cabarles laughed until Dorothy turned on him furiously.

"Cabarles, explain yourself," she demanded. "Why are you out here?"

"I just wanted to say hello before things got on edge. Apparently I'm a little late for that." His laughter skidded to a halt. "Dorothy," he continued in a soothing voice. "It is I, Cabarles. Your friend. You need not worry about me."

Covering her eyes with her hands, she took several deep breaths. "You're right. I'm just worried, that's all. I want this to go smoothly. No hiccups. Who's guarding the site while you're out here?"

"Jomo's on watch. The others rest blissfully in the dusty dank of the cave. I'm sure he's perfectly capable of sounding the alarm if the need arises. But you and I both know that won't happen while we stand out here. And we have the surrounding campfires to prove it."

"What is he talking about?" A trickle of sweat ran down the side of my cheek even though a cool wind blew. I felt exposed out in the open. I couldn't understand a word Darius told Dorothy, but I didn't need a translator to understand something spooked him. His hyper voice and the fear in his eyes told me everything. And then there were Dorothy's calloused words to Cabarles. Something wasn't right, and I wouldn't settle down until we moved safely inside.

"Yeah, I know you hate my guts right now, but you have to tell us something," Trendon said, standing next to me.

Dorothy watched Trendon for a moment, as she gnawed on the inside of the inside of her cheek. Then she seemed to relax a little. "I don't hate your guts, Trendon. Let's head toward the monastery and Cabarles can fill you in on everything you need to know."

"Those campfires belong to the Architects," Cabarles said as the four of us walked toward the mountain to where the wall ended and turned east. "There are four camps so far that I've counted. There may be more. I have no idea how many Architects are at each camp, but I'm willing to wager there are quite a few. Maybe more than a hundred altogether."

"More than a hundred? Ugh." Trendon grabbed his stomach. "I think I'm going to be sick."

I wanted to throw up as well. "How long have they been there?"

"They arrived yesterday afternoon," Cabarles said.

"Around the same time the previous Head of Restoration was breathing his last breath?" I asked.

"That's precisely why we don't feel right about this new monk. Things are being set in motion," Cabarles answered.

"It's okay. We knew they'd be here. This is not a surprise by any means. But time is still on our side." Dorothy held up her hand to stop us. After checking around the corner of the southern column, she motioned us forward, all the while holding her gun like a soldier.

"I never knew there'd be that many of them!" Trendon stared in the direction of one of the campfires as he walked. "What are we supposed to do once they all decide to come down for a visit?"

"I've told you that's not going to happen . . ." She stopped walking and I almost plowed into the back of her. Looking past her, I noticed movement by a spot near the foot of the mountain. Though a good distance away and despite the darkness, I could distinctly see two figures standing out against the landscape.

"Are those Architects?" I whispered anxiously. "Are they already here?"

"Hush!" Dorothy hissed. Aiming her weapon toward them, she pulled me behind her.

"What if they're just normal people?" Trendon asked. "What if you're just freaking out for no reason?"

"Be quiet!"

The motionless figures never moved toward us. What if Trendon was right? What if they were just a couple of people out for an early morning walk? Then again, if they were Architects planning to attack, Dorothy's tiny weapon didn't feel safe enough.

Dorothy held her aim. She kept one hand on my side, guarding me, and I could feel the tremble in her body. "Move. Keep going," she instructed and we began moving sideways. The figures remained motionless, like two statues. "Temel?" She spoke into her radio.

The walkie-talkie crackled and Temel's voice replied. "Go ahead."

"Do you know the spot just south of the city wall where those boulders surround a small stream from the mountain?"

Static. And then . . . "Yup. I know it."

"We may have a couple of tails following us, but I'm not sure. They could be scouts and I need you to find out."

"Uh-huh," Temel answered. The radio static died off.

Stumbling over every stray rock and unseen branch, I nearly fell multiple times as we continued toward the monastery because I kept watching for the figures to move. Eventually we lost sight of them and I began to wonder if what we all saw wasn't just a couple of shorter trees or rock formations. Fear played with my mind, conjuring up all sorts of horrible possibilities. Architects were gathered around the monastery, waiting for the right moment to strike, and it made sense to send scouts to check our progress. Though frightened and already regretting accepting Dorothy's invitation to Egypt, I took comfort in knowing the talented Temel felt right at home sneaking around in the shadows and checking things out.

7

"This is Jomo. Over there on the cot is Jackson and that's Ashleigh." Dorothy introduced us to her group. They all looked dirty and weary from working in cramped conditions.

"Jomo's originally from Kenya, earned his PhD from Berkley, and you wouldn't know it from his baby face, but he was just recently promoted to dean of students at La Trobe University in Australia."

My eyes widened at the mention of La Trobe, my dream university, and perhaps the best school for budding archaeologists.

"Baby face," Jomo repeated with a wide grin. He had ebony skin and thin, muscular arms. I heard him laughing at something Jackson said when we entered the room and I immediately fell in love with his rich, friendly voice.

"We're lucky to have him on loan for this project," Dorothy added.

"Yes, but not for much longer. My students await."

Next in line for introductions, Jackson wore a T-shirt wrapped around his head as a pillow. I could tell he was

American, especially after he greeted us with a southern drawl.

"Howdy!" He swung his legs to the side of his cot and sat up. "Welcome to the dungeon." Handsome and a sense of humor. I could see why Dorothy liked having him around. Then, as Jackson unwrapped the T-shirt from around his head, I noticed a similar tattoo to Dorothy's on his wrist.

Dorothy saw me eyeing the mark and cleared her throat. "Yes, I see you realized why we brought Jackson along for the ride. Don't let his lackadaisical attitude fool you. His skill for locating artifacts is unequalled."

"Pshaw, whatever. You're just trying to make me blush," Jackson said.

Dorothy knew how to pick her companions. The two men were most likely in their mid to late thirties. With the exception of Paulo who had yet to check out of the hospital, Ashleigh owned the title of the youngest in the group. Wearing a ribbed yellow tank top and baggy cargo pants, Ashleigh's hand opened and closed around a green object.

"It's a stress-relieving ball," she said when she saw me staring at her hand. "And I'm pretty stressed right now." The American's tiny waist, beautiful blonde hair, and eyes so penetratingly blue—I swore she wore contacts—immediately drew Trendon's attention. I caught him gawking at her several times during our introductions. How could *she* be working with Dorothy? She couldn't have been more than a few years older than me and Dorothy trusted her enough to bring her all the way to Egypt.

"This is us, minus Paulo, and you already met Darius briefly. Once he's finished occupying the monks, he'll join us. Small but efficient, and we're about ready to be done with this place, aren't we guys?" Dorothy asked. A murmur rippled through the group.

The nerve-racking three mile trek to the opening in the southern wall nearly pushed me over the edge. Every shadow played with my mind and I spent more time glancing over my shoulder, searching for signs of the Architects, than I did watching where we were walking. Dorothy did little to ease my nerves. She demanded we travel in complete silence and for once Trendon actually obeyed her wishes, which only made things worse. I missed his sense of humor, not to mention the fact when Trendon kept quiet, I had no way of knowing what he was thinking. Maybe that frightened me the most.

Dorothy led us through the monastery, keeping careful watch not to alert any unwanted attention from the monks as we slipped past the doors into the library unnoticed. Wooden tables and bookshelves stood along the walls brimmed with dark bonded books. Over a dozen glass boxes lined the library floor on pedestals. Each of the pedestals held decrepit books with waxy pages and gilded edges. From their weathered appearance, some of them had to be several hundred years old. Magnifying glasses hooked to chains that were bolted to the bases of the pedestals allowed readers a clear view of the script. But we had no time to examine any of the books.

On the center shelf of a credenza resting against the southern wall, Dorothy removed the key from under another glass case containing an old copy of the Bible, the Codex Sinaiticus. Then, down we climbed through a hidden door in the floor covered by a thick embroidered rug. It reminded me of a scene from *Indiana Jones and the Last Crusade.*

We walked approximately a half mile through a stretch of winding cavern, which ended at the room beneath the mountain. Several propane lanterns standing in every corner provided light to Dorothy's group, who had scattered around the room various pots, pans, and camping stoves; a few coolers of food and drinks; excavation equipment; and cots. Directly in the center, the floor sloped slightly, and I noticed a peculiar indentation. An outline of a closed casket in the smooth stone rose just a few inches above the level of the floor. A vibration hummed against my chest, and I pulled the glowing blue locator stone necklace out from my shirt.

"Whoa. That's it, isn't it?" Kneeling on the ground next to the unusual outline of the casket, I held my necklace closer to the floor and the stone glowed brighter. "The artifact is inside there."

"That's it? That looks like an ancient crime scene. Like someone carved around a murder victim." Trendon reached his hand toward it, checked to see if Dorothy would slap him away, and, when she didn't, pressed his fingers against the lid. "Are you sure the artifact's in the ground?"

"Yes, we think so."

"Let's just say you're wrong. And you're spending all this time kumbayaing around the wrong piece of junk?"

Ashleigh stood next to Trendon, and his hand dropped to his side, nervously fidgeting with his pants pocket. "Skeptic, huh?" she said. "Read the inscription." Still kneading her stress-relieving ball beneath her fingers, she leaned over Trendon's shoulder and pointed to the rim where the lid of the casket connected with the floor.

"Whu . . . what inscription?" he stammered.

"I don't see anything." I said, squeezing between them and playing it off as though I were searching for the words.

Ashleigh leered. "You don't because you don't know what to look for." She ran her finger over a groove in the stone. "Now do you see?"

No more than an inch thick, I saw tiny symbols embedded within the groove. Cartouches. Hieroglyphs. She held a magnifying glass over a portion of the groove and easily more than a hundred different glyphs expanded into view. I found it hard to make out all of them, but I could see a lion, a vulture, hands, feet, legs, a rope, and a snake. One right after another, the symbols filled the groove in the stone.

"What's it say?" I asked.

Ashleigh scrunched her eyebrows as she looked at Dorothy. "I thought you said they were promising archaeologists."

Dorothy never taught us how to read hieroglyphics, and I felt jealousy toward Ashleigh because she clearly understood them. And what was with the stupid stress ball anyway? Opening and closing her fingers faster than a hyper-beating heart, Ashleigh's toy provided quite the annoying distraction. Who used those things anymore? Was she trying to indicate she suffered more stress than the rest of us?

Once again, she placed the magnifying glass over the groove. "Some of it's no longer legible, but the main symbols are clear enough. *Beware to all who dare. Here lies the Wrath. Death's angel. Devourer of evil. Consumer of firstborns.*"

"Ah. Lovely." Trendon backed away from the box. "So who's buried in this thing?"

"We don't know yet. There's no name inscribed on the outside, which is typical procedure in ancient Egyptian burials. For all we know, the casket could just be an elaborate container for the actual artifact." The intensity of the moment must have eased, because Ashleigh finally stuck the stress ball into one of her pockets.

"Or there's an angry mummy in there ready to pop out like a jack-in-the-box," Trendon muttered.

"Ashleigh has a natural ability for translation and she's one of the top Egyptian hieroglyph translators in the world," Dorothy said.

"And one of the most obnoxious," Jackson added.

Ashleigh chucked a dirt clod at Jackson's head, which he barely managed to dodge as the dirt exploded against the wall.

"See?" Jackson said.

Jomo burst out laughing, his eyes closed, his hand bracing against the wall.

"Quit laughing. All of you!" Darius appeared in the opening of the room; his harsh words dispelling the jovial atmosphere. "You think this is funny? You think it a joke?" He held an unfriendly look in his eye as he stared me up and down. "So this is her?" he asked Dorothy, his eyes keeping their cold, steely glare. "This one?"

I didn't appreciate his tone and wondered what he knew about me.

The mood in the room sobered considerably. Dorothy squatted next to one of the cots and looked away from Darius. "We have a short amount of time. Anyone thirsty? I have water. Here." She tossed a bottle to Trendon and me.

The Egyptian sniffed the air, close to my hair, his eyes hardening. "I suppose I should be honored to meet you."

Something told me he found no honor in making my acquaintance.

"Honored, huh?" Trendon asked. "And why is that?" He flinched as Darius turned on him, a snarl hanging in his throat.

"Shut up, boy! I don't speak to you!" Bristling, Darius balled his hands into fists and his jaw clenched tight enough I could hear his molars grinding.

"Whoa, Rambo, I was just asking . . ." Trendon started to speak, but Darius cut him off.

"You think because you're children, you can do what you want? But I think different." His eyes narrowed as they left Trendon and returned to me. "Temel tells us stories of you. How you find things with your power. Is it true?"

Something had him wound tightly. I could hear the edge in his voice, and I didn't want to set him off. "I don't know about that. It's really not anything I'm doing."

"Don't lie to me!"

"Easy, easy." Cabarles, noticing the tension, slid in front of Darius. "Is this how it's going to be every time you open your mouth?" Darius's eyes flickered between Trendon and then to me, but when Cabarles waved his fingers in front of his face, his scowl softened slightly. "Come on. Let's not do this now. Why don't you and Jomo take a walk and patrol the cavern?" Cabarles suggested. He snapped his fingers at Jomo.

"Sounds good. I could use some fresh air. You

coming?" Jomo asked Darius. He threw the strap of his rifle over his shoulder and snagged a water bottle from Dorothy's bag.

Darius flashed his gaze at Jomo. "Fresh air? Is that another joke?"

Jomo sipped his bottle. "No more jokes."

"Sure." Darius shrugged. "I get it. Let's walk."

Trendon puffed out his cheeks, once the two men moved out of the cave. "What was that all about? Crazy looked like he was going to hit us!"

"Eh, Darius is always triggered up and ready for action. That's all. Been that way since we started," Jackson said. At some point during the confrontation, he rose from his cot and now held a shotgun in his hands.

I glanced at Trendon, who discreetly mouthed "psycho" before guzzling his bottle of water.

"We're all on edge. Don't worry about him," Cabarles added.

But I did worry and knew there was more to the Egyptian's behavior than the others were letting on. He didn't like me. That much was evident. Jackson offered me a seat on his cot and I gratefully accepted. I hadn't noticed it until then, but I felt woozy and disoriented. A few minutes of rest would be good for me. Surveying the room, I took note of the wide variety of dangerous weapons leaning against cots and rocks, evidence of Dorothy's preparation for battle. But would they be able to withstand once the Architects decided to attack?

"You know what would be great right now?" Trendon asked, sitting down next to me on the cot and finishing the last sip of his water.

With a faint smile, I thought before answering. "Pizza and some Mountain Dew?"

His eyes twinkled with delight. "I was going to say a big book on hieroglyphic translation, but I think I'm going to change my answer to yours. Mmmm. Stuffed crust with mushrooms and sausage. Oh, and . . ." He raised his eyebrows and snapped his fingers emphatically. "Zingers! Don't you just love Zingers? If I would have had more time to pack properly—"

Dorothy's walkie-talkie made a sound, which echoed in the tight confines of the cave and silenced Trendon's wishful thinking. She adjusted the volume knob and soon Temel's voice rang out through the receiver.

"Hey, boss, you copy?"

A flood of relief filled my chest. It was good to hear his voice, especially after the unusual mood brought on by Darius.

"Yes, what did you find out?" she responded.

"Nothing. Didn't see anything out of the ordinary. What was I supposed to be looking for?"

I recalled seeing the two figures by the mountain. Had they just been a figment of our imagination?

Dorothy's brow furrowed. "There were two of them. We all saw them. They must've left before you got there."

"I was already in the area when you radioed. Don't know where they would've gone in that short of time. Nothing here, though. Rocks. Water . . . Wait a minute." The radio chirped as static replaced Temel's voice. This went on for several seconds until his voice returned in an almost terse whisper. "Found something."

More static erupted from the radio. A full minute

passed with no response from Temel. Then another minute ticked away.

"Temel?" Dorothy spoke into the radio. "Do you copy?"

Cold fear replaced the relief I had felt only moments before. "What do you think is going on?" I asked anxiously. Temel was skilled at this sort of thing, but he was alone, and according to Cabarles, there could've been over a hundred Architects gathering in the mountains. Could they have ambushed him?

"Boss?" Temel's voice broke the stream of static. "You may have a problem. Found a pair of tracks that follow yours." I could hear Temel's heavy footfalls in the background as he panted.

Dorothy swore and squeezed the radio harder. "How much time do we have?"

"Dunno. I don't see anyone up ahead."

"Could they have gone elsewhere? Doubled back or walked past the opening?" Her voice sounded urgent, frightened.

"Don't think so," Temel answered.

"Are you coming here now?" She signaled to the others and the sound of arming weapons clattered throughout the cave.

"Yes. I should be there in the monastery in twenty, maybe thirty minutes, if nothing else goes wrong. But, boss, there's something else."

"What?" She checked the sight of her gun and clicked off the safety. I noticed Trendon eyeballing one of the spare guns lying on the ground next to the cots.

From somewhere out on the other end of the corridor, something growled. Everyone in the room spun around and aimed their weapons toward the opening of the cave. My breath caught in my throat as the growl increased in volume and transformed into what could only be described as the sound of a woman howling in agony. A breeze blew through the opening carrying with it the musty scent of a wet animal. In an instant, all the lanterns in the room dimmed to where I could barely see in front of me.

"The tracks aren't human," Temel said, right before Dorothy switched off the knob of the radio and the room plunged into silence.

8

It's okay, it's okay," Dorothy whispered as she pulled me away from the opening. Unwilling to let go of Trendon, I dragged him along behind me. "Stand here!"

"Is that what I think it is?" Trendon asked. "Those dumb monsters?" I squeezed his hand tighter in response. "Oh good. I've missed them."

The howling continued. I wanted to cover my ears to drown it out, but I didn't want to drop Trendon's hand. It was the only thing I felt secure about at the moment. We saw the Shomehr standing by the base of the mountain, watching us. Why were they following us? I had not seen them for almost a year, and my life had been pleasant without them. Dorothy rummaged around on the floor, and soon after, I heard the distinct click of the locks unlatching on one of the cases.

Gunshots thundered in the cavern and then . . . a scream, but not from the monsters.

"That was Jomo! Hold your fire!" Dorothy shouted angrily. "What are they doing? They shouldn't provoke them!"

The howling ceased abruptly, and the cavern fell silent. Over a minute passed by with no other noises until we heard the sound of someone running toward us, breathing heavy.

"Don't shoot! It's me!" Darius scrambled into the cave. Because of the poor lighting, I could only see his outline, but I could hear his wheezing.

"What happened?" Dorothy demanded. "Why did you fire your weapon?"

"They attacked me. I had no choice!" Darius explained.

I then saw the enormous gash in Darius' left arm. Three distinct grooves cut from the creature's claw zigzagged from his shoulder to his elbow. Darius's hand dangled limply at his side. Cabarles grabbed a container of first aid supplies and rushed over to doctor the wound.

"Leave it!" Darius spat. "I don't need medicine!"

"If we don't treat this, infection will set in, and you could lose your arm. Is that what you want?" Cabarles asked. Darius growled but didn't object when Cabarles applied antibiotic cream and gauze to the disgusting cut.

"Where's Jomo?" Dorothy demanded.

"Could be dead! Don't know! They struck him too!" Darius's voice escalated as he practically shouted every word.

"This is fantastic!" Trendon said. "Summer school rocks!"

"Shhh!" Dorothy gripped my wrist with her hand. "Are you ready for this?" Before I could answer, the familiar form of the Tebah Stick pressed against my skin.

My mind cleared, and the room brightened. I no longer stood in the cave with Dorothy and the others, but out in the cavern just down from the opening into the monastery. Jomo lay at my feet, still breathing, but unconscious with a deep gash across his chest. One of the Shomehr stood next to me, only its eyes visible behind a mask of hazy mist. Something warm dripped on my chest. Blood? No, not blood. Saliva. Kneeling, I dragged one of my fingers across Jomo's throat and watched as his jugular vein pulsed rapidly.

The Tebah Stick connected me with the Shomehr, and I realized that everything I saw appeared through the eyes of one of the creatures. The saliva I felt on my chest had actually dripped from its mouth.

"Stop!" I ordered, not knowing if I spoke the command out loud or only in my mind. "Don't touch him!"

The Shomehr's claw quivered, ready to strike a final blow.

Attacked us first. It deserves to die.

I heard it speak in my mind and felt my knees almost buckle. Just like the time before in Syria, the creature spoke with my voice.

I can make it quick and painless if you'd prefer.

"Leave him alone!" It took all my courage to be forceful, knowing how they could destroy me if they wanted to. I could feel their hatred toward me. They despised being forced to heed my commands, but I knew they would obey me.

Obediently, the Shomehr's hand dropped from Jomo's throat.

"Why have you come here?" I asked. "Why did you follow us?"

You called for us.

The simple response sent a shiver up my spine. When had I called for them? This was the first time I held the Tebah Stick in a year. Could they read my mind? Sherez told me I shared a connection with the Tebah Stick, just like what happened with Baeloc and the other artifact. But I didn't want those creatures inside my head.

I swallowed, calming my nerves. If they could understand my thoughts, perhaps this would be easier. "Okay then. You are not to harm any of my friends. Do you understand?" I waited for them to respond, but none came. Still, I knew they would obey. "I need you to do something for me. We need to get the artifact and get out of here quickly."

It would be unwise to open the tomb. It will place you in harm's way. All of you.

"I understand that, but I don't have a choice."

You have a choice. Hearing the Shomehr instruct me with my own calm voice felt wrong. It was as though my conscience had suddenly been given an opportunity to speak loudly.

"Will you help us or not?" I asked, but then regretted how harsh it sounded. They would heed my words, but how would they respond to bold commands?

All of you must leave the cave. It is not safe. When you are clear, we will do as you wish.

The Shomehr stood and, with the other, turned toward the cave. I heard their claws clacking against the stone floor as they walked, until my mind returned to my body and to the room. The warm vibrations of the Tebah Stick lit up my hand as Trendon held my other. Someone close by talked in a loud, angry voice. I couldn't understand it, but I recognized it as Darius, and he wasn't happy. Dorothy joined in the shouting match and then Cabarles. As I blinked my eyes into focus, I saw Darius pointing his gun . . . at me. The rest of the group seemed torn between aiming at Darius and at the opening into the cave.

"You brought evil here!" The gun in Darius's hand shook as his finger hovered over the trigger; his other arm was hanging at his side, half enveloped in the bandages of Cabarles's unfinished work.

"Point that gun somewhere else, you dumb idiot!" Trendon slid in front of me to disrupt Darius's aim.

"I'll shoot you both. Don't think I won't!"

"If you don't lower your weapon this instant, we will shoot you!" Dorothy's voice sounded serious.

How did this happen? How long had my mind been gone?

"Jomo is dead because of her! Look at my arm. It's because of her! You'd shoot me instead of her? Me?" Darius's eyes filled with tears, and he gnashed his teeth up and down on his lower lip.

"Jomo's dead because of you, not her," Cabarles added. "And, yes, I'd shoot you in a heartbeat if it meant saving Amber."

"He's not dead," I said meekly.

"She speaks!" Trendon spun around, his back still blocking Darius. "She's not completely brain dead!"

"Jomo's hurt, but he's still alive in there. The Shomehr won't kill him. I promise. But they'll be here any minute, and we have to leave the room."

Darius lowered his gun. Before he could change his mind, Jackson sprang on top of him and wrestled it from his hand. "Not cool, Dari-o. Thought you were going to shoot the kid. What's a matter with you?"

"Was going to shoot her," Darius mumbled. His eyes glazed slightly, and he didn't struggle as Jackson hoisted him to his feet and backed him over the far wall of the room.

Dorothy lowered her gun and looked into my eyes. "Amber, what do they want? Did they tell you anything?"

"They want to help," I answered. "But they said we can't stay in the corridor while they get the artifact. We'll have to move out to the library, I guess."

"The library?" She wiped her mouth.

"That's ridiculous! It's a half mile through the corridor." Ashleigh eyed me suspiciously. "We'd be wasting too much time. Why do they want us to go there?"

"They didn't go into detail," I explained.

"Well, ask them!" she snapped.

My pulse quickened, agitated by her disrespect. Yeah, I was younger than her and she was gorgeous and brilliant, but it gave her no right to treat me like a worthless kid. "Do you want to ask them? Because I'm not going to bring it up and I don't think we should go against their wishes. They definitely said it would be dangerous if we didn't leave the cave."

"Just the cave though?" Jackson clarified. "They didn't say go above ground into the monastery specifically, right?"

It felt as though no one believed me. "I . . . I can't remember, but wouldn't it be better to get as far away as possible while they open the box? If you want to stay around because you're too tired to walk, be my guest."

One corner of Jackson's mouth pulled upward

condescendingly. "That's not what we're saying at all now, is it? We're being practical, not lazy. And leading our whole group up to the monastery would be too big a risk without a definite reason."

"Why is that a risk?" Trendon asked, coming to my side.

"Well, son, what if we get spotted by a monk. They patrol the library nightly and we'd have no alibi as to why we were just sitting there staring at the walls." Jackson watched me from time to time, but for the majority while he talked, he kept his focus on Dorothy. "We're not supposed to be here. Darius has done a good job covering our tracks and keeping the local law enforcement clueless as to our business, but if one of those monks raises the alarm, we'll be spending the next few months in an Egyptian prison while my boys in 'Bama try to expedite my safe return home. Heck, if that happens, might as well give the Architects all three weapons and be done with it."

"And let's say the Architects swarm the monastery," Ashleigh added. "What then?"

"Yep." Jackson pointed at her in agreement. "We'd have to hoof it back underground a half mile to the cave, and then turn tail and try to make it out without getting shot."

"I think Amber is being wise, and we should trust her," Cabarles said, holding his finger up to quell the argument.

"I agree with all of you. Everyone makes valid points. This is not going exactly as I had planned, but we'll have to improvise," Dorothy said. "We'll move away from the room and take our chances halfway into the corridor. Are you okay with that?" she asked me.

"That's fine. Whatever the group wants." I offered the Tebah Stick to Dorothy, raising it up and letting the wooden handle roll from my palm, but she held her hands back in surprise.

"No, you're not finished yet. I still need you to keep them under control."

"I don't think I need this anymore," I said.

She blinked in confusion. "What are you talking about?"

"Never mind," I said, dismissing the discussion.

With his gun pressed against Darius's back, Jackson moved out of the room and Cabarles followed.

"We're seriously going to go out there with those things?" Trendon asked.

"Would you rather stay in here with those things?" Ashleigh responded.

Her words caught Trendon off guard, and his head swiveled in her direction. "Hey! Have you ever seen a Shomehr before?"

"Nope. But Temel and Dorothy have described them quite vividly."

"Yeah, well. That ain't nothing. Describing them is one thing, but seeing them in action is completely different. Just wait till they start slicing everyone up with their razor claws. I could show you my scar to prove it."

Rolling her eyes, she brushed past Trendon into the corridor. "I think I'll pass, but thanks."

"Oh, I was just . . . uh . . . I didn't mean I'd actually show you . . . I was only . . . ," he stammered, and I dug my fingernails into his hand. "Ouch! What?"

"How can you act like that around her?" I whispered. "Didn't you see how she treated me? And she's, like, four years older than you and thinks you're a moron. So quit slobbering over her."

Trendon tilted sideways to see where Ashleigh stood in the cavern, before ramming his finger into his lips and hushing me. "I'm not slobbering over her!" his voice squeaked. "She's barf, man! Not my type."

I fixed him with a cynical glare and then realized we were still holding hands. He noticed as well, because he stared down at our interlocked fingers, and his cheeks flushed red. We both let go, and he casually massaged the marks from my fingernails in his skin.

"What happened with Darius? Why did he go nuts like that?" I asked, wiping my sweaty palms against my pants.

"You kinda freaked everyone out back there."

"How?"

"You started mumbling weird stuff. Talking to yourself and answering back. It was like you were having a conversation with one of those things. Your voice was way different though. Creepy."

"Have I done that before?" I could recall holding the Tebah Stick and controlling the Shomehr while Trendon watched in Syria. He never mentioned me acting in any peculiar way.

"No. That was a first for everyone." Trendon kicked a rock as we followed Ashleigh out of the room.

"Why do you think that is?"

"You got me. But you're still holding it now, and you're not loopy, so I guess that's a good thing." He warily eyed the artifact in my hand.

"I'm not in their heads right now. That's why."

"Yeah, well, make sure you keep them happy. I don't need another injury."

"There's something else I should tell you," I whispered,

nudging close until my shoulder pressed against his arm. "I don't need the Tebah Stick anymore to control them."

He cocked an eyebrow, wearing a skeptical smirk. "Are you trying to be funny? Because you've never been really good at that."

"I can be funny!" I said, objecting to his comment. "But it's not a joke. I'm connected with them now. With or without the artifact."

Trendon stared at the ground. "That's perfect."

We walked for a couple of minutes into the corridor before stopping, the cave opening still visible from where we stood. I could see the stone box in the center as I checked over my shoulder and knew we had not reached the halfway point of the corridor. Dorothy held her hand up to silence us and pointed to where the two Shomehr, faces still shrouded in mist, stood in the hallway.

One in front of the other, their bodies tall and rigid, they moved toward us. Everyone turned away or looked at the floor as they walked and eventually stood in front of me.

You will need to join us, they spoke in my mind.

"Me? Why?" Accompanying the two monsters through the dark corridor wouldn't have been my first choice.

We will show you how to open it.

"Can't you just open it for me? I give you permission."

The Shomehr didn't respond, but one of the creatures turned and began walking in the direction of the room. As I stood, still hoping they would change their minds about needing my assistance, I noticed the other Shomehr was waiting for me to move. I didn't like it, but I could sense it wasn't up for negotiations. I walked between them, a few paces behind the first with the second close behind me, the rhythmic cadence of its claws clacking against the ground. My arms shook, though I knew I had nothing to fear. They would never harm me as long as I controlled them and I looked down at the Tebah Stick held in my hands for security. At that moment, I remembered the dream I experienced in Amman a year ago. In my dream, I discovered myself following one of the Shomehr in a mysterious cave, while the other trailed behind me. The Tebah Stick was also in my possession, controlling the creatures as they led me to some unknown spot beneath the mountain. I never realized the dream had been more of a premonition of things to come, but as I walked, casting fleeting glances at the tight, claustrophobic walls of the cavern, an eerie wave of déjà vu settled under my skin. The only thing missing was Abelish, and I wondered about Dorothy's companion, one of the last known Destroyers in the world.

The locator stone around my neck began to glow as the lead Shomehr crossed beneath the opening of the cave and knelt beside the casket lid. Watching me with its eyes, the creature dragged its claw along the outer lining of the lid where earlier, Ashleigh revealed the row of tiny glyphs etched in the stone. I followed its finger as it slowly worked its away around, touching each of the glyphs until it finally rested upon a single symbol.

A ram's head.

Be mindful of the poison within. We cannot open the casket for you, the Shomehrs' voices spoke in my mind and the flesh on my neck prickled. *But we won't be far should you require it.* Having said that, the Shomehr left me alone in the room.

9

Ten minutes passed before I quietly approached the group after the Shomehr had left the cavern. Temel stood at the end of the corridor lowering Jomo to the ground. Jomo's gash ran deep, but the bleeding had started to coagulate.

Cabarles rushed passed me into the room in search of his first aid supplies and returned with bandages, medicine, and a sewing kit. Crouching, he began tending to Jomo's wound while the rest of us watched helplessly.

"Took you longer than a few minutes to get here, huh? You better have stopped for snacks," Trendon said, slugging Temel in the arm.

"No snacks, bro. What did I miss?" Temel asked.

"Oh, you're a comedian too, huh?" Trendon folded his arms, but I could see it was an attempt to keep them from shaking. "Did you see them?"

After checking back down the corridor, Temel nodded. "Just two, right?"

"Yes, there are only two left," I said. "Baeloc killed the others in Syria." A fleeting image of Baeloc manipulating fire from the sky and torching the Shomehr returned to my memory.

Sucking on his toothpick, Temel peered over his sunglasses at me. "What did they want?"

"Goodwill toward men," Trendon said. "And doggy shampoo, I think. It's hard to know exactly. I don't speak . . . beast."

After a few stitches, Cabarles looked up at Temel. "And what of our Architect friends in the mountain? Any news?"

"The campfires have all burned out. They'll be coming soon." Temel gnawed his toothpick into two pieces and chewed both in either corner of his mouth.

Dorothy rubbed her temples but stopped when Cabarles grabbed her wrist. "I know you're eager to get the artifact, and as important as we all feel it is to ensure Jomo's safety, we won't do him much good if we don't get out of here fast." Releasing her wrist, he snipped the thread with a pair of scissors.

She pursed her lips together and stared into the room. "What did the Shomehr show you?" she asked me. "Do you know how to open the casket?"

"I think so," I said, remembering the symbol of the ram.

"Good. Come with me, then." Her eyes seemed distant until they focused on mine, and I could see her exhaustion. She offered me her hand, and I followed her toward the cave. But we only made it a few steps before she stopped walking.

"This will just be me and her. You don't need to come along," Dorothy said, not looking back. "She'll be safe."

I had to look and saw Trendon standing less than a yard behind me.

"Sorry, Ms. H., but we're a packaged deal."

"It's okay. I'll be fine." I didn't need him to guard my every step, but even with my persistent reassurance, he wouldn't budge. "Seriously, you don't have to come along. Stay with them." I pointed at Cabarles and Temel, but Trendon hesitated as he stared at our friends, the corners of his eyes crinkling.

"Nope. She bought my ticket too. I should be able to come."

Was that really what he wanted? To be a part of the discovery?

Dorothy exhaled loudly. "Fine. Just don't touch anything."

It took less than a minute to find the symbol of the ram in the stone and point it out to Dorothy. "This is the one," I said. "It touched this and then it warned me about the poison within. Should we be worried about that?"

Dorothy's nostrils flared as she pressed her thumb against the symbol, ignoring my question. Her eyes widened as the sound of grinding stone echoed in the room.

"Poison?" Trendon asked, content to stand in the opening of the cave without taking another step closer to the casket. "Maybe we should be wearing hazmat suits."

Dorothy worked rapidly, digging her fingers under the lid as it unlatched.

"Help me," she whispered.

Leery of what we would find inside, I reluctantly offered my help, and exerting all our energy, the two of us heaved the lid off the casket. The stone slammed against the ground, and I leapt back as musty air escaped the opening.

My breath caught in my throat as I peered at the dark skeleton lying on its back. Sunken sockets and a fleshless face stared back at us from the coffin. A part of me expected to see its teeth suddenly begin to chatter. Bits and pieces of blue-gray fabric clung to its bones. Time had rotted away almost the entire person lying in the casket, but then I noticed something within one of the skeleton's hands held close to its hollow rib cage.

"Ah, yuck! That dude's dead. Who is that?" Trendon demanded.

Dorothy didn't answer as she stared at the thing resting beneath the skeleton's bony fingers. Carved out of what looked like bronze, the object resembled a small statue of an Egyptian Pharaoh. The figure wore an elaborate gold and purple headdress. Wide eyes gazed blankly beneath thin black eyebrows, and a long colorful beard jutted down from its chin.

"It's King Tut!" Trendon exclaimed.

"Shut up, Trendon. It's not King Tut," Dorothy responded sourly.

The statue was beautiful and looked as though the sculptor made a great effort to carve it with intricate detail. Dorothy's eyes widened with delight and she knelt down next to the hole.

"Seriously, who is that? Do you think he wants you to take his toy?" Trendon pressed.

"Trendon, this man is dead. He doesn't care anymore about the artifact. And I don't know who he is. I will though. See that placard above him?" She pointed to a stone square attached to the coffin directly above the skeleton's skull with two rows of hieroglyphs etched into the stone, the top row containing much larger characters. "Those are Egyptian, which will probably tell us who he is."

"You can't read that?" Trendon pressed.

"I'm not well versed, no. But Ashleigh can and that's what we'll ask her to do first thing. Right now, you just need to settle down and let me handle this."

"What does it do?" I held my necklace, noting the intense humming in my fingers as the stone glowed bright blue.

"It's hard to say, Amber. Before Baeloc became involved in our lives, I had never heard of the Wrath. We've done much research on it since then, but the exact measures of its power are a mystery." She had yet to touch the artifact.

"Why is it called the Wrath?" Trendon's head tilted to one side, examining the artifact from a distance.

"Did you not hear what I just said?" she barked. "I don't know. It's dangerous and if the powers of the previous two Weapons of Might give any indication, then you should assume this artifact could be the most deadly item on earth."

I watched Trendon for a reaction to Dorothy's harsh words, and part of me wondered if she ever intended for him to be there with us in Egypt. Sure, she bought him an airline ticket and instructed me to go persuade him, but maybe that was just a ruse to convince me to come. Maybe she secretly hoped he would refuse because of the summer break, and she wouldn't have to deal with him anymore.

"What do you think?" she asked me, her eyes filled with wonder. "This is it. The final artifact. I've waited so long to find it and now it's right at our fingertips. Are you as excited as I am?"

I didn't know how to respond. Excited for what? The Architects had extinguished their campfires, which probably meant they could already be swarming the monastery. Discovering an ancient item provided plenty of thrills, but this was not the time to stop and enjoy it.

"Not to spoil the mood or anything, but I'm pretty sure Jomo needs a checkup and the rest of you need a bath. We still have to walk forever because somebody thought it would be a good idea to park in another zip code," Trendon said, voicing a few of my own thoughts.

Dorothy's eyes snapped toward him and she opened her mouth, but shook her head to rethink her response. "Why don't you make yourself useful instead of just cowering over there? There are two empty metal boxes in the corner. One is for the Tebah Stick and this artifact should fit nicely in the other."

Reluctantly, Trendon followed her instruction. Placing the Tebah Stick into the box, I closed the latches and ran my thumb over the three combination locks to securely fasten it.

Dorothy opened the other container. "Now, let's get out of here. Go ahead, Amber."

Not wanting to let her down, but disgusted nonetheless to touch the skeleton, I picked up a chisel from off the floor and pried it under the fingers of the skeleton's right hand. With focused effort, I pulled up on the chisel, trying to wiggle the artifact free. The force snapped off three of the skeleton's fingers.

"Oh my gosh!" A feeling of nausea struck my gut.

"It's okay. Don't think about it. It's just a rock. You're not hurting it," Dorothy coaxed. "Try again."

Puffing out my cheeks in concentration, I again worked the chisel under the remaining fingers. Using less strength than before, I pried up the thumb and forefinger and the artifact rolled free. Gasping with relief, I tossed the chisel aside and reached into the casket for the artifact.

"Wait!" Trendon shouted before I could touch it.

"What?" I snapped, closing my eyes in frustration.

"Remember what happened the last time you touched an artifact?"

Dorothy's eyes narrowed. "We don't have time for another one of your pointless jokes."

"I'm not joking," he said, standing his ground despite her toxic stare. "I don't think Amber should be the one to pick it up. She's already messed up because of the Tebah Stick, and we saw on a video what Baeloc's doing now that he touched the Axe. What if this artifact does something horrible to her? Like it turns her into a bird? Amber, do you want to eat worms for the rest of your life?"

My fingers were mere inches away from touching the artifact, but I closed them into a fist and lowered my hand out of reach. I didn't want anything else to mess with my mind. It was bad enough having the Shomehr as my companions. And Baeloc could spontaneously combust into fire in his prison cell. These artifacts left their mark on all who touched them, and I could live without any more surprises.

"I think he's right," I said to Dorothy. Though she appeared disappointed, she kept silent.

"I'll do it," Trendon said. "If someone has to, I'll pick it up."

"You don't want to do that. You don't even want to be here," I said.

"So what? I think you've done enough. You big glory hog! Maybe we could use some gloves or something."

"Turn her into a bird?" Dorothy muttered. It wasn't her voice that startled me, but her sudden burst of giggling. Within moments she erupted with laughter, buckling over and nearly dropping the container. I kept expecting the laughter to transform into something else like spitting rage, but it became evident she genuinely found Trendon's words to be funny.

I couldn't help myself. I laughed as well. Trendon eyed us both as though we had lost our minds, but then a smirk broke the surface of his mouth, and he too joined in the noise. I could only imagine what the others thought as they listened out in the corridor. Would they think the artifact had brought on the outburst of laughter? That made me laugh even more, and I actually snorted for good measure.

"I wasn't trying to be funny. Honestly," Trendon said, once the laughter finally stopped.

"Oh, my dear Trendon, I've been too hard on you, haven't I?" Dorothy wiped the tears from her eyes. "I'm so sorry for the way I've treated you lately. Try not to take it personally. I've been that way with everyone. My head hasn't been clear in more than a year and I just want this over with. Don't you?"

Both Trendon and I nodded. More than anything, I wanted it to be over. No more hiding from Architects. No more voices of the Shomehr whispering in my mind.

"All I'm saying, Ms. H., is that I don't want Amber touching something else that could hurt her." I could hear the sincerity in Trendon's voice.

"I don't think it will hurt her..." Dorothy began to say.

"But you don't know for sure," Trendon blurted.

She sighed and closed her eyes in exhaustion. "Let me finish, Trendon. What I was trying to say was that I don't think it will hurt her, but you're absolutely right. Amber shouldn't be touching the artifact. She's done enough already and it's time someone else stepped up and handled things. And that shouldn't be you either." She handed the metal container to Trendon, and before either one of us could object, she grasped the artifact with both hands and gingerly lifted it off the skeleton's chest.

Holding my breath, I waited for some drastic change to come over her and tried to rid my mind of the image of Dorothy transforming into a giant bird. Why did Trendon have to say such weird things? His lips were pressed tight, his nostrils flaring with each exhale.

Dorothy rotated the statue in her hands and then held it close to her eyes as she inspected it. Judging by how easily she hefted it, the statue was lightweight. The golden object took on an hauntingly blue color as it reflected the light from my locator stone necklace. Running her fingers over the Egyptian design, she lightly shook it, listening for any sounds. Nothing happened.

"Anything?" Trendon asked. "Does it feel weird?"

Her lips curled in concentration. "I don't think so. Should it?"

"Uh . . . yeah. I guess," I answered, glancing over at the Tebah Stick resting quietly in its box. I remembered the sensation of holding it. How it eliminated all other sounds and distractions and allowed my mind to unite with the Shomehr. Because we were below the mountain, I had no idea what was going on outside. Perhaps storm clouds were gathering, like when Baeloc first grabbed Elijah's Fire.

"Well, it doesn't. That's a good thing, right?" She waited for my approval and I halfheartedly agreed. "Okay then. That's that." As she was about to place the artifact in Trendon's container, she stopped and once again brought the artifact close to her eyes. "That's interesting. Take a look at this." She focused her gaze on a spot just below the figure's gaunt chin where its purple beard extended. "I think this was made to open."

Dorothy twisting her fingers in a counterclockwise motion, and the head of the small statue swiveled. A sharp hiss leaked out as pressurized gas sprayed from its mouth directly into her face.

10

"Support her head!" I ordered to Trendon.

Fumbling over the mess of spelunking gear, Trendon moved behind Dorothy's prostrated body and gently lifted her head from off the ground. The point-blank burst of mist couldn't have been any more powerful than the projection from a can of hair spray, but the shock of it hitting her directly in the face sent her tumbling backwards. Her head struck the stone lid of the casket and she now lay motionless on the cold cavern floor. I found her pulse, saw the distinct movement of her chest, and breathed a brief sigh of relief.

"She's not dead. She's just unconscious. I think." Using my shirtsleeve, I tried to wipe away any of the spray from around her nose and mouth, but the clear, sticky liquid had already begun to evaporate.

"Don't touch that stuff!" Trendon slapped my hands away from her face. "You don't know what that is! Could be like ancient mummy battery acid. Or poison. Or—"

I bit my lip in frustration and shook my fist at him. "Stop it! Stop talking! I'm trying to help her, and all you're doing is freaking me out!"

Temel entered the room and hurried over to where we tended to Dorothy. Cabarles entered, and the others followed supporting Jomo, who appeared to be in an enormous amount of pain, grimacing and pressing his hand against his bandaged wound. Now we had two casualties on our hands. The cave would soon have more patients than an ICU.

"What happened to her?" Temel asked, splitting his attention between Dorothy and the rotted skeleton lying in the floor.

"The artifact sprayed her in the face," Trendon explained. "She turned its head and then its mouth opened and spat on her."

"It didn't spit on her," I corrected. "You're just exaggerating."

"Whatever." Trendon glared at me. "That doesn't matter. It poisoned her. It's like a Russian nesting doll, only it's not Russian, I don't think."

"Booby-trapped perhaps." Temel removed his sunglasses, a rare gesture, and began his inspection of Dorothy. Gently holding her chin, he moved her head from side to side. He checked her pulse in her wrist, timed it against his watch, and seemed contented. "She's breathing fine— from what I can tell."

"Yeah, for now. Wait till the poison kicks in," Trendon said, his curly hair forcing its way between us and hindering our view of Dorothy.

"Seriously, stop spazzing out!" I pushed him out of the way.

Temel stuck his hand in his jacket pocket and rummaged for a bit.

"You're not gonna make a gum bandage again, are you?" Trendon asked, referring to the time Temel used grape Big League Chew and rubbing alcohol as treatment for when I had a piece of glass stuck in my shoulder.

Disregarding Trendon's question, Temel found his flashlight, clicked it on and off a couple of times to test its strength, and peeled back one of Dorothy's eyelids with his dirty finger to inspect her pupil. The action made her jolt, and she sat up suddenly, causing both Ashleigh and Trendon to scream in near harmony.

"What was that?" Dorothy sounded loud and hyper. Pressing her hand against her chest, she tried to catch her breath but struggled to do so. "Did you see what happened?" She reached out and clasped my hand. "I saw something. Some sort of . . . thing . . . It was there!" She pointed to the corner of the room. "Right after the voice."

"What voice?" Trendon's eyes doubled in size.

"You didn't hear it? It was so loud. Like a storm." She smacked her lips together as she tried to moisten them with her tongue.

"Relax, boss," Temel said. "Take a minute to breathe."

"No, I don't want to. We need to get out of here . . . we need to move . . . it's not safe!" She rambled on and on, compelling Cabarles to join Temel in calming her down. "Get everyone away from here! It's coming!"

I looked at Trendon and felt an unsettling chill swoop through the room. I never heard a voice. No sounds, just the spray from the artifact. What was the "it" she was talking about? The Architects? There was more than just one of them, so that eliminated that possibility.

"Listen to us, Dorothy. Do you know where you are right now?" Cabarles placed his hand on her shoulder.

Her eyes darted around the room, never making contact with the others. "Of course I know where I'm at. I'm in . . . wait." She slapped the side of her head, violently attempting to disperse her confusion. "Am I in Egypt?" Her voice grew quiet as she asked the question and Cabarles confirmed it with a nod. "Cabarles? Is that you?"

"Handsome as ever, so I hear."

She relaxed visibly, and Temel gently coaxed her into lying back down on the ground to rest.

My whole body trembled from fear. I honestly thought the spray had killed her and then to see her react in such a frightfully panicked manner . . . it was too much.

Trendon raided the water cooler, and I heard him cheer to himself when he discovered an ice-cold package of Hershey's chocolate bars. "Who's are these?"

"Those are Paulo's," Temel said.

"Oh." Trendon nonchalantly removed the wrapper from one of the candy bars and looked away from Temel as he placed several sections into his mouth. "I'll just put it back then."

With Dorothy resting, Ashleigh and Jackson began to examine the skeleton more closely.

"So who are we dealing with?" Jackson removed a piece of the tattered fabric from the skeleton's bones. "He's got to be old. What do you think? Three or four thousand?"

"Well, Moses lived around 1400 BC," Ashleigh said. "You do the math."

"Moses?" I asked. "What did this guy have to do with Moses?"

Ashleigh ran her finger under the placard. "That's what this says. This translates as Moses."

Jackson whistled through his teeth, appearing impressed by Ashleigh's discovery. "Get out of town. Did we really just uncover the grave plot of Moses? The one and only?"

"Shut up! That's not Moses," Trendon said. "Moses had a beard and a staff. You're just messing with us."

"Then who is it?" Ashleigh asked derisively. "Was there someone else named Moses who happened to live in Egypt and visited Mount Sinai?"

Jackson now looked doubtful. "I have to agree with the kid. I don't see any other indicators of his title. You sure you know what that translates into?"

"I know how to read Egyptian, okay? And that says Moses. Look it up if you don't believe me."

"What does the other line say?" Trendon asked, pointing to the row of characters beneath the larger ones.

"It's not important." She turned her back to Trendon. Curling his lower lip in thought, Trendon quietly removed his phone from his pocket.

"How can this be Moses, the great prophet?" Jackson scratched his head. "The one from all the stories? Surely, the people would've shown him more respect. They would have mummified him."

"Maybe he is someone else," I said. "Maybe that sign wasn't intended for this man."

"Maybe you should let us handle this." Ashleigh glared at me.

Annoyed but refusing to let her disrespect bother me, I turned my attention to the casket lid lying on the ground next to the hole. No one had bothered to examine it yet. Running my fingers across the surface, I noticed a powdery substance coating the stone and it reminded me of what I discovered lining Elisha's tomb in Syria. Doing my best to be discreet, I brushed the powder clear with my hand and, in doing so, revealed a small row of symbols etched into the stone, each hieroglyph no bigger than the nail on my pinkie finger. I should've announced my discovery to the others, but I convinced myself if they didn't value my opinion, why should I waste my breath showing them what I discovered? Leaning closer, I made a mental note of the symbols. There were seven of them: a large bird like a hawk, an eye, another hawk, a smaller bird like a sparrow, a squiggly line, yet another hawk, and a twisted rope. Maybe they had no significance, but I logged them into my memory nonetheless.

Jackson and Ashleigh's discussion began to rise in volume, with Jackson continuing his doubts about the skeleton belonging to Moses.

"It just doesn't add up," he persisted. "The burial of a prophet or a holy man would demand some sort of wealth deposit. Even religious leaders were buried with their most treasured possessions. All this guy had was the artifact. Oh, wait a minute." He bent forward, dropping his head into the tomb. "Jackpot!" The sound of crackling bones announced Jackson's movement of the skeleton. Curious, I watched him twist the arm lying at its side and remove a leather pouch from beneath its hand. The bone popped from the force and he hefted the pouch from its fingers. "That's it? That's like two pounds, wouldn't you say?" He passed the small bag to Ashleigh who tested its weight.

"Yup. Give or take. And . . ." She pulled open the bag and frowned. "Ah, man! I was hoping for gold. This is a sad haul for weeks of hard labor." Several dozen hexagonal silver pieces clinked together as Ashleigh sifted them through her fingers.

"Is that real silver?" Trendon asked, suddenly more interested in the bag of treasure than his research on his phone.

"No, it's fake. It's plastic." Ashleigh snickered and flicked one of the pieces at Trendon. "Yes, it's real silver. What did you think?"

"Is this worth anything?"

"It could be. The silver isn't worth more than maybe a hundred bucks, but it might have some value seeing how old it is." Ashleigh closed the pouch of silver and dropped it in one of the pockets of her baggy cargo pants.

"Hey! Half that's mine," Jackson said.

"Don't worry. You'll get your cut." She winked.

"What do you think you're doing with that?" Dorothy asked, rising up into a sitting position. She looked angry, even shocked as she confronted the two thieves.

"We were just, well . . . we just thought . . ." Ashleigh backpedaled.

"Put that back," Dorothy ordered. "You can't take that with you!"

"Ah, come on. It's just a little bag of silver." Jackson cajoled. "It wouldn't hurt to—"

"I said put it back! We came for one thing and one thing only." Dorothy's chest heaved as she breathed. "We're not grave robbers."

Awkwardly checking with Jackson first to see if he agreed, Ashleigh jabbed her hand into her pocket and tossed the pouch into the tomb.

With several hands supporting her, Dorothy stood on her feet and appeared to have fully recovered from the incident. "Where's the artifact?"

During the commotion, the statue fell and rolled beneath one of the cots. As I reached down to pick it up, Trendon chucked his wadded-up wrapper toward me and it struck me in the ear.

"Ouch! What's the matter with you?" I exclaimed more out of surprise than actual pain from his projectile.

"Are you stupid?" he asked, the corners of his mouth laced in chocolate. "Did you not just see what happened to Ms. H., and now you're about to pick that thing up?"

Dorothy hurriedly rushed to where it lay and gathered the artifact in her hands. "The actual artifact is inside. That's the reason why I didn't feel anything when I touched it." Holding it beneath her waist, she once again attempted to twist the statue's head.

"Do you think that's wise?" Cabarles asked, carefully pulling me out of range of the artifact. "We still don't know what it was that sprayed you. It could be some sort of slow-reacting chemical. For all we know, there could be more in there and you could endanger everyone in this room."

She smirked. "I'm fine. It tasted like water, nothing else."

"You tasted it?" Trendon gagged but still managed to unwrap and devour another chocolate bar.

"Yeah, boss, could be a booby trap," Temel repeated his suggestion from earlier.

Concern rarely registered on his face, but he wore it then as he eyed her carefully.

"What kind of poison can withstand two or three thousand years of lying dormant? Do you know of one? The Egyptians were basic chemists, using only chemicals to aid in mummification. You know this, Cabarles, as do you, Darius. What do you think?" She stared at the Egyptian no longer under Jackson's watchful guard. Darius looked uncomfortable as though being anywhere miles from that cave, including the camp of the Architects, offered a more ideal location. "Well?" she pressed.

"Probably not poison," Darius muttered, wincing from the pain in his arm.

"Still, Dorothy, you and I have both seen some strange things in our days. Things that defy logic and reason," Jackson said, throwing his opinion into the mix. "I wouldn't be surprised if some of these ancient characters found a way to weaponize a chemical. It would make sense to safeguard this artifact against anyone who dared touch it. We need to get you inspected, and I agree with the others that you shouldn't be messing with it anymore. Let's just put it in the box and move out."

Dorothy clenched her jaw tightly. "I told you I'm fine, and we need to make sure we have what we're looking for. Rule number one when collecting an artifact: Always guarantee the item in question is indeed worthy of collection."

Jackson snickered. "No way did you just toss out a rule. That's uncharacteristic."

"Rules? What rules? There are rules?" Trendon asked in between chomping chocolate.

Temel's brow furrowed when he noticed the debris of

candy bar wrappers littering the ground at Trendon's feet. "Hey! I said those were Paulo's!"

Unfazed by Temel's accusatory stare, Trendon casually placed another chocolate wedge into his mouth. "I'll buy him another pack if we ever get out of this alive."

I didn't know where I stood on the matter. I definitely agreed with Dorothy's friends, but I also felt the urgency of making sure we had what we needed. Enduring all that work to dig up the ancient cave and not securing the artifact would be a tremendous waste of their time.

Defiant to their pleading, Dorothy once again twisted the artifact and the small hooded head popped off. No other mist expelled from the opening and nothing else dramatic happened. But as she looked inside the statue, her countenance dropped.

"It's empty." She shook the artifact upside down into her palm. "It's empty!" she repeated with venom.

"Let me see." Cabarles offered, and she slapped the artifact into his hand. After his thorough examination, he too looked grim. "She's right. There's nothing in there."

"Nothing?" I asked. "Well, then maybe the statue itself is the actual artifact. Maybe there's not supposed to be anything inside." It certainly seemed mysterious. Why couldn't it be the artifact?

Dorothy shook her head. "No, this is a Canopic jar. I didn't know it at first because it's not fashioned in the usual designs and I wasn't expecting to find one here, but there's no mistaking it now."

"What the crud's a Canopic jar?" Trendon asked.

"Of course you wouldn't know," Dorothy growled. "I only discussed it year after year in class and it was on multiple tests and assignments. Naturally, you'd have no idea what Canopic jars were."

"Oh, chill out!" He wiped the chocolate from his mouth. "Humor me!"

"Canopic jars were used in ancient Egypt during the mummification process," I explained. "They held the internal organs of the person being mummified."

Puffing his cheeks out, Trendon mimicked throwing up in his mouth. "So you're saying Dorothy just got sprayed in the face by some ancient lung butter?"

"Cut out the sarcasm! I don't need it right now! Canopic jars have also been used as protective containers for smaller artifacts." Dorothy turned her tirade onto Ashleigh. "You! Why isn't it here?"

Ashleigh flinched. "How should I know?"

Dorothy leapt at her, her hand almost striking Ashleigh, who barely avoided the blow only because Jackson and Cabarles restrained Dorothy. "How should you know? You were the one who translated the inscription. We trusted your judgment! Now we have nothing! We're back to square one and it's all because your incompetence led us on a wild goose chase."

"Don't blame this on me!" Ashleigh fired back from the safe distance of the cave entrance. "You understand most hieroglyphics, and both you and Jomo confirmed my findings. Sorry, Jomo," she quickly added an apology to the injured Kenyan.

"Don't be. You're right. We did confirm the translations," he muttered, grimacing in pain.

"See?" Ashleigh shouted indignantly. "This is not just my fault. If anything, it's mostly your fault!"

All at once, everyone with the exception of Trendon and myself began arguing and pointing fingers. Temel clearly had Dorothy's back, but how could he possibly know where the mistakes were made that led them to the wrong location? Darius jabbered in Egyptian, but by the way he remained near Ashleigh, I could tell where his allegiance lay. Jackson argued with Cabarles about some sort of papyrus scrolls they discovered in Syria and how that could've been where things turned sour. I wanted to side with Dorothy, but I didn't know enough about all the measures they took to locate the artifact to add my opinion. Blaming Ashleigh seemed like the best option, because I didn't like her attitude, but how could it just be her fault? Everyone's tempers flared beyond agitation and who could blame them? We were in the wrong spot. If the artifact wasn't here, then where could it be?

Trendon watched the commotion with one obnoxious eyebrow raised. After finishing off the remaining chocolate bars, he picked up two cooking pans and loudly banged them together until the arguing stopped.

"Can I say something?" he asked. Before Dorothy could reject him, he banged the pans together again. "No, it's my turn to speak." Perhaps it was his bold statement, or the way he stood his ground in opposition of Dorothy. Perhaps it was due to the fact he held two cast iron pans, which could easily be used for striking. Regardless of the reason, Trendon immediately garnered the full attention of the group. "Now, there are two things everyone has seemed to have forgotten in the past thirty seconds." He dropped one of the pans and held up his index finger. "One, we still have Architects all over the place surrounding the monastery. There are hundreds, right?" He looked at Cabarles for confirmation. "Maybe all of them. That's a pretty good sign we're in the right spot, don't you think? But if you need more proof, then here's number two. The dumb Shomehr opened this box for Amber. Why would they do that if they didn't think there was an artifact inside?"

"That doesn't mean anything," Jackson said. "The Architects could be just following our lead. We've known of their spies all along. Naturally, once we found a place of interest, they would alert the others of our position and surround us, thus our current predicament. Without Baeloc at the helm, they don't have the means to do the legwork. As for the Shomehr, how can we possibly know what motivates them?"

A murmur rippled through the group. Trendon's reasoning stifled their argument, but they all agreed with Jackson.

"He's right," I said.

"See? Even Amber concurs." Jackson snapped his fingers.

"No, I didn't mean you. Trendon's right."

"Booyah!" Trendon snapped his fingers back at Jackson mockingly.

"No one truly understands the Shomehr like I do. I'm not happy about it, but I know they wouldn't have opened that tomb if the real artifact wasn't supposed to be inside. That's not how they work."

"Then where is it?" Ashleigh asked, her voice still carrying a condescending tone. "Do you think someone got here first?"

"That can't be the reason," Trendon said.

"Don't act like you possibly know what's going on here," Ashleigh fired at him scathingly. "You haven't been involved in this line of work long enough to merit an opinion."

"Uh, excuse me. Now should I show you my scar?" Trendon patted his chest.

"An accidental injury doesn't mean anything. You've been on what? Two digs? That gives you this much experience." She pinched her thumb and forefinger together for a visual. "There is always the possibility that someone gets there first."

I braced myself for whatever insults Trendon was about to unleash. However, instead of verbal slams, he calmly leveled his eyes on Ashleigh. "So what you're saying is someone else, the Architects perhaps, who happen to have a couple of monsters at their disposal, got here before we did and ran off with the actual artifact."

Blank stares filled the room as everyone attempted to digest his statement.

"Am I the only one who listens?" He groaned with frustration. "I thought the Shomehr had to be used in order to locate these artifacts, and, unless I've missed something, Amber's the only one who can control them."

Dorothy looked dumbfounded as if Trendon offering sage words to the situation was more shocking than anything else she witnessed in the cave. I, on the other hand, had grown to accept Trendon's ability to be at one minute completely disconnected from the world around him and then the next be a beacon of light and truth. Once again, he was absolutely right. I controlled the Shomehr. They worked for me and if they alone possessed the ability to

open the stone casket, then it was impossible for anyone to
have stolen the artifact before us.

"So . . ." Trendon continued after he allowed his words
to sink in. "That means, the Canopic jar *is* the artifact
and you just opened it. And not to point out any more
of your flaws, sweetheart," he batted his eyes mockingly
at Ashleigh, "but I looked up the second line in the tomb.
You know, the one you said that wasn't important. And it
says 'my place of refuge.' And it's not Moses. It's Moriah.
Check your translation next time."

Ashleigh glared at him, but I noticed her glancing at
the stone container, most likely inwardly confirming Trendon's facts. Oh, how I loved that boy!

"Is he right?" Jackson asked her.

"You found the translation on your phone?" Ashleigh
looked skeptical.

"I can find anything on my phone."

"How did you get reception down here?" Cabarles
scratched his ear.

Trendon scoffed. "Please. Let's not go there."

"But there are different characters you have to consider,"
Ashleigh rambled. "Some are Hebraic, and others are—"

"Be quiet! It's not important anymore!" Dorothy stared
down at the figurine in her hands and then scanned the
floor of the cave. "Could something have fallen out? Did
you notice anything?" she asked me.

"Nothing came out of it." *Just the mist,* I reminded myself.
"Are you sure you feel all right?" Whatever that spray was,
some of it had entered her nose. She actually swallowed
some.

From out in the corridor arose the sound of footsteps.

Temel pulled out his gun and stepped in front of the opening, aiming into the cavern. Cautiously, I leaned forward to look as well.

"Uh, that's interesting," Temel muttered as we caught a glimpse of something small and white flapping in the darkness.

It looked like a handkerchief.

11

D on't shoot! Hold your fire!" a voice announced from beyond the opening.

Immediately I recognized the owner of that voice and deeply inhaled when Joseph appeared in the room. Where had Joseph come from? What was he doing down beneath the mountain? How did he even know where to find us? I had so many questions, but I was unable to ask them. It seemed clear no one else in our group could talk either. Joseph had his blond hair uncharacteristically trimmed short. He also wore unusual clothing: a crimson silk shirt and olive green dress slacks. Had he really hiked through the cavern wearing that?

"Please don't shoot me!" His eyes met mine for but a second and then settled on Dorothy.

"Joseph?" Dorothy asked, the metallic click of her gun cocking in her hand. "What are you doing here?"

"This is going to be difficult to explain, but I'm hoping you'll trust me."

Since our last conversation a year ago in Jordan, I finally convinced myself to once again trust Joseph.

He betrayed Dorothy and me so long before, but he worked hard to earn back my confidence. Partly due to his help, we defeated Baeloc in Syria. I couldn't deny how I once wanted to have a relationship with him, but if he cared about me, he would have worked hard to stay in contact over the last year. Not once did he call or text or send a letter. Then there was the mysterious way he left us from Dorothy's compound. Where had he gone? What had he done while Trendon and I attended school and tried to piece back together our lives? Despite all that, I couldn't pull my eyes away from his face. It was Joseph, handsome as ever, and my heart picked up its rhythm.

"Who is this kid?" Jackson asked. "Friend of yours?"

Dorothy hesitated before answering, "Yes, he's our friend. What's going on, Joseph? We need answers. "

"I know you do, but I can't be the one that gives you the answers. The new Head of Restoration will be doing that."

A murmur of confused voices rippled through the cave. "Here? He's coming here, right now?" Dorothy's head jerked as she looked at Temel.

"What are you talking about?" I asked anxiously. "How do you know the Head of Restoration?"

A faint smile flickered on Joseph's lips. "Hey, Amber. Good to see you. Like I said, you'll have all the answers you need shortly. But, first, everyone needs to lower your weapons. Put them away."

"I think not." Temel spat his toothpick out on the floor.

"Please! This can't get heated. The Head of Restoration is a peaceful man now. He no longer wants violence.

And you are running out of time. Please!" Joseph repeated, focusing on Dorothy. "Dorothy, tell them to listen to me."

Dorothy's face held a mixture of perplexity and surprise. She seemed unsure of what to do. Joseph stood firm in the opening, nodding his head in reassurance, and finally she conceded. "Put them away."

"Boss?" Temel looked shock.

"Yeah, Dorothy, I'm with Temel on this one," Jackson added. "I think putting away our—"

"Just do it!" she commanded. Temel, Jackson, and the others grudgingly holstered their weapons.

"Thank you. I'll be back in a few minutes," Joseph said as he exited the cave.

"What's going on here?" Jackson asked incredulously. "Who's this Joseph? And how do the monks even know we're here right now? Is it because of you? ' He pointed at Temel.

Scratching his moustache, Temel tilted his head to one side. "Me?"

"Yeah, you were the last one down here. Didn't you cover your tracks?"

"Come on, man. You think I don't know how to sneak?"

"Then how?" Ashleigh demanded.

A knowing look registered in Cabarles's eyes as he turned and stared at Darius. "Do you have something to do with this?" A similar look formed on the others as they joined Cabarles in confronting Darius.

Relaxed and unflinching, Darius boldly stared Cabarles down. "Of course I don't. I've never met the new Head of Restoration, and I don't know who that kid is. But she knows." He flicked his chin at Dorothy. "And so does Amber."

"Did you tell Joseph about what we were doing?" Dorothy asked me, her voice masking a hint of outrage.

"Of course not! I haven't spoken to him since Jordan."

"Then how could he know about us and this place? How does he know the new Head of Restoration?"

"And, once again, no one seems to pick up on the details," Trendon chimed in. "Why did Joseph say the new Head of Restoration was a peaceful man *now*? And how he no longer likes violence?"

Dorothy's eyes narrowed as she took in Trendon's words.

"That's because I wasn't always a peaceful man." The voice belonged to the man standing just beyond the opening. Tall with dark skin, clean-shaven, and wearing a glimmering red robe and a white scarf around his neck, the man looked out of place in the dingy cave. A few wrinkles etched the creases by his dark eyes, but he looked healthy and vibrant, which was a problem considering the man standing in the cave had died last year.

"Kendell Jasher?" Dorothy immediately reached for her gun, as did the others.

"Oh my! Always quick to shoot and ask questions later, aren't we?" Jasher asked, his voice smooth.

Jasher was dead. Baeloc killed him. How could he be standing there talking to us? Behind him, several other faces emerged from the darkness. They too wore varying colored robes but made no attempt to rush past their leader. All of them appeared to be unarmed. Then Joseph stepped in next to his uncle and something in my mind clicked. Joseph told us his uncle had been killed. No one actually saw the body.

"You said he died! You told me Baeloc had killed Jasher!" I shouted. Trendon held my arms, and if it weren't for his restraint, I might have attacked Joseph.

"Don't blame my nephew so quickly. He wasn't entirely deceiving," Jasher said, sounding calm despite the array of gun barrels aimed at his body. "Part of me was killed by Baeloc."

"Oh brother! Here we go again with this nonsense," Trendon said. "Somebody shoot him." My head spun and I glared at Trendon. "What?" Trendon asked, recoiling from me. "He's an evil dude! What do you think we should do? Have a tea party?"

"Please." Jasher held up a ringed finger. "There's no need to shoot me."

"Start explaining then, nice and slow, and don't leave anything important out." Jackson leveled his gun directly at Jasher's chest. "You're only going to get one chance at swaying my finger." His eyes flickered toward Dorothy, and she didn't tell him to stand down.

"I've been called as the new Head of Restoration of the library, which makes me the highest current authority on staff."

"How did you accomplish that?" Cabarles asked. "Did you buy your way into the monastery?"

Jasher chuckled. "I'm very good at what I do. You're not the only ones who have a love of archaeology and discovery. I have means and resources at my disposal, and the brethren saw fit to offer me the position."

"But you have to be a monk, don't you?" Trendon asked. "Or is that just a superstition?"

"I am a monk. Have been for over a year now." Jasher

wrapped his arm around Joseph's shoulders and pulled him close to his side.

"What?" My mind spun. "You . . . you've been working with the enemy since the beginning!"

"And I have suffered for my sins." Jasher bowed his head. "Perhaps I'm not worthy of your forgiveness. But I have tried to help you. Remember, Amber? In the restaurant just below your campus? I did my best to warn you. I even sent you those books with clues. All of that was my way of turning over a new leaf."

Before Syria, I received two leather-bound volumes containing the first and second books of Kings in the Old Testament from an unknown source. In them, someone circled specific verses that matched up with the mapping coordinates of Baeloc's fortress. I went through a number of possibilities of who sent me those books, Dorothy and Joseph being the top choices. But in the end, I realized Jasher was the one, and I never understood why until now.

"Surely Baeloc knows of your deceit. You couldn't have become completely invisible." Cabarles watched Jasher closely, waiting for him to make some move.

Jasher scratched the corner of his mouth with his pinkie and then wiped his fingers on the lapel of his robe. "Did you have any idea of my deceit?" he asked directly to Dorothy. "Baeloc is in prison, if I'm not mistaken. You, on the contrary, have been quite involved here beneath the monastery." His eyes darted around the room. "Where I've been . . . . serving for many months. Yet I firmly believe my appearance is a shock to all of you. Am I wrong?"

Dorothy waited until she released several breaths before

subtly shaking her head. Jasher then clapped his hands together once to emphasize his point.

"And you're just . . . a monk now?" Trendon rubbed his eyes, shaking his head in disbelief.

"Yes. I'm but a humble servant who has learned all about your quest to remove the artifact known as the Wrath from our guard."

Everyone's weapons had begun to lower during Jasher's speech. At the mention of the Wrath, they snapped back up.

"How long have you known about that?" Dorothy shot daggers from her eyes at Jasher as she spoke.

Jasher's focus momentarily rested on Dorothy's gun and, more important, her quivering trigger finger. "This is my home, Ms. Holcomb, and the master knows all of what goes on in his house. Did you think you were the only ones who knew of its existence?"

Had Jasher and the monks been waiting all this time for us to open the casket to remove the artifact? Could they be working with the Architects? I couldn't read Joseph's body language, and it made my stomach tighten. Peering over Jasher's shoulder into the corridor, I tried to determine our chances of escape, but I had no way of knowing how many monks filed in line behind their leader. Maybe they did have weapons concealed beneath their robes.

"Let's get this over with then!" Temel snarled and stepped through to the front of our group.

"Yes, let's." Jasher nodded. "We have set up barricades on both the east and west walls, and I have involved some of the more trustworthy of the local authorities to ward off a direct attack on the monastery gates. You are welcome to stay here and hide. I have set aside several rooms in the living quarters to accommodate your needs, and you will have full access to our library to pursue your research on the artifact. If there are books on the subject of the Wrath, they will most likely be hidden within our shelves. I gather, however, from your aggressive behavior, you'll probably pass on that option. Your southern entrance should be the best route for you to take. It would be foolish to try and collect your vehicle from the outskirts of the city since I've been informed your enemies have already compromised it. I will provide you with a vehicle to transport your group, but I cannot offer you a driver. I hope you understand. My involvement in this must remain clandestine. I would not want to compromise my new position as Head of Restoration."

Jasher pressed his fingertips together and placed them beneath his lips as he spoke. "The Catherine Pass will lead you to the Nuweiba Highway. Head northeast for sixty kilometers until you see the directional signs for the Gulf of Aqaba. I've made all the arrangements for you to travel by way of boat. They won't ask questions and can pass through the borders of whatever land you wish to travel, regardless of passport or customs. Like I said, my resources come in handy from time to time. From there, I'm sure you can take care of yourselves the rest of your journey. Any questions?"

"You're going to help us?" Dorothy asked, skeptically.

"Of course." Jasher blinked. "Any others?"

"You're just going to let all of us leave? Just like that?" Trendon scratched his head.

"Just like that. Except I must request your two injured friends should spend a day or two in our infirmary." He gestured to Darius's arm and then to Jomo lying with his back against the cave wall. "We have sufficient medical capabilities to clean their wounds. They look quite nasty and without antibiotics, those injuries could fester and place them in grave danger."

"Why should we trust you?" Temel asked.

"What choice do you have? I have offered you two options. Sanctuary in our sacred monastery or the safest passage I can provide out of the country. If you can think of a better solution, by all means, feel free. But the clock is ticking, and your Architects are already on the precipice."

"At least tell us why you're so willing to help us. Give us some reason," I said, not wanting to let the issue go.

Sighing, Jasher appraised me with a focused gaze. "I may be an evil man, but I value my life. I want to live it with fullness, enjoying all of my treasures and wealth. Baeloc's mission would end that. It would end everything. How could I agree to destroy this earth when I don't share his hatred for humanity? My ancestors weren't cursed. When I truly learned what Baeloc intended to do with the Weapons of Might, my priorities changed. And now, here you've come to eliminate this hideous artifact. I'd be a fool not to provide you with assistance. So unless there are more pressing questions, I suggest . . ." His words sputtered to a halt as he finally noticed the open Canopic jar in Dorothy's hands. Jasher opened his mouth, and though no words came out, there was no mistaking his panic.

"No more discussion!" he spoke hastily. "You must leave at once!"

12

At least a dozen monks stood solemnly in the library when we surfaced through the secret opening. Others sat along tables examining manuscript pages through enormous magnifying glasses. Each of them stopped their work long enough to watch us as we passed, but they made no attempt to stop us from leaving. The heavy weight of the Tebah Stick and its metal container slowed my advance, but I felt better being the one who carried it. Dorothy and Cabarles each carried one of the metal containers holding the Wrath and Elijah's Fire as they hurried along at the front, directing us through the monastery now buzzing with activity.

We arrived to the southern entrance and shielded our eyes from the blaring light outside. The sun shone from above and a quick glance at Trendon's phone confirmed the time was after seven in the morning. As Jasher promised, a dusty blue SUV rested less than twenty yards from the entrance. Still a skeptic of Jasher's legitimate offering of help, no one immediately rushed to the vehicle. It could be a trap. Maybe the monks rigged the SUV with explosives. I had made too many mistakes trusting people I knew to be crooked, and I wasn't about to take the first step out into the open. Greed and the desire for power once fueled Jasher's actions. How could one year in a monastery change that?

Then there was Joseph. Why hadn't he just told me the truth about his uncle? Would I have listened? I hated Jasher and knew Joseph's attempt to convince me otherwise would be hopeless, but did that make it right for him to lie about Jasher's death? Pondering those questions would have to wait.

"What do you think?" I asked Trendon.

Trendon stared around the group and shrugged. "I think we look like a bunch of morons standing here in the doorway."

"Agreed," Cabarles said. "I'm not saying we should trust Jasher completely, but we have no where else to go and that vehicle looks like a promising escape."

At first, the coast seemed clear of any Architects, but as the seven of us, minus Darius and Jomo, climbed into the SUV, Temel raised the alarm from the driver's seat.

"Coming up fast! Looks to be just one for now." He adjusted the rearview mirror. Immediately spinning around, I caught sight of a flash as sunlight reflected off the windshield of a bright white off-road vehicle barreling toward us.

"Floor it!" Dorothy demanded from the front passenger seat. Temel stepped on the gas pedal, churning up clouds of dirt and sand in his wake.

Not even five seconds passed before the Architects rammed the back of our SUV, sending a jarring concussion that sent everyone plowing into the seat in front of them.

"Hang on!" Temel shouted as the vehicle hit an invisible divot in the ground, and we momentarily took flight before crashing back to earth. Miraculously, Temel kept us righted, but two of our hubcaps shot off like rogue saw blades tearing up the ground.

Glass exploded from behind. I thought they started shooting at us but then realized Jackson had only kicked out the back window. Leaning over the tailgate, he aimed at the Architects and released a tremendous noise from his shotgun, muting all other sounds in our vehicle. Each time he fired, a chunk of the SUV disappeared. A part of the front bumper. Both headlights. The side mirror. Despite the steady diminishment of their vehicle from the constant spray of Jackson's shotgun, the Architects would not be deterred. For thousands of years, the descendants of the original architect of the Tower of Babel, had suffered from their curse. Unable to speak and plagued by a tormenting pain in their throats and shamed as outcasts from the rest of the world, the Architects had developed a pure hatred for mankind. Now, with all three Weapons of Might in our possession and their leader, Baeloc, showing signs of invincibility, the Architects would stop at nothing to kill us and fulfill their destiny of destroying the entire human race.

One of the Architects emerged from the sunroof, pale skin almost blending in with the white paint of the SUV. His black hair flapped in the wind and his head looked almost comical as it bounced up and down with every dip and rise in the rough road.

"What's he doing?" Trendon shouted. A pause in the cacophony of blasting gunshots while Jackson reloaded made it possible for him to hear the question. Glancing up, he leaned forward for a better look, and we all watched in horror as the Architect heaved a massive machine gun up through the sunroof. Hitched to some sort of rigging, the weapon appeared to be anchored to the vehicle.

"Mini-gun! Take cover!" Jackson dropped below the smashed-in window and gave us just enough warning to do the same.

My right jaw smacked against the floor mat as both Trendon and Cabarles collapsed on top of me. Unable to see and breathe because of the suffocating weight, I could only listen as what seemed like an endless amount of ammunition peppered the SUV. Glass showered down, stinging my neck and arms. Bullets clanged the metal frame like the trilling sound of a fire alarm. My throat felt shredded and hoarse from my constant screaming, though it was impossible to hear my voice above the bombardment. I had no way of knowing how long the machine gun continued to fire upon us, but when we finally received a break, I poked my head up and prepared myself to witness the bloody remains of my friends.

"Is everyone all right?" Jackson asked as he resurfaced from the floor.

Frantically I patted my chest and stomach down for injuries and then did the same on Trendon. I didn't see any blood, but the SUV had more holes in it than a colander.

"Quit tickling me!" Trendon said, unleashing desperate giggles. "I'm fine. I'm fine! Are you okay?"

Tears filled my eyes. "How about everyone else?" I searched the faces of the others. No one was lying in a heap, and they all appeared to have survived.

"How's that possible?" Trendon dug his finger into a bullet hole in Temel's headrest and winced. "That's still dang hot!"

"It's a miracle we're not all dead right now," Cabarles said, dusting glass from off his shoulder.

Half of us started to laugh. It was a miracle! How did all those bullets miss?

Jackson whistled sharply. "Save your miracle talk until after round two. These jerks are about to try again!" He fired off another couple rounds and the driver of the SUV veered to avoid his gunshots. Scowling, the Architect struck the mini-gun with his hand and yanked on a lever jutting out from the side. Apparently, it had jammed and he labored with it, trying to fire once more.

Ashleigh smacked Jackson on his shoulder to get his attention. "We won't get lucky again. You've got to take out those tires!"

"What do you think I've been trying to do?" More gunshots and more pieces of white metal vanished from the blasts. Jackson aimed lower, but his next shot only succeeded in removing the grill. With the mini-gun functioning again, the Architect once more pointed the barrel at us and his emerald eyes sparkled.

"Get out of the way!" Ashleigh pulled out her pistol, a laughably tiny comparison to Jackson's shotgun.

"That won't make a dent . . ." Jackson began to argue, but with Ashleigh's first shot, the front tire burst and the white SUV swerved too sharply to correct its direction. The blown out tire spun as the Architects tried to resume their pursuit, but the shredded rubber and the off-road terrain proved to be the perfect combination. Their vehicle soon became a white blur as Temel put a wide distance between us.

"Good night!" Trendon eyed Ashleigh's gun in awe. "Nice shooting!"

Ashleigh blew on the nozzle tip and reholstered her weapon, her brilliant shooting no doubt damaging Jackson's ego.

A cell phone rang from inside Dorothy's bag near Cabarles's feet, and he pulled it from one of the pockets. "It's Darius," he said as he answered it. "Tell us good news, my brother." He listened as the voice on the other end spoke. "Are you sure? Well, that is good news." Cabarles covered the bottom of the cell phone and pulled it away from his ear. "Jasher and the police have most of the Architects on the run. Nuweiba Highway should be clear all the way to the Gulf."

An eruption of cheering filled the SUV. If he hadn't have shown up when he did, no way would we be where we were. Jasher literally saved our lives.

Cabarles continued his conversation with Darius. "Do not trouble yourself anymore, Darius. You are forgiven. We were all acting impulsively." I knew they were discussing the incident when Darius almost shot me. I wished I could see his face because I couldn't imagine what he looked like when he apologized. "How's Jomo?" Cabarles paused and then pressed his lips together. "Good, good. That's not too horrible. Jomo has most likely felt worse. Rest well tonight. We shall see you soon."

"No more freaks?" Trendon asked once Cabarles hung up the phone.

"I'm afraid not. It looks like Jasher has become somewhat of an ally."

"Yeah, right. Let's not get crazy." Trendon plopped his head into his hands and dragged his fingers down his eyelids.

"Still, better reload and do an ammo check," Jackson grunted as he fed several dark green shells into his shotgun. "Five bucks says the moment we let our guard down, we'll have more company than coasters."

"Coasters?" Trendon grabbed for a box of ammunition, but Ashleigh moved it out of reach. "Is that a Southern expression?"

"It's a Jackson expression," Cabarles said. "He's full of them."

As I watched the others reload, Temel's movement from the driver seat caught my eye. His right hand squeezed Dorothy's shoulder, his attention torn between watching the distant Nuweiba highway grow steadily closer and checking to see if she was all right.

"What's wrong?" I climbed over Trendon and grabbed Dorothy's seat.

"Hey, boss? You still with us?" Temel shook her and her head drooped forward until her chin dug into her chest.

"Has she been shot?" Flustered, I pushed my way in between the two front seats, consequently cutting off Temel's ability to shake her, and began a frenzied inspection of her body for wounds. I knew our surviving the Architect's onslaught of machine gun fire had been too good to be true. Those bullets ripped through the SUV like a swarm of hornets, but it took only a few seconds to realize her body appeared to be intact. No wounds. No bullet holes. No blood.

Dorothy once again fell into a comatose-type state.

Though I could only see her eyes behind her half-closed lids, they looked glazed over completely. I gently pulled her head back from off her chest and tried to lay it against the headrest.

"She's burning up with fever!" I yelled. Her forehead felt almost too hot to touch. "We've got to cool her off!"

"What are you yelling about? Oh man! What's wrong with her?" Trendon recoiled from the sight of Dorothy.

"She's not any better. I think that spray from the artifact is doing something to her." I heaved a backpack from the floor at her feet and found a half-filled bottle of water stowed inside. Ripping off a piece of my shirtsleeve, I doused it with lukewarm water, and pressed it against her head.

Temel continued to watch her, checking for progress. "Yo, Cabarles! Is this poison?" he demanded.

Cabarles felt her head beneath the torn fabric and his eyes expanded with fear. "She's way too hot! This fever could kill her! It very well may be poison. I'm afraid the artifact could have been laced with a high concentration of some sort of toxic material. Mercury exposure can cause extremely high fevers. Dorothy should've known better than to open it like she did! She needs medicine—a high dosage of a fever combatant to reduce her temperature." Ducking away from the front, Cabarles searched the vehicle floor. "No good! We left the first-aid kit in the cave."

A rush of emotion swept over me. "We have to stop!" I said. Dorothy needed immediate medical attention and though I expected everyone in the vehicle to argue with me, I knew the best place to take her. "We can go back to the monastery. They have an infirmary and can help her!" Of course Dorothy's safety was my primary reason for wanting to go back, but I had a second reason as well. Maybe Jasher still had evil motives, but he did help us escape and he offered the library to use. If time was against us, we needed an immediate place to research. A safe place. A location right at the heart of the final artifact.

Temel began to ease off the gas pedal.

"That's a bad idea. Don't listen to her," Ashleigh ordered, sounding cold and impassive from behind me.

"Why is that a bad idea?" I asked, my voice shaky from crying.

"Just keep driving, Temel. Don't stop until we're at the Gulf."

Unable to calm my anger, I spun and faced Ashleigh. "Why don't you do everyone a favor and be quiet!"

Ashleigh leaned forward wearing an ugly frown. "Letting you call the shots is not doing anyone a favor. You're just a child, and you're acting irrational."

"I'm not being irrational! Saving Dorothy's life is not irrational! Darius told us Jasher and the police have gotten rid of the Architects."

Ignoring me, Ashleigh reasoned with the others. Cabarles took up half the responsibility of dabbing Dorothy's scorching forehead with wet pieces of fabric, but he gave Ashleigh his partial focus as she spoke. "We narrowly escaped back there, and most of you don't really trust Jasher. If we go back, we will all get caught and killed. The Architects get all three Weapons and we fail. You know this, Cabarles. And as much as I hate seeing Dorothy suffer, I'm not about to let Amber control our lives or the lives of everyone on this planet for that matter. Or have you all forgotten what will happen if the Architects unite all three artifacts?" She scanned everyone's faces, passing over mine with clear indifference. "Temel, did you hear me? Do not turn this car around. Dorothy wouldn't want that."

Temel watched her through the rearview mirror but kept silent. Why wouldn't he say something? She was talking condescendingly to all of us.

"Don't act like you know what Dorothy wants," I said. "She's only ever talked about Temel and Cabarles and has never said a word about any of you. I think we know what Dorothy wants more than you!"

Ashleigh's smirk widened. "You gonna let her insult you like that, Jackson? Haven't you known Dorothy for fifteen years?" Like Temel, Jackson didn't participate in the conversation, satisfied to listen and watch the argument unfold between us. I knew Jackson would side with Ashleigh on this, but what about the others? Cabarles? Temel? Didn't they want to help Dorothy? "Admit it, Amber. You know you're wrong. You don't know Dorothy at all. You were her student. That's it. These type of decisions need to made by adults."

Another insult pointed directly at my age, but no one stepped up to defend me. It then dawned on me why they weren't saying anything: I was wrong, and Ashleigh was right. My thoughts were focused only on helping Dorothy. In doing so, we could jeopardize the whole mission. I didn't want to admit it, but if Temel followed my command, I would lead us straight to the Architects. I *was* being irrational, but watching Ashleigh arrogantly take control of the situation was too much to handle. I wanted so badly to punch her in the mouth, but getting physical with her would definitely be considered irrational.

"You're a jerk. You know that?" It took all my will-power to keep the trembling out of my voice. "Fine. I'll admit it. Going back to the monastery would be a mistake."

Ashleigh smiled. "Good girl."

"But there's something I won't admit." My voice rose as I cut her off before she could say any other snide remark. "I won't admit you know Dorothy like I do. Especially you. You're still just trying to cover up your mistake. Dorothy trusted you to translate the inscription and you messed up. All you're trying to do is avoid the real problem." I could instantly see the effects of my words and had we not been in the company of the others, I wondered if Ashleigh would point her gun at me.

After a few moments of fuming, she opened her mouth. "You better watch yourself from here on out. I will hit a kid if I have to."

"Oh, give me a break!" Trendon finally turned on Ashleigh. "Just because you can read scribbles better than most and you probably have the highest score on *Duck Hunt*, it doesn't make you any more important than the rest of us. I bet you're barely out of high school. And if any of us were in danger and we had to choose between you and Amber to save us, we'd pick Amber any day of the week. With or without her walking doggie friends."

"Hear, hear!" Temel nodded his head emphatically and winked at me from behind his sunglasses.

Now they decided to show their support. Regardless, hearing Trendon rip on Ashleigh and then having Temel agree was worth taking her advice in the end.

"There is time to help her, but we need to get to the gulf and pray they have sufficient medical supplies on our boat." Cabarles patted Temel's shoulder. "I don't think I need to remind you, but speed is of the essence, my friend."

Temel gave one last glance at Dorothy slumped in the passenger seat, inserted another toothpick in the corner of his mouth, and pressed his foot on the gas pedal. Outside, beyond the shattered windows of the SUV, the scenery whipped by in a blur as he accelerated.

13

Almost nine hours had elapsed since we arrived at the Northstar Saad Hospital in Tabuk, Saudi Arabia. After showering and changing back into our dingy clothes, most of the others stashed their belongings—their backpacks, supplies, and radios—in the corner of the room. They kept their weapons, of course, and went looking for dinner, leaving Temel to prowl the hospital as security and Trendon and me in the room to keep watch over Dorothy. Trendon slept on the floor by my feet, his head on a pillow with his ear buds dangling from each ear.

Dorothy's fever stayed constant at a hundred and six degrees, the threshold before bodily organs shut down. Veins bulged on her forehead and her eyes remained closed, though they remained perfectly still behind her lids. I wondered if she dreamed in her current state. Lying on a cot, head propped up by several flat pillows, she looked far worse than I could remember seeing her. When Abelish used Adino's Spear against the Architects in Syria, the exploding artifact knocked Dorothy unconscious. I could still remember her drooling into her lap, but that Dorothy looked healthy compared to the one lying dormant in front of me in the room.

An IV fed fluids into the top of her hand and a mess of complex medical equipment hummed, beeped, and chirped next to the bed. I sat on an uncomfortable metal chair, leafing through a magazine, while I watched her sleep.

After arriving at the Gulf of Aqaba, we boarded a small ferry, which took us on a two-hour journey across a blue-gray window of water. Cabarles made the decision to enter Saudi Arabia. The option to travel to Jordan had been on the table, but he explained how Dorothy's compound in Amman had been shut down after the incident in Syria. Her relationship with her Jordanian contacts no longer carried any weight, and with that part of the Middle East still considered Architect territory, it would be wiser to lie low in a new location. Since Cabarles knew the area better than any of Dorothy's group, no one objected.

A soft knock sounded at the hospital door, and I looked up from my magazine as Cabarles stepped in holding a bag of food.

"Hungry?" he asked, shaking the bag. "It's not much. Bread and some cheese."

I eyed the bag hungrily, but my appetite dissipated as quickly as it surfaced. I couldn't eat thinking about Dorothy.

"Where are the others?" I looked into the hall.

"They found a restaurant nearby. Any improvement?"

Green lines flickered across the monitor like a primitive drawing of a mountain range and Dorothy's skin appeared flushed as though the blood beneath it simmered from tremendous heat and pressure.

"She won't wake up." I hugged my arms. "She's made no sounds or movement since this all started."

Cabarles read the medicinal information on her IV bag and checked the folder next to her pillow. Tenderly, he touched the top of her hand where the needle entered her vein and gradually exhaled through his nostrils. "She will. She's tough. You know that."

I felt the tears welling up in my eyes and tried desperately to hold them back. "This is different though, isn't it? She seems really bad."

"You should eat. The bread's a little chewy, but . . ." His eyes took on a playful look when he spotted Trendon snoring on the ground. Holding his finger to his lips for quiet, Cabarles knelt down, peering beneath the chair.

"Quick, Trendon, hide! The monsters have come!" he shouted.

Trendon immediately shot up smacking the bottom of the seat. "What the?" he yelped, furiously rubbing his head. "Oh, it's you. Joy." Slugging his pillow, Trendon plopped back down and tried to get comfortable.

"Impressive reflexes." Cabarles clapped in amusement. "The way you flew up, I would've thought you had been attacked by a hooded cobra."

I giggled but felt sorry for Trendon, who looked so peaceful while sleeping.

Wiping the corners of his mouth, Trendon clenched his jaw. "Ha. That's so good. You're a real peach."

Cabarles offered his hand in greeting. After staring at his fingers, Trendon grudgingly took it. Before he had time to protest, Cabarles hoisted my best friend to his feet.

"Come on, man! Give me a warning, at least!" Trendon

growled as his iPhone dangled precariously from the head-
phones still rammed in his ears. "Does no one believe in
beauty rest anymore?"

"You don't need it. You're already beautiful." Trendon
opened his mouth to fire back an insult, but Cabarles cut
him off. "I brought you a snack. Truce?"

Trendon's eyes fell upon the bag, and he leaned forward
to see inside. "Yeah, whatever."

"Cabarles? I've been wanting to talk to you about Jasher,"
I said.

Cabarles fished a roll from the bag and broke it in two
pieces. "We can eat while we talk."

Hesitantly, I took the roll and nibbled the crust. "How
do you feel about him? Does it seem weird to you?"

"People can change," he muttered.

"So you think we should trust him?"

Cabarles promptly shook his head. "No. I think he
was being honest when he said he was an evil man. We
cannot ignore his motivations. Greed. Wealth. Power. He
and Baeloc didn't see eye to eye on the Weapons of Might.
That doesn't mean Jasher won't find other ways to combat
our cause in the future. We should count ourselves lucky
to have escaped so easily."

"But he helped us. We wouldn't have made it here without him."

"Yet here we sit with our dear friend, Dorothy, in this
alarming state."

"You think Jasher did some sort of voodoo on Dorothy?"
Trendon asked.

"I don't know. I wasn't there in the room with you to see
for myself. I find it hard to believe there was nothing else

inside the Canopic jar. You are certain nothing fell out?"

"It's not a normal Canopic jar," Trendon said, trying to sound as though he had known about Canopic jars for most of his life. "The container is the artifact."

Cabarles shook his head slowly. "But that doesn't make sense."

"When has any of this made any sense?" Trendon asked. "Noah used a big stick to herd elephants. Elijah used an axe to control lightning. Why couldn't this last artifact just be an ancient Pez dispenser?"

Cabarles tapped his lips with his finger and watched Dorothy lying still and quiet on the bed. "The Weapons of Might are connected, each piece constructed so as to be joined with the others. Baeloc knew of this, as did Dorothy and myself. Together they make one weapon."

"Could that be figuratively?" I asked, understanding why Cabarles struggled with confusion. The other two artifacts, though different in ability, shared similar characteristics. Both of them had a handle and both could be easily used as an actual weapon. The Wrath owned a completely unique design.

"I don't believe so. I think there needs to be a way to combine them."

Trendon went to work on his iPhone and, within a few seconds, pulled an image of several Canopic jars up on the screen. Disgusted, he read through the information. "Which one of these held the liver, I wonder?" He handed me the phone. The Canopic jars featured in that article looked much different than the one we discovered in the monastery. There were four: a jackal, a lion, a hawk, and a man with a pointed beard. The man was the closest in comparison to Dorothy's artifact, but the jar from the tomb was more detailed and colorful, unlike the picture on Trendon's phone.

"So I'm no expert, but why couldn't a Canopic jar join the other two artifacts together?" Trendon asked.

"How could that work?" I scrolled to the bottom of the article and then handed him back his phone. "The other pieces are wider and bigger in size."

"Yeah, but maybe there's a way to screw the Wrath onto the bottom of one of them. Maybe it has a hinge and it opens in the middle. We didn't really look at it long enough to find out. Who knows? Maybe it's built like with Egyptian Legos. Hey, I'm just saying we don't know," he defended when I stared at him skeptically.

"Trendon's right," Cabarles agreed. "We need to take a closer look at the artifact to be sure."

Beyond the thin pane of window in Dorothy's room, the city of Tabuk slipped into darkness. Three enormous palm trees grew in a cluster next to the window; their wide leaves fanning out like fingers. Streetlights and the illuminated signs of a few shops and restaurants lit the sidewalk as groups of people milled about. From my vantage point on the fifth floor of the hospital, I could see the dark gravelly rooftops of other buildings, and several air conditioning units with fans no longer needing to spin due to the cold desert air, standing out despite the darkness. I watched people walk in and out of the shops, bags in hand, pausing at the edge of the road to hail taxis, and suspiciously I wondered about their intentions. Did any of them have a clue we were five floors up in the hospital with the most deadly artifacts in the world in our possession?

We stowed the three metal containers beneath a blanket in Dorothy's bathroom. It was by no means the best hiding place, but it was only temporary. Each container weighed differently, the one holding the Wrath being the lightest. Carefully, I placed the box on the chair and rotated the numbers on the three combination dials: one, eight, four.

The latches popped opened, but the lid remained shut, waiting for me to lift it up. Looking at the final Weapon of Might in the hospital felt more dangerous and terrifying. Even the creepy setting of the cave under Mount Catherine felt strangely safer. Maybe Dorothy's condition, brought on from handling the artifact, made the hollow pit build in my stomach, but dangerous didn't quite do it justice. The Wrath was deadly.

"How do you know the combination?" Trendon whispered.

I tapped my finger against my temple. "Good memory that's all." One, eight, four had been the combination to Dorothy's apartment safe in West Virginia. It stood for Genesis, chapter eight, verse four.

And the ark rested in the seventh month, on the seventeenth day of the month, upon the mountain of Ararat.

Since opening that safe and learning that scripture, which began my involvement in the deadly race to find the Weapons of Might, my life would never again be the same. Dorothy told me once a year ago how she would always use that combination from then on and she kept her promise.

"Before you lift the lid, let's lay out some important

rules," Cabarles said cautiously. "Only I should touch it. Not you two."

"Why only you?" I asked.

"Shut up. That's a good idea," Trendon said under his breath.

"I am much older and more prepared for these things than you." Cabarles removed a pair of gloves from his pants pocket.

"Gloves," Trendon mouthed. "That was my idea."

"If this is indeed the Wrath, these thin leather gloves will offer no protection. But . . ." He placed the gloves over his hands. "It makes me feel a little safer. Okay, Amber. Open the lid."

Slowly, I lifted the lid of and leaned back against Trendon, who held my shoulders in his hands.

Inside the box, the statue had disappeared and in its place stood a pile of ash.

14

I s this the wrong case?" Cabarles stared at me and then back into the opened box.

"That's the right one, and it hasn't been out of our hands since the monastery. What is that stuff?" I gripped the edge and lowered the box so I could better see the contents.

"Do you think it . . . it melted?" Trendon asked.

Undoubtedly, he was trying to be both funny and pose a legitimate question at the same time. Since I didn't think anyone in our group would be able to steal the artifact out from under our watchful guard, I began to wonder if the Wrath did indeed change into some other form. Melting would imply intense heat, which could have meant the artifact negatively reacted to the outside air.

"Maybe when it shot that mist into Dorothy's face, it was just starting to break down. Maybe we just did the world a favor by accidentally destroying it." Trendon snapped a picture of the gray ash with his phone. "I'm just gonna try something online, but don't hold your breath."

"If you're thinking of uploading that picture on the Internet, I wouldn't recommend it," Cabarles said.

"Why? It's not like the Architects are watching for a pile of junk to show up online. Besides, there's no way they could know all of my alternate handles."

"What if they're tracking your phone?" he suggested. "The moment you upload something could alert them of our location."

Trendon smiled at the absurdity of Cabarles's suggestion, but his smile vanished as he changed his mind. "You make a valid point, Cabarlicious."

"Which brings us back to our initial problem," I said, returning the focus of the conversation. "How is the artifact gone?"

A low cackle arose from the hospital bed as Dorothy's eyes opened. Her soft laughter died off. "Not gone," Dorothy said. "It's not gone."

"Dorothy! You're awake!" I scrambled to my feet, temporarily forgetting about the missing artifact. However, I backed away from her. Her natural color had yet to return to her skin, and beads of moisture dotted her chest and arms. But by far the worst feature was her eyes. A charcoal-gray coating now covered them so that even the whites surrounding her irises were no longer visible. It looked as though two solid, dark marbles quivered beneath her lids.

"You won't find it in there, Amber." Her lips pulled up until the top of her cheekbones stretched wide. "It's in here." She patted her chest. "Inside of me."

"You ate it?" Trendon asked in disbelief.

"What are you talking about?" Cabarles straightened, his hands clenching at his sides.

With a quick unnatural motion, Dorothy's head snapped in his direction. "Ahhh, Cabarles Godoy, my old friend.

143

Have you been trying to figure me out? Fit the pieces together? Does it not make sense?"

Stepping in front of me, Cabarles reached for the remote lying across her lap to summon the nurse. "We'll get you some more meds. You're not yourself right now."

Another ripple of laughter parted her lips. "On the contrary, I'm very much myself, Cabarles. I've never felt more alive, which is more than I can say for the three of you. You look sickly. Pale. Let me put my hands upon you."

"Enough!" Cabarles tossed the remote aside without pressing it, a snarl hanging in his throat. "You're not Dorothy!"

"She's knocked a screw loose!" Trendon pulled me back toward the window. "What kind of medicine is she on?"

"It's not the medicine." Cabarles stole a glance at the medicine bag dripping into her IV as if considering Trendon's idea but then looked back at Dorothy. "This is something else. Get out of here! Both of you! Take the boxes," he ordered, pointing at the bathroom. Following his command, Trendon and I collected the remaining two artifacts and moved toward the exit. My heart pounded against my chest, aching with each beat.

Outside the window, the night sky lit up with a bright, orange light. Despite my concern for Dorothy, the light drew me to the glass, and it took only a fleeting glimpse to recognize the source of the fire.

Baeloc stood on the rooftop of the nearest building, his army of Architects, too numerous to count, stood behind him, with a row of vehicles engulfed in a blaze in the outdoor hospital parking lot below. By the look of the high-reaching flames of the parking lot fire, the leader of the

Architects had sufficiently trained his body to control the power of Elijah's artifact.

"I told you that dude was a freak! How did he find us so quickly?" Trendon kicked open the bedroom door just as the hospital fire alarm unleashed an ear-splitting roar. As we stepped through the door, a group of orderlies dressed in muted green scrubs nearly ran us down as they raced to the other end of the hallway, followed by several security officers toting machine guns, squawking into their radios. "This place has gone nuts. How are we supposed to sift through that mess?" He leaped back as more people darted past. My body tensed as a sudden crash sounded in the hospital room behind us. "Are you coming with us or what?" Trendon turned to check the status of Cabarles and his mouth dropped open. I didn't want to look, but I couldn't prevent myself.

Dorothy stood on the bed, ridding her arms of the tubes and needles connected to her, the gown flapping around her body like a cape. For only a second, remorse flashed across her face as she turned and stared to where a gaping hole penetrated the window. The heat from the parking lot fire at ground level wafted through the massive opening in the glass.

"Where is he?" I demanded when I realized Cabarles no longer stood in the room. "What happened to him?"

Dorothy continued to watch the window, a mixture of rage and sadness appearing as her eyes contorted, and I finally understood. Dorothy had thrown Cabarles through the window! The feat would be impossible for someone with tremendous strength, but Dorothy weighed less than I did and her illness had withered her body down to almost nothing. How could she have done that unless something had indeed taken control of her? Just like my ability to command the Shomehr or Baeloc's manipulation of fire without our controlling or handling our artifacts, a similar change had happened to Dorothy.

My first urge propelled me toward the window, but Trendon held me back.

"Nope! Nothing we can do for him now. She's coming for us next!" He dragged me into the hallway as Dorothy stepped off the bed, her bare feet thudding softly on the linoleum floor.

Chaos struck the hospital. Patients wearing gowns and carrying their belongings filled the halls, all of them scrapping their way toward the elevators. I knew that would be the worst place for us to go. We needed a better place to hide. A place with another way out. Weaving our way through the crowd, we bypassed the row of elevators, and slipped into the stairwell.

"Is she still behind us?" Trendon asked, gasping for breath.

I peered through a small crack in the doorway and amid the confusion of people crowding the hallway, caught a glimpse of Dorothy standing just outside her room. With her arms dangling limply at her sides and her shoulders slumped forward, she looked more like a zombie than my archaeology teacher. Slowly, her head turned in our direction and our eyes met.

"I think she's coming!" I leaped back from the door, slamming it shut.

"I'm gonna smack that woman! Do we go down or up?" Trendon jerked his head between the two options in the stairwell.

"I don't know. What's up? Is there another way out of the hospital?"

He pressed his lips together as he thought. "Probably not. I think there are like four or five more floors, but maybe there's like a fire escape. What do you think?" When I didn't answer, Trendon continued rambling. "There's probably a lot of rooms up there we could hide in."

"You want to stay in the hospital? With Dorothy and Baeloc hunting us?"

"Maybe there's a maintenance closet, or better yet, a cafeteria." In typical fashion, his instincts directed him toward food.

"She threw Cabarles through the window! Think about what will happen when she unites with Baeloc. They'll burn this hospital to the ground!"

"Down it is!" Trendon finally agreed.

Our feet pounded the metal stairs, echoing as we descended. The artifacts felt heavy especially carrying them in their protective boxes, but abandoning them in the stairwell wasn't an option. After passing three exits leading to other floors of the hospital, we stopped just beyond the door marked with an "L" for the main level. The stairs continued down, wrapping around out of sight.

Trendon quietly opened the door and stuck his head out. After checking in both directions, he reappeared. "Okay. I can see mostly doctors and normal-looking people. I don't see any Architects, and I definitely don't see old baldy! I say we take a chance and head for the exit. Maybe we'll blend in with the rest of the crowd and Baeloc will miss us." He allowed the door to close completely and waited for me to answer. "Come on, Amber, you're gonna have to decide. I've got nothing."

Were we ready to make a run for it? Charging directly toward the Architects would be like playing chicken with a thousand cars at once. It was as though I had a huge target on my back.

Both our heads snapped up as we heard a door a few floors up fling open. The sound of heavy footsteps pounded on the stairs. It could've been anyone—more patients, or security guards—but I felt almost a hundred percent positive it was someone coming for us, and there was no way I wanted to risk finding out.

"We gotta go now!" Trendon once again turned the door handle and inched it open.

Feeling an overwhelming impulse take hold of me, I slammed my hand against the door and latched it shut.

"No? You don't think we should?" he asked, eyes desperately waiting for me to give the order.

"Not that way," I answered. Grabbing his hand, I led him down the stairs. "The hospital also has an indoor parking garage underneath. There will be other exits and maybe more places to hide. Can you hot-wire a car?"

He actually laughed as he fished his phone out of his pocket. "Can I hot-wire a car? No, but I can find out fast enough." In less than a minute, his eyes gleamed, as he found the information he needed to complete the task.

The parking garage spiraled down four levels beneath the hospital, but we didn't want to take the chance of getting stuck that far underground. On the first level of the garage, Trendon burst through the door and his head swiveled as he looked for the perfect car to test out his hot-wiring skills. Clapping his hands once he found one, he raced toward a red BMW parked a few stalls over in one of the reserved lots.

"Not that one!" I shouted.

Feet skidding to a halt, Trendon's knees buckled, sending him crashing to the ground. "Good grief! Why not? It's a Beamer, man!"

"Yeah, and it probably has an alarm system. And it's bright red! Why don't we just announce to the world where we are?"

Rubbing his rear end from where he fell, Trendon got to his feet and shrugged. "Good point. What then? A station wagon? A minivan? Something with one of those stupid stick-figure family window decals?"

"Do they have those in Saudi Arabia?"

"How should I know?"

I pointed to a four-door sedan with a large ding in the bumper and a busted taillight. I had no idea if breaking into that car would set off an alarm, but I believed it a better choice than Trendon's BMW.

After testing all the doors and not finding one unlocked, Trendon sat the container holding the artifact on the ground and tried shattering the window with his palm. By the third thud with no results other than Trendon nearly swearing from the pain, I climbed onto the hood and sat with my legs dangling over the edge above the back passenger window.

"I'd get back and cover your eyes if I were you," I said.

Counting to three, I kicked my foot out and brought my heel down solidly on the window. Though the glass didn't shatter, I felt it spider web and give way under the pressure of my foot. By the second blow, the window caved in.

Using a screwdriver we found from a toolkit in the glove compartment, Trendon removed a panel on the steering wheel column. Then, referring to the website on his iPhone, he masterfully hot-wired the car. Pumping the gas pedal, the engine roared as Baeloc stepped through the door into the garage.

"Drive! We've got to get out of here!" I screamed.

Trendon slammed the car in reverse and the tires squealed on the smooth concrete. Baeloc's hands ignited, sparking with fire. Extending his fingers, the flames shot out and immediately enveloped our car. Though not powerful enough to burn us, the fire settled on the trunk, licking at the rear window and threatening to ignite the gas tank. Trendon yanked on the windshield wiper handle and an insignificant jet of water spritzed out.

"That was worthless," he hissed as he changed the gear of the car into drive and once again spun the tires.

"Don't worry about the fire! Just get us out of here!"

Another more powerful blast from Baeloc's fingers shot toward us as Trendon finally willed the car forward. The fire missed and instead connected with a motorcycle in the stall next to where our car had been parked only moments before. The motorcycle toppled over to one side and, as the heat intensified, exploded.

Trendon slammed on the gas and the gust of wind extinguished the fire by the back window. As we picked up speed, leaving Baeloc behind us, I watched as several more Architects emerged from the door, joining their leader in the road. By the looks of it, no one was in any rush to charge after us. I wouldn't fully relax until we reached the street, but I calmed down just enough to realize how horribly my hands were shaking.

Trendon only slowed down around the turns but didn't stop even at the parking lot pay terminal. Instead, he floored the pedal and rammed the car through the fiberglass bar. The broken piece cracked the windshield and thudded as it bounced across the hood and disappeared beneath the car.

Pulling out onto the main road just outside of the hospital, I saw Baeloc's handiwork burning out of control. More than twenty vehicles were ablaze in the external parking lot, but at least the fire department had arrived to try and regain control to the chaotic scene.

"Okay, slow down a little," I said. "We don't want to get pulled over by any cops. Just play it normal."

Trendon promptly eased off the gas pedal and then remembered to turn on the headlights. We filed in line behind a row of slow moving cars, the drivers rubbernecking as they surveyed the disaster area. A mob of people, probably the drivers of the charred vehicles, stood behind a barricade shouting—their voices loud and foreign, and extremely angry—at several police officers with flashlights.

"I think we lost them," I said, once we finally moved away from the danger zone.

Trendon looked terrified. "Yeah, maybe."

"Are you okay? Can you still drive?"

He didn't answer at first but then swallowed slowly. "I'm fine. Don't hate me, okay."

"I don't hate you. You saved us! You were brilliant. Why would I hate you?" I promptly leaned over and kissed him on the cheek. Apparently, he hadn't shaved in quite some time and his stubbly whiskers tickled my lips. Trendon shaving? I never would've imagined it.

"Just don't hit me, that's all," he mumbled, unfazed by my kiss.

Doubt began to fill my mind. What was he talking about? I stared at the box in my lap and ran my fingers over the combination dials. I then searched the floor at my feet and turned to examine the backseat.

"Trendon?" My voice increased in volume as alarm replaced the doubt I had just been feeling.

"Ah crap!"

"Where's your box?"

15

I couldn't keep the humiliating thought of an ecstatic Baeloc discovering his long lost artifact in the parking lot out of my mind. Somehow, I controlled my rage by not hitting Trendon. Had he not asked me so sincerely not to, I would've certainly pounded him.

"What happened? Where is it?" I craned my neck to watch the road behind our car. "Slow down and start talking!"

"I . . . I just sat it down when I was trying to break the window, remember?" Trendon stammered. "And then I forgot about it. I'm so sorry, Amber. Should we go back and get it?" He pressed on the brake and slowed the car as we approached a red light.

"Go back?" I couldn't keep my voice low. "That would be suicide. All we would accomplish is handing them the final artifact!" We had it in our hands! We actually made it out of the hospital, only to find out we had failed miserably.

"Yeah, you're right. What then? Where should we go? Do we try to find the others? Go to the police? Bury the Tebah Stick somewhere? What?"

"I don't know! Stop asking so many questions and let me think!" I closed my eyes and blew a mouthful of air from my cheeks. It wasn't Trendon's fault. It could've happened to anyone, but the timing couldn't have been worse. "I'm sorry, Trendon. I shouldn't yell at you."

"Yeah, you should. Yelling hurts a heck of a lot less than punching. I'll take yelling any day of the week."

Suddenly, I felt guilty. How many times had I punched Trendon? It had always been my first response to ball up my fist and slug him in the shoulder. But I was a girl and though he wasn't in the best of shape, Trendon was impressively strong. Had I really caused him pain?

"My punches never really hurt, do they?" I asked.

"Only when you land them. Admittedly, that doesn't happen too often." He snickered but eyed my hands cautiously.

I hefted the container holding the Tebah Stick into my lap. "I guess I'm kind of a bully to you, aren't I?"

Trendon pulled over to the curb but left the car idling. "Are you being serious or is this just some trick to make me lower my guard right before you pounce? Because I'll hit you back. Don't think I won't." When I didn't respond, he tilted his head to one side and looked at me. "Do you really feel bad about being mean to me?"

"Well, yeah. I don't want to hurt you. You're my best friend. You've always been there for me. This isn't your fault. It's Dorothy's fault." I covered my mouth with my hand as a surge of emotion striking me in the throat. Dorothy! What had become of her? What was that thing inside of her controlling her mind? "Oh my gosh! Cabarles! I can't believe he's dead!" Cabarles had helped us with our search for the Tebah Stick in the Philippines, had been there to comfort me in Syria throughout my interrogations with Baeloc, and had become a permanent fixture in my mind of trustworthiness and security. Now he was gone.

Trendon shifted awkwardly in his seat. I knew he handled his struggles differently than I did, but I wanted to hear him say something about it. "I know," he muttered, checking the rearview mirror. "I can't believe it either. Let's not talk about it anymore. We just need to decide where to go."

Choking back a sob, I pushed the image of the gaping hole in the hospital window out of my mind. There would be time to dwell on the sadness of losing Cabarles, but now we had to stay focused. We needed to make a smart choice of our destination, but I had never been to Saudi Arabia. I didn't know my way around nor did we have any maps at our disposal. Driving down the road blindly could lead us into a trap or even worse, right back to the hospital.

"Should I ask for directions in there?" Trendon pointed to a building next to the curb.

"What if they don't speak English? What good would that do?" I stared at the ground, wiping at my eyes in an attempt to dry them.

"I bet they know a little. Probably enough to take my order."

"Your order?" I looked out the window and groaned at the sight of a bright neon sign. Though written in a foreign language, I recognized the familiar logo of the Domino's Pizza restaurant. "Are you really that hungry?"

"Aren't you? Getting chased by a demon woman always works up my appetite. I'll ask for directions to someplace safe, and then I'll eat while we drive." Trendon kept the car running as he hopped out on the road.

"No anchovies," I said.

A look of disappointment flashed across his face. "What? Why not? They're just little fishies."

"Yes, exactly!"

Ten minutes later, the smell of pepperoni, sausage, and mushrooms filled the car as Trendon dropped three different pizza boxes in my lap.

"So that was pointless. They didn't help us at all," I said, dabbing my chin with a napkin as Trendon continued driving on the main strip of road.

"Oh, they helped us plenty. This sauce is awesome!" Chomping a mouthful of pizza, Trendon winced a little with each bite. "But I don't think these are peppers. It tastes like some sort of pickle." He spat something out in his hand and held it close to the dashboard to examine it.

"Watch the road!" I shouted. A half-eaten slice rested on top of the three boxes in my lap. "And where are you taking us?"

"I don't know. I'm just trying to get as far away from the hospital as possible. Don't you think that's a good idea?"

A car horn blared behind us, and I spun around, tipping the pizza boxes so half of the pieces dropped out of my lap.

"You spaz! Pick 'em up!" Trendon screamed. He braked and, with the car still in the middle of the road, leaned over to salvage as many pieces as he could from the floor mat. "This is our dinner, Amber!" Frantically, he picked dirt and grime from amid the toppings, but I paid him no attention.

A pair of headlights flashed our rear window as the car behind us swerved into the next lane and sped up beside us, screeching to a halt. With no time to react and with Trendon too preoccupied with cleaning pizza slices, I gripped the door handle, ready to make a run for it. Who else would recognize us out on the road but the Architects? Then I saw Ashleigh staring back at me from the passenger seat of the other car.

"You guys all right?" She poked her head through the opened window. I leaned to the side and recognized the driver.

"Hey there! I get one little appendicitis and look what happens." Paulo looked weak and exhausted but genuinely happy to see us.

Empty pizza boxes and plastic water bottles littered the hotel floor. Figuring she had the least contact with the Architects, making her the most difficult one to track, Ashleigh used her credit card and purchased a room for the four of us. Trendon and I had just finished describing in detail what had happened in Dorothy's hospital room. How she changed. How something seemed to control her. Neither Paulo nor Ashleigh took the news lightly.

"Are you sure she wasn't just hallucinating?" Paulo stood by the window, peering through a crack in the closed curtains.

"It was no hallucination, Pablo. She tossed Cabarles like he was a stuffed animal. Chucked him right out the window." Trendon ate the bulk of the pizza after I explained to the others how I dropped the pieces on the floor mat. Now, had we dropped the pizza on the hospital floor, Trendon would've reacted quite differently.

"She wouldn't have done that to him," Ashleigh said, glaring at Trendon. "Cabarles is one of her closest friends."

"And I'm telling you, she did. The artifact made her do it. Cabarles is dead!" Trendon said.

"Can we go on?" I pleaded. I didn't want to relive the nightmare of Cabarles's death, especially knowing Dorothy's directly involvement. Just as Ashleigh said, he *was* one of her closest friends. She trusted him and he trusted her. How could she have done that to him?

"So where's Jackson and Temel?" Trendon asked.

"We don't know. Our group separated," Ashleigh said, her voice harsh and filled with anger. Sitting on one of the queen beds, she cleaned her handgun, working a brush in and out of the chambers. "There were Architects everywhere and the police. I didn't want to split up, but it wasn't my idea."

"Yes, it's not her fault," Paulo added, glancing down from the window. "Temel went into the hospital to look for you and Dorothy. When he returned unsuccessful, he instructed us to head in different directions to search. Temel and Jackson headed west. We headed east. And we found you."

"So where do we meet up now that you found us?" Trendon tossed the last bit of pizza crust into one of the boxes.

Paulo looked at Ashleigh, who scowled. "We don't have a rendezvous point," he said.

"Why not? That's dumb!" Trendon tossed his hands up in frustration. "Shouldn't that have been the first thing you did? Set a rally spot?"

"We had no time to think!" Ashleigh growled. "Cars

were blowing up. Architects swarming the hospital. Temel made the decision and we went our separate ways!"

"Well, call someone then," I said, confused why they hadn't thought to do that yet.

"With what?" Ashleigh glared at me. "All of our supplies were in Dorothy's room. Our cell phones. Our radios. Everything! We have no way to contact each other."

The gravity of our situation settled in the room, and I rubbed beneath my eyes with my fingers. We were on our own. Lost in an unfamiliar city with the enemy tracking us down as we sat surrounded by empty pizza boxes. I would never voice this out loud as to not hurt Paulo's feelings, but more than anything else, I wished he and Ashleigh had traveled west instead of east. Temel, a professional in this line of work, knew his way around almost any country. And like Dorothy, Jackson was a Collector with similar skills. Instead, we had Paulo and Ashleigh, the two youngest members of Dorothy's group. Regardless of how much experience Ashleigh boasted, I honestly felt better off without her. After sitting quietly for several painful minutes, Trendon finally broke the silence.

"You always bring your cell phone. That's the most important thing you own." He held up his phone to emphasize the point. "There's no way to get in touch with them now. We might as well head back to the hospital and turn ourselves over to the Architects."

Paulo's eyes blinked rapidly. "It's not our fault. We were just following orders. When Temel told us—"

"You can call him Dad now, you know? It's not a mystery anymore." Trendon rolled his eyes.

Paulo winced in surprise, as did Ashleigh

Baffled, Ashleigh began to laugh. "Call him Dad? Wait!" She pointed her finger at Paulo. "Temel's your father?"

Paulo looked at his hands nervously and returned to peering through a crack in the curtains.

"Were we not supposed to tell?" Had we just released Paulo's big secret? I thought everyone but us knew that fact. Apparently, I was wrong.

"I can't believe this!" Ashleigh looked angry. "How long have we worked together? Ten months? And I'm just finding this out now? Nice, Paulo. Real nice. And how is it you two know this?"

Though I appreciated knowing something Ashleigh had previously been oblivious to, I once again hated the way she treated Trendon and I like worthless imbeciles.

Trendon scraped a glob of cheese from the bottom of one of the pizza boxes and tossed it in his mouth. "That's funny. I guess we're really good at picking up on things right in front of our noses. We weeded through the translation. Understood the facts. You know. Basic stuff. You should practice that a little. Maybe we wouldn't be in this mess right now had you picked up on the details."

"Watch it, boy," Ashleigh snapped, but instead of pursuing an argument, she gathered up her cleaning supplies and dropped her gun into her holster.

"Thank goodness!" Trendon grunted. "I thought that the gun would go off the way you were scrubbing it."

"I know how to use a gun. It wouldn't have gone off, okay? I'm just really stressed right now." She stood and unfolded a map of Saudi Arabia, spreading it across the bedside table.

Why hadn't Paulo told her? Or Jackson? Or Darius and

Jomo? And why had Dorothy chosen to reveal that secret to us? Maybe she knew we would figure it out eventually. The similarities between Paulo and Temel were uncanny, but maybe she trusted us more than Ashleigh. That seemed to be the right answer. Especially after the blow-up in the cave when Dorothy accused Ashleigh of messing everything up. Maybe Dorothy hated the fact she needed Ashleigh's help with translation. Dorothy played the role of an extremely independent woman. Yet she never felt bad about asking for my help. Why was that? I would have loved to ask her personally, but would the real Dorothy ever return?

Using a black permanent marker, Ashleigh circled our approximate location on the map. "We're here, which is too close to Baeloc. By now, they've moved on from the hospital and are searching for you in the area. Thanks to Trendon, they have not one, but two of the artifacts." Trendon simmered next to the bed but refused to speak. It *was* partially his fault after all. "The Tabuk airport will be compromised. I'm certain Baeloc will have some of his Architects keeping watch, so there's no way we can take a flight from there. And we have to get out of the country. I think we should drive southeast until we hit Riyadh." She dragged her finger quite a distance along the map and tapped on the black star next to Riyadh, the capital of Saudi Arabia.

Trendon snagged the map, found the mile distance graph on the lower left-hand corner, and measured the mileage between Tabuk and Riyadh with his thumb and forefinger. "That's like fifteen hours away!" He kicked one of the boxes. "Why there?"

"Well, it's not west. And west is where Baeloc is," Paulo said.

"Thank you." Ashleigh beamed. "And Riyadh is heavily populated. There are airports and a United States embassy. We can get back to the States, get you guys home, and then Paulo and I can figure things out from there. We'll find a smart location to hide the artifact and wait this thing out."

Though he had yet to stop glowering, I could see a change coming over Trendon. Ashleigh's words started to sound good to him. I thought about the many great things Riyadh had to offer. The more people there were, the better chance we had of blending in, and I couldn't help but agree with Ashleigh on the dangers of the Tabuk airport. Plus, there was something comforting about the words "United States embassy" and "going home." I wanted my parents beside me. They could make things better. Safer. Maybe I could forget about everything and just let Ashleigh and the rest of the Society of the Seraphic Scroll handle what to do with the artifacts while I enjoyed the rest of my summer. As quickly as those comforting thoughts entered my mind, I dismissed them. My parents couldn't make things safer. No one could. Not while the three Weapons of Might existed. Baeloc would come and find me no matter where we went, and going home would only endanger the people I loved most. So as great as Ashleigh made Riyadh sound from her explanation, it wasn't enough to convince me. Since discovering Jasher was still alive, I continued to think about him and, more important, about the library.

"I think we should go back to the monastery," I whispered.

Ashleigh smiled but she looked almost in pain, which made her slightly unattractive. It was a good look for her. "Go back to the monastery? Is that your brilliant plan?"

"Yes, it is." I folded my arms defiantly. "Would you like to know why?"

"Oh man." Trendon closed his mouth and softly shook his head. Was he disappointed in my suggestion too?

"It's the best place to go," I said, defending my choice. "Jasher offered us his help, and we need to use the library to research what to do next."

Ashleigh paused before visibly controlling an outburst. "No, Amber, we're not going back there. That's idiotic. For starters, that's west, and if by some miracle we manage to get through the Architects unspotted, how are we supposed to travel to the monastery? By boat? We don't have the connections like your friend Jasher. There's no airport and it would take us two or three days to go around the Gulf of Aqaba if we drove. Stop being immature and start using that brain of yours to help us!"

"I am using my brain! If we keep running, we'll get caught. We need to figure out how to destroy the Wrath and we can't do that on the run." When Ashleigh persisted in shaking her head, I felt my skin flush with anger. "I'll go without you. You don't have to be my escort."

"Oh no. I'm not letting you take that artifact out of here. And look around, Amber. Whoever has the gun is in charge."

Ashleigh had to be the most annoying person I had ever worked with and I had met some real characters as of late. Gritting my teeth, I did my best to keep calm. "Fine. You leave me with no choice. I'll just summon my friends, the Shomehr, and let them eat you, and then I'll take your gun."

Though her eyes quivered with rage, she looked incapable of a response. From the window, Paulo snickered. "What are you laughing at?" she snapped.

Paulo shrugged. "I'd listen to her if I were you. Tem . . . I mean my father tells me Amber is not one to be messed with."

Ashleigh's left eyelid twitched. "So you're siding with her now?"

"I was always on her side and you should do the same. There's a reason why she's here, and I don't believe it's only because of her ability to control the monsters." Paulo left the window and knelt next to me beside the bed. "If she thinks we need to use the library, then I believe we should go there. It seems like a good reason to risk it."

"That's not the reason," Trendon said.

"What are you talking about?" I asked warily. He had been quietly watching the argument unfold between Ashleigh and me. Something bothered him, making it difficult for him to look me in the eye.

"Amber has had a crush on Joseph for as long as I can remember. She's in love with him." Still refusing to make eye contact, Trendon fidgeted with his shoelace.

I felt like laughing, but what escaped my mouth sounded more like a bird screeching. "Are you serious? Is that what you really think?" How could Trendon say those things? He didn't know how I truly felt about Joseph and I thought he sided with me. "I don't . . . um . . . have a crush on Joseph."

"Come on." Trendon finally looked up from the floor. "I saw the way you changed when Joseph came into the cave."

"I was shocked to see him! So were you!" I couldn't keep myself from shouting.

"Yeah, but I didn't bat my eyes at him. At least I hope I didn't." He reared back when he noticed me baring my teeth. "Anyway, she thinks he's some amazing guy, but I can't understand why. All he's done is cause trouble and basically bring about the beginning of the end with these artifacts. The dude's evil."

My jaw practically unhinged with shock. "He's not evil." My eyes moved to Paulo and Ashleigh, who were tight-lipped. "Joseph has made some bad choices, but he's not evil, and I think he still wants to help us. But I don't even care about him. That's not why I want to go back to the monastery at all." Of all the statements made, I felt positive that one was true. How could I jeopardize everyone I cared about to pursue a crush that didn't exist? "Trendon, I don't love him. I never did. Okay, maybe I liked him, but . . . that all changed when the real Joseph showed up. And I haven't talked to him in forever." I pursed my lips together. "I didn't know you felt this way about him. Why didn't you say something to me before?"

"It's no big deal. What do I care? You can like whoever you want, but if that's the only reason why we're heading back to the monastery, you can count me out." Gathering up the pizza boxes in his arms, Trendon stood and headed for the door. "I'm just going to throw these away." Trendon left me speechless on the hotel bed as he shut the door behind him.

16

Outside, a lone dog barked in the distance, its throaty voice echoing as I descended the stairs to the bottom level in search of Trendon. More than a half hour had passed since he left the room to take out the trash, and I began to worry about him. Maybe he needed his space or some alone time to think about things, but it was too dangerous to be outside in the open, especially with the threat of the Architects in the area. Ashleigh and Paulo stayed behind in the room, but the plan was to leave as soon as I brought Trendon back.

Exiting the stairs, I stepped into the parking lot and cast a cautious glance toward the check-in office. Beyond the window, fluorescent light lit up the small room where a few leafy ferns grew from pots next to the door and a flat-screen television hung from a wall mount in the corner. A young man, possibly in his early twenties, leaned across the counter on his elbows watching the television as images from the hospital fire flashed across the screen. I craned my neck to see if possibly Trendon could have been sitting in one of the cushioned chairs in the lobby, but it looked empty. A few cars down from the stairwell, right across from the office, an older man wearing a pale blue sport coat stood leaning with his back against a yellow pickup truck as he talked on his cell phone. Occasionally, he would use an English word intermixed with his Arabic. He noticed me creeping along the sidewalk and narrowed his eyes suspiciously as he lowered his conversation.

"Sorry," I said timidly.

The entrance to the hotel parking lot connected with a busy road, where all sorts of vehicles zoomed past the opening. On the opposite side of the road, a spacious stretch of desert spanned for miles. Goats grazed upon the meager offering of plants jutting up from the sand and in the distance, dozens of motorized oil pump jacks bobbed up and down. I had seen pump jacks in California, like odd-shaped metal birds pecking at the ground, while the machine extracted oil from deep below. The desert looked desolate. Empty. I didn't remember seeing any places for someone to walk next to the road and some of those drivers drove recklessly. I also couldn't recall any restaurants close by, which would be the only reason I could see Trendon risking a walk at night.

Deciding to look elsewhere, I turned around and faced a block of other hotel complexes rising up to the rear beyond the parking lot opposite of the road to the south. A few of them stood more than five or six stories tall and had outdoor swimming pools. A chain-link fence surrounded the parking lot, but a small opening led into an alley in between two of the rear hotels. At the end of the alley I could see the neon lights of what looked like a grocery store across the road.

Bingo. There would be snacks there. Drinks, candy, chips. The perfect hideout for my best friend. Picking up the pace, I crossed the parking lot and cautiously stepped through the fence into the alley. No exterior lights lit the narrow walkway and I could barely make out a dumpster standing about halfway between the parking lot and the road ahead. On the opposite side of the dumpster, steps lead up to a door in one of the buildings. Perhaps a service entrance for hotel employees. I imagined anyone could easily slip into that alley unnoticed. If Trendon would hesitate stepping onto a busy road at night in search of food, would he really enter a dark, creepy alley? Swallowing, I whispered, trying to make my voice carry. "Trendon, are you in there?"

No one answered, and I contemplated going to our hotel room to have Paulo join the search. From the neighboring swimming pool arose the sound of children giggling and splashing. Just a normal night for them. Perhaps a vacation.

"Don't be stupid," I told myself. "No one's in there."

I stepped into the alley, hugging my arms, and passed briskly into the darkness. Keeping my eyes glued to the neon sign of the grocery store as my guide, I stepped one foot in front of the other, not even slowing when my shoes splashed through a cool puddle of water. Only when I reached the dumpster at the halfway point through the alley did I stop.

Bending down, I strained my eyes to see if anyone could've been hiding beneath it. Behind me, the mystery dog continued to bark for some unknown reason. The distant sound of its call made me feel very much alone. What was I doing walking through a dark alley in Saudi Arabia?

Had I lost my mind? The dumpster looked clear, but as I straightened and readied to run for the store, an uncomfortable prickling traveled across my shoulders.

"Trendon?" I asked again, this time louder than before. "Are you here?"

The door up the small flight of steps burst open and I didn't have time to turn and see who came out of it, as a clammy hand covered my mouth and someone dragged me up the stairs.

I screamed into the palm, but my voice stifled from the pressure. Kicking and flailing about, trying to free myself from the strong limbs dragging me backwards, I grabbed hold of an arm and felt thick, wet fur beneath my fingers. The door slammed closed, latched shut, thrusting me into complete blackness.

The hand covering my mouth released me, and I gasped for breath as my legs gave out and I fell to the floor.

You must be quiet now, Amber. The voice of the Shomehr rang out in my mind.

I smelled them and could sense at least one of them less than a few feet from where I lay. Fingers shaking, I furiously tried to wipe the musty, sour taste off my mouth. The Shomehr reeked of the smell of wet animal. Something else tingled in the air, like the humid moisture in a sauna. I imagined the tell-tale mist of the Shomehr clinging to its face, preventing all from seeing its true likeness, now gathering around me in a supernatural fog.

"What do you want with me?" I demanded, finding a way to talk. From the far corner of the room, I heard the sound of a muffled voice, struggling to speak. "Who is that?"

Not out loud. Stay quiet now, the Shomehr insisted.

Regulating my breathing, I sat up and tried to adjust my eyes to the dark room.

Where am I? I asked in my mind.

At the moment, out of danger. But only just.

What does that mean?

It means you are safe for now, but you must listen to us closely. Do exactly as we say.

Why are you doing this? In Syria, one of the creatures came to my room and beckoned me to follow it out of Baeloc's fortress and even dragged me under a river to search for the artifact. But as terrifying as that was, this felt much worse. I hadn't called for the monsters to come to my side. What made them act on their own? *You can't just grab me like that! I don't like it! I don't want you touching me. Ever!*

We are trying to keep you out of harm, they reasoned.

Out of harm? How was I in danger?

But they didn't offer the explanation. From just outside the door in the alley, the distinct sound of footsteps ascended the stairs and I heard the soft tapping of a finger against the door.

"Amber, honey, are you in there?"

A whimper caught in my throat. Covering my mouth with my hand, I quietly slid away from the door.

"Can you let me in?" Somehow Dorothy had found me. The knob jiggled and once again four taps of her finger announced her desire to enter. "Why don't you answer me? I know you're close."

What do we do? I asked, pleading with the creatures for help.

Do nothing. Stay quiet. If fate will have it, this shall pass.

That was their instruction? Sit there and be quiet while the psycho formally known as Dorothy tried to break in?

I couldn't see anything in the pitch-black room and I had no way of knowing if another way out existed. Standing, I readied my legs to bolt through the door, should she find a way to open it. Maybe I could knock her down. Surprise was pretty much my only option.

"Am . . . ber?" she sang my name with chilling melody. "You need not fear me. I would never hurt you . . . hmmm." She sounded amused as she continued, "Or Trendon. I love you both. We've been through so much together."

I grabbed my arms to keep them from shaking.

"I'm still alone, but soon Baeloc will join me when I'm ready for him. Once the transformation is complete, the artifact will unite with him completely. Just like you and the Source. But I won't let him harm you. I promise." She paused long enough to jiggle the doorknob and test the lock. She, however, did not break it open. "This must be so confusing for you, but it has never been more clear to me." She then hummed some unknown tune and when she spoke again, it took all my willpower not to scream out. "Will you help me one last time?" Her voice changed into something else, something sinister. A man's voice— deep, rough. Backing away from the door, I stepped into an enormous warm body behind me and the Shomehr steadied my shoulders with its claws. Standing that close, I could feel its breath dampening my neck, but I didn't want to move away from it. I felt security from the creature, and suddenly, a new thought entered my mind. I had seen what the Shomehr could do when I commanded them. They could keep Dorothy away from me or even better, they could grab her and we could find out what had happened to her.

Can you capture her? I asked. *And take her back to my hotel room?*

Before I finished my second question, I knew what their answer would be.

We cannot touch the Finisher.

The Finisher? What did that mean? From the way they spoke, I could sense them bristling with fear. I didn't ask them outright, but I questioned what would happen to them if they touched Dorothy. If the creatures refused to obey my order because it involved laying their hands upon Dorothy, what would happen if she touched me?

"Very well, Amber." Dorothy's voice returned to its normal pitch. "I won't be far from you, but I'll give you time to decide on your own." The footsteps on the stairs announced her departure and after a minute of silently waiting, I felt capable of breathing normal again.

17

I s it safe for me to go out there now?" I asked after several minutes.

It is safe now.

"You said you couldn't touch the Finisher. What did you mean by that?"

Dorothy has power to take any life she chooses, simply by touching them. We are no different and would share the same fate as you.

Once again I heard someone else struggling to talk in the room but being prevented. "Who is that? Who else is in here?" I heard that mumbling when I first entered the room and now I felt certain the Shomehr had brought along company.

We kept him safe, the Shomehr explained.

I heard a deep intake of air and then, "Worst day of my life!" Trendon blurted.

"You're here?" I felt along in the darkness and caught hold of his shirt collar. Pulling him close, I squeezed him in my arms. "How did you get here?"

"Same as you." Trendon stood rigid and unwelcoming.

"I was just minding my own business, heading over for some snacks, and the next thing I know, I'm being manhandled by the Chupacabra!"

"Shh! Don't insult them," I warned. "They saved our lives." I felt Trendon shrug, but he didn't disagree. "Can we go now?" I asked the Shomehr.

She will follow you. She knows you're here and will attack soon. Perhaps within the hour. If you leave, you must go far from this place, but it won't last forever. Eventually, she will find you.

"Then what do we do? We can't just stay here. Should we go back to the monastery in St. Catherine?"

There's not a place she won't find you now that she's become the Finisher.

"What are they saying?" Trendon asked. "Remember? I can't read their minds like you."

I blew a strand of hair out of my eyes. "Basically, Dorothy is going to find us no matter what. We're marked. Well . . . I guess I'm marked and the artifact sends off some sort of signal. We can't go anywhere without her being able to track us." I let go of Trendon and felt around once again in the darkness. Sensing my searching, the creatures moved out of the way as I brushed past.

"What are you doing now?" Trendon asked.

"I'm looking for a light switch."

"Don't turn on the lights!" His voice carried through the room and I promptly shushed him. "Don't turn on the lights," he repeated in a more measured tone.

"Why not? It's too dark." I found the switch but waited to flick on the light.

"I'd rather it be dark then have to see these things. No offense to them, but they creep me out."

They creeped me out too. Following Trendon's advice, I left the lights off.

"Also, I don't think we should walk out the door until we know exactly what we're going to do," Trendon added. "If she's out there and she's coming for us, she probably already knows where we're staying."

Had Dorothy already paid a visit to Paulo and Ashleigh? "We should go there then and warn the others. We'll be able to put some distance between us and her if we drive back to the monastery."

"You still want to go there, huh?"

"I do, but not for the reason you said. I don't care about Joseph that way. Not anymore, and I think you owe it to me to trust me on that." I imagined Trendon squirming, trying to think of the snarkiest remark he could muster, but knowing full well I was right.

"Fair enough," he eventually conceded.

"There's something I haven't told anyone yet—something I think is important for us to look for. I found some hieroglyphs under the lid of the tomb from the cave. Ashleigh and Jackson didn't see them and I didn't have time to tell anyone about them yet. I'm not sure, but I think they have something to do with the skeleton in the tomb and I'm guessing with the final artifact as well."

"What kind of symbols were they?"

Closing my eyes, I sorted through my memories. "There were seven of them. There was a hawk, an eye, another hawk, a sparrow, a squiggly line, another hawk, and a twisted rope. Maybe the line means water or a staircase or something like that. They were very small and covered in dust."

A soft glow appeared across the room as Trendon powered up his iPhone. The glow concentrated around his hand and waist, but gave off just enough light where I could make out the shadowy outline of the two creatures standing farther away from us, next to the wall. I watched them as Trendon worked and a thought of werewolves entered my mind. Why did I have to think of that? The Shomehr were difficult enough to look at without labeling them as werewolves. I began to wonder what manner of creature they truly were. Did they exist before the flood? Were they regular animals roaming about or did they just appear to guard the Tebah Stick? And if that were true, who sent them? How did they come to be?

They walked upright, they were covered in thick fur like an animal, but they had far greater intelligence than any animal I had ever known about. Though the mist always cloaked their faces, making it impossible to see their true image, I recalled the time I watched them floating in the Orontes river in Syria. The moonlight almost illuminated them and the mist pulled away just long enough for me to notice the human-like quality of their faces.

You feel threatened by us. The Shomehr spoke in my mind, startling me. Could they understand my thoughts whenever they wanted?

No, I don't. I don't feel that way at all, I answered. *You saved us.*

Yet you think us evil.

Not evil. Different. Honestly, I don't know what your intentions are or why you're here. Why you continue to help me.

We follow our master. That has always been our task. We shall never harm you.

But that wouldn't have been the case had I not touched the Tebah Stick first. I knew I was nothing special. It was all just a matter of coincidence. Had Trendon or Dorothy been the one to take hold of the Tebah Stick in the Philippines, they would've earned the Shomehr's allegiance instead of me. What I wouldn't give to have let someone else be the one with the burden of controlling them. Someone who understood what needed to be done and could make the tough decisions to ensure the safety of everyone that mattered. Being the hero never suited me. That type of responsibility fit better with someone like Dorothy or Temel.

"Okay, you still there?" Trendon held up his phone and the light shone across my face. "Thought you fell asleep or something."

"I'm here. What did you find?" Standing next to him, I peered down at the small screen.

"Would you recognize the symbols if you saw them?" he asked.

"Yes," I answered without hesitation.

Trendon then showed me the web page with the ancient Egyptian alphabet he used to prove Ashleigh wrong. Several different symbols appeared on a colorful screen. "It's possible the symbols you saw represented words, but I thought we'd start with the alphabet. Recognize any of them? That one there looks kinda like a twisted rope." He pointed to the letter *H*.

"That's it. And there are the others!" My voice carried a hint of excitement as we searched the screen. It took us only a few seconds to find all seven symbols and spell out their meaning. The hawk stood for *A*, the eye for *R*, the sparrow a *U*, the squiggly line an *N*, and the twisted rope an *H*.

"ARAUNAH. The word is *Araunah*," I whispered.

"Does it mean anything to you?" Trendon opened another browser window on his phone and navigated to Google.

Dorothy had never mentioned it in school or I would've remembered. Most memories from her class stuck around permanently in my mind and *Araunah* would've been no different. But I had no recollection of it.

"Doesn't look like there's much online about it," I said as Trendon scrolled through the pages.

"Yep, and you can't just trust any of these sources. A lot of them don't know what they're talking about."

"Look it up in the Bible," I suggested. "The Old Testament search."

Trendon nodded and found an online version of the King James Bible. After typing "Araunah" in the search field, nine possible hits appeared on the screen, all of them found in the Second book of Samuel.

"Araunah the Jebusite," Trendon said, but then fell silent as we read the verses.

Only one Araunah existed in the Bible, and all the verses dealt with one specific story. Araunah was a simple farmer who sold his property to King David. David then built an altar on the land. In the sixteenth verse in the twenty-fourth chapter of Samuel, we discovered a significant link.

And God sent an angel unto Jerusalem to destroy it: and as he was destroying, the Lord beheld, and he repented him of the evil, and said to the angel that destroyed, It is enough, stay now thine hand. *And the angel of the Lord stood by the threshingfloor of Araunah the Jebusite.*

"What's a threshingfloor?" Trendon opened another browser, researched the word *threshingfloor*, and brought up an image of a flat circular piece of concrete on which farmers laid their grain upon to thresh and remove the husks.

I reread the words in the sixteenth verse. "David built an altar on the land he purchased and that's where the Destroying Angel rested. Next to Araunah the Jebusite." The last words hung in the air and a cold hollowness filled my chest.

With nimble fingers, Trendon highlighted *Araunah* on his phone and checked it against an online encyclopedia. He typed in the word *Egypt* after the name, but that resulted in zero matches. Next, he tried tomb. Again nothing.

"Help me out here," he asked.

"Um . . . try Mount Sinai."

He did, but nothing came up.

"Are you misspelling the name?" I asked.

Trendon scoffed. "Please give me a little credit. I am an honor student after all."

"Try Moses, or Wrath, or Finisher."

"Finisher? That's a weird one."

"Just try it."

Again, like the other searches, all of my suggestions came up with zero matches. "Weird. Check this out. According to this site, Araunah also went by another name. Ornan the Jebusite. There's the exact same story in the first book of Chronicles."

As I read in Chronicles, the story unfolded identically

to the one in second Samuel, only with Araunah's name changed to Ornan.

"Same guy. Same story," Trendon said. "I wonder why they wrote it again?"

"That's not that strange. The Bible has multiple retellings of stories."

"Yeah, I guess, but I'm not finding anything of value with this Araunah guy. Are you sure you remembered the symbols correctly?"

Reworking the images in my mind, I saw them reappear on the bottom of the lid as I dusted them clean. I then remembered the other inscriptions above the skeleton's head. "Try Moriah," I whispered.

This time, Trendon found a match in Second Chronicles, chapter three, verse one.

Then Solomon began to build the house of the Lord at Jerusalem in mount Moriah, where the Lord appeared unto David his father, in the place that David had prepared in the threshing floor of Ornan the Jebusite.

"Araunah was from Moriah!" I felt an excited chill. "Just like it said in the tomb."

"Where's Moriah?" Trendon scrunched his nose.

"Look it up."

We soon discovered Mount Moriah was also named the Temple Mount located in Jerusalem, the original location of the Jebusite fortress, but more important, the place where Abraham almost offered his son, Isaac, as a sacrifice.

"But Jerusalem is five hundred miles away from Mount Catherine. How did Araunah or Ornan or whatever you want to call him end up in Egypt?"

"I don't know, but I think it's important to find out. The

Bible describes Araunah as not a wealthy man. Just someone who David bought land from. That would explain
why Jackson was so confused by the skeleton. He wasn't
mummified. He didn't have any belongings."

"Just that bag of silver."

"Yet he was there under the mountain buried with the
artifact. Araunah had to be someone of importance. What
about that translation?" I squinted and pulled the words
off Dorothy's page from my memory. " 'Thus allowing the
final protector time to make certain no unsanctified hand
unleashed the Fury of Har Megiddon.' What if Araunah
was the final protector?"

He wasn't someone I would immediately link with the
Weapons of Might like Noah or Elijah or even Moses, but
we found him holding the final artifact. A chilling thought
struck me. If the final protector was dead and rotted, did
that mean no one could stop Dorothy from unleashing
Armageddon?

The Finisher's Fury. I heard the Shomehr mutter in mind.
It sounded so clear, they could've spoken it out loud, and it
wouldn't have been any different. Glancing in their direction, though unable to see them because of the darkness, I
knew they watched us intently.

"Trendon, earlier the Shomehr told me the artifact rests
within Dorothy. They called her the 'Finisher.' I don't
know what that means exactly, but it kind of makes me
think she has the ability to finish . . . things. She'll finish
the work Baeloc started with the Weapons of Might, but
she could also finish people."

"Finish people?"

"Yeah. Like the Destroying Angel." I turned toward the

door and my thoughts immediately switched to Paulo and Ashleigh in the hotel. So much time had passed since I left to look for Trendon and they would no doubt be searching for us. If they happened to come across Dorothy while they were looking . . . "We have to go now! We have to warn the others!"

"Whoa, whoa, whoa!" Trendon grabbed my arm as I headed for the door. "If this is real and Dorothy can kill us just by touching us, we can't just go running out there without a plan."

"I don't think she'll do that to us."

"Then she wouldn't do it to the others either," Trendon reasoned.

I hesitated as I considered his suggestion. "Yeah, but Ashleigh is dangerous. She has a gun and she's already ticked off at Dorothy. I think she'll do something stupid if we don't get to her first and stop her. If she tries to shoot Dorothy or use force, I think both Ashleigh and Paulo could get killed."

"What's to stop Dorothy from doing the same thing to us?"

"She wouldn't kill us."

"She's not herself anymore. And don't you remember what she did to Cabarles?"

"That was different. I don't think she meant for him to die."

"Right. Because falling off a building is a normal thing to do nowadays."

I broke free and reached the door. The two Shomehr still stood by the far wall and I could see their outline as they waited for my command. "Dorothy could've easily broken in here earlier and killed us both, but she didn't. And it's like you said," I continued, "she threw a grown man out a window from across the room and yet a brass doorknob and a cheap lock kept her away from us. She had her chance, but she didn't come in."

"That's because we have two Sasquatch bodyguards."

"No, you don't understand. I told the Shomehr to grab her. To capture her so that we could try to figure out how to get her back, and they wouldn't do it. They were afraid to touch her. They knew if they put their hands on her they would die. Dorothy must know that too. The artifact inside of her is driving her actions, so she would have to know she had the power to do whatever she wanted." Breathing from the excitement, I recalled what Dorothy told me through the door. About Baeloc and how he had yet to fully master the power of the artifact. Was that some sort of clue I was supposed to pick up on? Why would she give us that information? I turned once more and stared in the direction of the Shomehr. "Could you look out for her and let us know if she gets close?" I asked them.

"Now that's a brilliant idea!" Trendon agreed.

If that is your command, we will obey. But we shall not come close to her.

"Okay, they'll do it. They'll watch our backs while we go get the others."

"And then we head back to the monastery?" Trendon said.

"Yep. Araunah the Jebusite is hiding something back there. I just know it. It might be something we overlooked in the tomb or in the library, but it's the only thing we've got going for us right now, and we have to find out why he traveled so far from his home to die in that cave."

Turning the knob, I shoved the door open a crack. Though the alley wasn't lit by any streetlights, my vision improved drastically than from when we were inside the dark room. Pushing the door open wide, I crept out onto the steps and scanned both directions for any sign of Dorothy. When I couldn't see her, I dropped to the ground and Trendon followed.

18

The Architects swarmed the hotel parking lot. They were everywhere—guarding the hotel lobby, patrolling all three floors, moving in and out of rooms, and flashing lights into car windows. Armed with machine guns and radios, the constant chatter of their voices filled the air reminding me of the sound the cicada insects made in West Virginia. A constant *ch-ch-ch-ch-ch* sound rising in volume. I watched them from the edge of the alley, horrified of what they might be doing to Paulo or Ashleigh at that very instant. How would they question them? Would it involve torture?

Baeloc stood by the parking lot entrance, staring at the passing cars; his bald head gleamed in the glow from an overhead street light. Next to him, two police officers in light tan uniforms pointed to a map and signaled to another group being pulled behind by enormous dogs on leashes. It looked like the beginning of a manhunt.

"We knew Baeloc had connections," Trendon whispered. "I wonder if he owns all the police or just a small squad of them here in Saudi Arabia."

I didn't want to think about it. My eyes kept returning to the open door of our hotel room. A few Architects walked out and leaned over the balcony, barking into their radios. Scanning the parking lot, I didn't see Paulo or Ashleigh out there. I looked once again at Baeloc, still standing by the entrance and realized he wasn't holding the case containing the Tebah Stick, which meant he hadn't found it yet.

A quick flash of light turned my attention to the back of the hotel where I saw something flickering inside a massive bush next to the rear entrance. Paulo peered through the branches, and behind him, Ashleigh clicked her flashlight on and off in short bursts.

"Over there!" I squeezed Trendon's arm and pointed to the bush. Ashleigh continued to turn her light on and off.

"Can they see us?" Trendon asked.

"I think they're trying to signal us."

The Architects hadn't noticed their position yet, but I didn't dare step out of the alley to acknowledge them. Trendon discreetly flashed his phone in their direction and Ashleigh extinguished her light.

"Now that we've made contact, what do we do next?" Trendon asked, pocketing his phone. "That's too far to go creeping across the parking lot."

I bit my lip in concentration. At the front of the hotel, the police officers with their K-9 units eagerly dragging them along began walking toward the opposite end.

"Those dogs will catch them! We have to help them somehow!"

"What do you suggest we do? Maybe I could SOS them with my phone. I think there's an app for that."

"Don't do anything that would bring the dogs over here. We need a distraction."

"I'm all ears." Trendon stared at me, eyes wide.

"Why do I always have to think this stuff up?" I glared back at him.

"Because you're good at it."

"Fine. The parking lot's filled with cars. We could sneak along and try to set off some alarms to draw their attention away from Paulo and Ashleigh."

Trendon chuckled. "That's the stupidest idea ever! Where the heck are we gonna go after we set off the alarms? Can you outrun a German shepherd?"

I groaned. "We have to do something!"

A total of three K-9 units spanned out, searching every area of the lot. They sniffed beneath cars and in flower beds. And then something caught their attention as the dogs' heads perked up and began to growl, sending off an alert, but they weren't growling in our direction. They had their noses pointed upward, toward the higher floors of the hotel. At least a dozen Architects filed out of the rooms on the second and third floors and spread out along the balconies, turning their attention to the roof.

"What's going on?" I asked. "What are they looking at?"

It happened fast and without warning.

A dark blur leaped from the roof and landed in the middle of the Architects on the third floor. Gunshots exploded and then screaming. One of the Shomehr slashed his way through the group, tossing a few of them over the edge. The dogs' barking turned into wild yelping and whining as they tried to free themselves from their masters holding them back. Most of the Architects on the lower levels just stared dumbfounded at the scene, unsure of where to aim their guns.

Baeloc raced away from the entrance, his hands brightening as fire blazed from his fingertips and shot out toward the monster, engulfing it in flames. Then the awful moaning of the Shomehr filled my ears, overpowering the sound of gunshots and howling dogs. I had no way of knowing if everyone else could hear the sound or if only I could hear it in my mind. The Shomehr scrambled up the wall, grasping hold of the overhead awning, and pulled its burned body back onto the roof.

Some of the Architects on the third floor still moved somewhat, alive for now. Baeloc snarled and pointed to them, instructing the others on the ground level to rush to their aid. Then the other Shomehr stepped out of the lobby, its face obscured by the unnatural mist, and lashed out with its claws. One of the Architects yelled a warning as the Shomehr dragged him back into the lobby, but the sound of the man's screaming snuffed out completely.

"Let's go!" Trendon grabbed my arm, and without thinking, we raced across the parking lot unnoticed and hopped behind the bush with Paulo and Ashleigh.

"What is making all that noise?" Paulo asked, keeping his eyes glued to the road through a space in the bush. Next to him on the ground, I saw the metal case containing the Tebah Stick, and I closed my eyes in relief.

"The Shomehr are attacking the Architects, but Baeloc burned one of them. Is it dying, Amber?" Trendon asked.

I searched my thoughts and sensed the pain the creature felt, but it wasn't dead or dying. It was angry and preparing to strike again.

"It's still alive," I said.

"I've never seen anything like it. Not even in a movie. That thing jumped off the roof and started slicing up everyone. Then the other stepped out of the lobby like a scene from *Friday the 13th*. It was absolute chaos!" Trendon rambled. "Nice job on the distraction, though." He gave me a thumbs-up. "That's better than what I could've come up with."

"I didn't do that. That wasn't me."

"Really?" Trendon asked.

I shook my head, but doubt took hold of my thoughts. I had just been thinking we needed a way to distract the Architects when the Shomehr sprung from the shadows. Were they acting out my wishes without me commanding them? Once again, I allowed my mind to connect with the Shomehr. The one on the roof slid to the edge of the front awning and crouched ready to spring upon a group of Architects. The one inside the lobby hid behind the counter, a body lying at its feet. I wondered about the hotel employee I had seen earlier watching television. Had the Shomehr attacked him too?

Don't kill anymore, I spoke to the Shomehr in my mind.

You asked us to protect you, they answered. *They will show you no mercy.*

I don't care. I don't want you killing anyone unless I tell you to.

If they attack us, we'll have no choice but to defend ourselves.

I clenched my jaw together. *Okay, I understand that, but only if you have no other choice.*

More rapid gunshots fired from the front of the hotel parking lot. The guttural shouting of Architects filled the air.

"We need to hit the road." Trendon's voice brought me back to reality as he pointed to one of the cars in the parking lot. "I can totally hot-wire that car now."

"Are you crazy?" Ashleigh held her gun next to her cheek, finger on the trigger, ready to point at anyone who came close to the bush. "They're everywhere. And they have the police and the military with them too. There's no back entrance to this place."

"They have the military?" Trendon asked in disbelief.

"Did you not see the soldiers?" Paulo knelt beside me. "Or the helicopter?"

"Shut up!" Reaching over, Trendon yanked Paulo's binoculars off his waist and stuck his head out the side of the bush. "Where did they get that chopper?" He pointed to a spot in the desert just beyond the highway where the rotating blade of a black helicopter distorted the sky behind it.

"Lucky we heard it," Paulo said. "We would've been still in the room when the Architects attacked."

"How does Baeloc have all that on his side? Don't they know what he plans to do with the artifacts?" I nervously gnawed on my fingernails. I felt hot and red in the face, despite the cool breeze of the desert air.

"Of course they don't know. Baeloc has money and power and that's enough to fuel corruption. I wouldn't be surprised if he owned half the city of Tabuk," Ashleigh said.

"So we'll probably have to ram through some dudes to get out of here," Trendon said. "I'm cool with that."

"You're not listening. The roads are blocked. There are police vehicles, and they've set up a barricade right in the middle of the highway. We can't go that way. And if we all go together in one car, we're as good as dead. We need to split up. Two of us should take the artifact far from here. Try to hide it somewhere they wouldn't think to look."

"We were split up," Trendon said. "And then you called us all back together."

"We only wanted to make sure you didn't go looking for us in the room," Paulo explained. "Ashleigh is right. If we go together, it gives them one target. If we split up, we make it harder."

"Fine. You two take that gold minivan right there and Amber and I will hijack that gray pickup truck. I have my phone, so you can call me whenever you're clear of the Architects and then we can meet up somewhere safe." Trendon patted his pants pocket.

"You two shouldn't go together. You have the least amount of experience. Trendon and I will take the artifact and go on foot back down that alley you came from. Paulo will take Amber," Ashleigh said. "Maybe lay low here until there's a break in the chaos and then try to work your way out onto the main road. There could be just enough commotion to allow you to slip past the barricade. Hitchhike if you have to. Just don't get spotted by anyone of authority."

"I'm not leaving her with Pablo. No offense, buddy, but I'm the only one I trust to keep her safe." Trendon folded his arms defiantly.

"And I'm not letting the Tebah Stick out of my sight," I added. I felt absolute accountability for the artifact and I didn't trust Ashleigh to make the right decisions when it came to protecting it.

"You guys aren't thinking clearly!" Ashleigh lowered

her gun and wiped her eyes in frustration. "Our lives mean nothing. Please, Amber, listen to reason!"

I ignored her pleading as something Dorothy told me reappeared in my memory. I thought about Baeloc standing at the opening, wielding the fire from his hands as if it no longer required any of his concentration. Dorothy said the transformation was complete. That the artifact had transferred its essence to Baeloc just as it had done with me. She mentioned the Source. The Tebah Stick. Why did she say that? If Baeloc now had Elijah's Fire in his possession, why wasn't he using it to call up the fire? These questions clouded my mind, blocking out the argument between Trendon and Ashleigh, as I stared at the case by Paulo's feet. Bending over, I undid the combination locks on the case, and the brass hinges popped open.

"Amber?" I faintly heard Paulo ask, but I didn't answer him. I needed to see something. To either put my mind at ease or confirm my worst fears.

The confirmation came immediately as I raised the lid of the container and saw the pile of ash resting in the center; the Tebah Stick had disintegrated into useless dust. As I ran my fingers through the pile, watching it crumble and spread, I realized we no longer needed to split up. The artifact was gone.

19

Ashleigh's face contorted with confusion. "I don't understand," she muttered, staring at the scattered dust. "How can it be gone?"

"It's just like the Wrath," I said. "That artifact, however, transferred its essence much quicker than this one though. Now all Dorothy has to do is connect with Baeloc and me and that's it. Together, we'll bring about the end of the world." Closing the lid and snapping the latches back in place, I scooted the container away on the ground. I then hugged my arms, suddenly feeling cold.

"You're speaking gibberish." Trendon snapped his fingers in front of my face. "Where did it transfer its essence?" He swallowed, appearing to comprehend. "Into you?"

"Where else?" I asked. "Don't you get it? Even if you hadn't dropped the artifact back at the hospital, Trendon, it wouldn't have mattered. I'm positive Baeloc's case is holding another pile of ash where Elijah's Fire had been. That's because Baeloc absorbed it. Dorothy absorbed the Wrath and now the same thing happened to me. Honestly, if you think about it, I'm lucky the Tebah Stick took as long as it did to transfer."

I should've recognized the change earlier. How I so easily connected with the Shomehr. How they followed my inner thoughts before I could even attempt to utter them out loud. I had become the final Weapon of Might.

"Okay." Trendon squared his shoulders. "Let's say you're right. You've somehow absorbed the artifact. Why didn't it happen to Noah or Elijah?"

Trendon definitely made a valid point, but my thoughts cleared. "We had all of the Weapons with us when we dug up the Wrath. I think that has something to do with it. We set things in motion. Started the linking between the three artifacts. Noah and Elijah never crossed paths in their lives, and because of that, they could use their weapons for a single purpose." It made sense. Everyone stared at me, the gravity of the situation finally sinking in. The ash inside the container provided the strongest evidence. Once again, my thoughts turned to the monastery. Araunah's tomb perhaps held the only answers to our predicament, but now we were hours away.

"Why did we leave the monastery?" I asked to no one in particular. "We could've stayed there and maybe found the answer."

"We were being attacked by the Architects," Ashleigh explained, her voice soft and controlled. "We had no choice."

"We had a choice, but our first reaction was to run away, which was the worst thing we could have done. We could've stayed hidden so we could research and discover a way to destroy the Weapons, but now the monastery could be on the other side of the planet and it would feel the same."

Trendon shook his head. "I'm going to disagree with you. Dorothy's stomping around out there like a crazed lunatic and so is Baeloc. They were going to become these things regardless, and if we would've stayed at the monastery, we would have had to deal with them eventually. Let's stop feeling sorry for ourselves and get you out of here. I say we all head for the alley and then go—"

"Go where?" I interrupted him. "Baeloc's closed the roads. He has roadblocks set up."

"We could hide in one of the other hotels," Ashleigh suggested. "Try to wait this out."

I gave her a "you're pathetic" look. "And how long do you think that will last? Dorothy will find me. She probably already knows where I am."

Trendon's eyes widened and his head snapped toward Paulo as if formulating a plan. "Hold up! Hold up just a second! Oh man. You're Temel's son, right?" he asked Paulo.

Paulo glanced sideways at him and then at me, uncertain of how to answer. "Uh . . . yes."

"You do everything with Temel. You've worked alongside of him your whole life. And would you say you were an exact copy of your dad?"

"Haven't we already established this?" Paulo asked.

"An exact copy?" Trendon clarified. "Like anything he can do you can do also?"

Paulo shrugged. "Yeah, I suppose. Why?"

"I'm just going to assume that means you probably have some explosives somewhere on you right this instant, don't you?"

Puckering his lips, Paulo nodded his head from side to side in agreement. "A little. Not enough to do much damage, but—"

"Enough to turn some heads?" Trendon pressed. "Enough to get ol' baldy's attention?"

"Ah . . . sure . . . yeah, I have enough," Paulo stammered. "What did you have in mind?"

Beaming from excitement, Trendon ran his tongue across his lips. "Can you plant some stuff on a few of those cars to create a big explosion?" He pointed to the rear of the parking lot to where several vehicles were parked next to the chain link fence surrounding the hotel. Paulo followed Trendon's finger, nonchalantly scratched his nose, and then fished out several small, brown packages.

"Ah yeah! That's C4, baby! Plastic explosives! Am I right?" Trendon grew overly excited, rubbing his hands together with sinister intentions.

"But what's that going to do?" I asked. Though doubtful, I joined them by the edge of the bush as Trendon picked three lucky cars from the lot to assist in his plan. Ashleigh kept watch from the other side, but for the moment, the Shomehr occupied the full attention of Baeloc and his minions near the front of the hotel. "Even if we had enough explosives to blow up the whole parking lot, we have no way to get through the barricades. Baeloc owns the police and the military. There's no way for us to slip past them in the road. It's pointless."

Trendon raised his eyebrow. "Which brings us to part two of my plan." Hurrying over next to Ashleigh, he poked his head through the bush and pumped his fist in victory. "Yes! It's still there and there's hardly anyone near it!"

"What are you talking about?" I took the chance to peer out of the bush from over Trendon's head, but couldn't see anything that should cause him to be so happy. "What are you looking at?"

"Paulo? Best buddy?" Trendon asked, his head still half-way out from our hiding place. I noticed how he called Paulo by his real name and not by Pablo. What caused this change? Gesturing wildly at a spot on the main road, Trendon finally succeeded in alerting us of the second part of the plan as he pointed to the helicopter. "Please tell me your daddy taught you how to fly."

20

Following my orders, the Shomehr fell back into hiding to await my next command. They had succeeded in injuring many Architects and enraged Baeloc beyond comprehension. Half the hotel building was burning out of control because of his anger.

Wait until I give you the signal, I reminded the Shomehr.

We needed to create absolute mayhem. A scene where no one knew where to turn and look. At least a hundred yards stood between our bush and the helicopter perched in the field across the main highway. A hundred yards seemed an impossible distance to travel without being spotted, but if we played it right, we felt we had an honest chance of making it. Paulo had flown a helicopter similar to Baeloc's several times before and knew exactly how to operate it. We just needed to get him there and to give him enough time to get off the ground.

"Brace yourself." Paulo clasped the remote in his hand. "This might be a little bit loud." With Trendon's assistance, Paulo planted the brown squares of C4 on three separate vehicles near the back of the parking lot, equipping each of the bombs with a detonator no bigger than a cell phone battery. His remote could signal the explosion in all three cars simultaneously. Burying my face in Trendon's chest, I plugged my ears and braced myself as Paulo flipped up a lever and pressed down on the yellow button with his thumb.

The parking lot erupted as the trunks of three cars blew open. Though the explosion's shock wave slammed against us, peppering our skin with dirt and gravel from the parking lot, the sound and overall damage wasn't quite as destructive as I expected. My ears rattled and a cloud of smoke billowed from the devastated cars, but I easily cleared my mind when the sound of rushing footsteps and agitated chatter approached from the side of the hotel.

Now! I commanded.

The Shomehr reacted without hesitation, dropping down from the roof amid the group of Architects and scattering them once more. Again, the night filled with the sound of gunfire and screaming.

Trendon held his breath, checking through the edge of the bush. "Those losers are everywhere, but we have somewhat of a straight path to the helicopter!"

Leaping to my feet, we broke into an all-out sprint as we raced across the parking lot. My chest ached from the running and I could hear my breathing echoing in my ears. Trendon's speed surprised me. Had he not been holding my hand, he could have easily surged ahead of the group. Paulo ran just off my right side, never looking anywhere but straight ahead at the helicopter. Ashleigh brought up the rear, covering our backs, as three of the Architects hiding near the lobby broke away and tried to grab us. One by one, each of them dropped to the ground with the sound of gunfire. Stunned by the suddenness of their fall, I checked over my shoulder and saw Ashleigh lagging behind, reloading her gun. A black ammunition cartridge dropped from her hand as she slid another one in its place.

"Stay with us!" I screamed.

She waved me on and opened fire once more on another group, slowing down altogether to take better aim. Windows shattered from her onslaught as Architects dove behind battered vehicles. Ashleigh dropped to one knee and fired six times at a car from where they hid, but one of the Architects returned her fire, hitting her on the arm. Her shoulder jolted back from the impact, and she dropped immediately, falling face forward to the concrete.

"No!" I screamed, skidding to a halt. Trendon refused to let go of my hand, literally dragging me forward through the parking lot. "They shot her! Ashleigh's been shot!" I repeated over and over as we ran, but he wouldn't stop.

"We have to keep running! We can't stop!" His eyes were wet with tears, but that could've been from the smoke saturating the air. "We're almost th—ah, suck!"

Baeloc stepped into our path, blocking our escape through the parking lot entrance. His hands blazed and he shot a bolt of fire right at Paulo. Trendon dove sideways, knocking Paulo to the ground just as the fire screamed overhead.

Help us! You have to stop Baeloc! I needed the Shomehr to force him out of our way. One of the creatures sped past me, a shadowy rocket that struck Baeloc before he could release another bolt of fire.

"Yeah! Rip his head off!" Trendon cheered.

The Shomehr pinned Baeloc to the ground; its powerful claw, capable of slicing through almost anything, hovered in the air waiting for me to give the word.

"Don't stop! Kill him!" I heard Trendon demand.

I hesitated, not certain if I should give the command to have it destroy my enemy. Could Baeloc be killed like that? Now that he had the power of the artifact inside of him?

I shall end this for you, the creature spoke.

Before I could decide, flames burst from Baeloc's body, enveloping both he and the Shomehr perched upon him. The blaze burned blinding white, and I shielded my eyes as the Shomehr fell silent.

No howling. No final words.

I knew with a certainty, it was dead. Looking back, I saw the other creature standing alone next to the lobby door. I could see scorched skin on its arms and legs from where it received the brunt of Baeloc's initial attack. Though the mist covered its face, I saw its eyes staring out at the fire where its brother had been only seconds before.

"The road is clear!" Paulo shouted. "Get to the helicopter!"

More gunshots rang out and bullets whizzed by us as the other Architects pulled away from the final Shomehr and opened fire. Crossing the road, we reached the helicopter and Paulo went to work, flipping switches and strapping on a headset. He found two other headsets and tossed them to each of us as the massive rotor spun into life.

"What about Ashleigh?" I spoke into the mouthpiece. "We can't just leave her there."

"They shot her, Amber," Trendon said, strapping on

his headset. "We can't go back and get her." He ducked low to avoid the bullets clanking against the side of the machine.

"We may not get very far if they keep shooting," Paulo said, gripping the joystick as the helicopter steadily rose.

The last thing we needed was to drop from the sky in a huge hunk of metal. I scanned the parking lot as the ground shrunk away. Baeloc still lay on the ground near the entrance, but he slowly rose, shoving the charred heap of the dead Shomehr off to the side, and looked up at the helicopter.

"Baeloc is getting up!" I warned the others. "We have to fly faster!"

"Sorry, Amber. I can't make it go any faster. Once we gain altitude, I can speed up," Paulo explained. I felt awful for opening my mouth. Of course we needed to fly faster, but I knew Paulo was trying his best.

A bullet pierced my seat just below my leg and another splintered the helicopter's windshield. At only a hundred feet from the ground, we were easily still in range for the Architects' weapons. Then I saw Dorothy step out of the hotel and felt my pulse quicken. No longer wearing the thin fabric hospital gown, she had changed into something more familiar: blue jeans, an off-white T-shirt, and brown boots. With her hair pulled back out of her eyes, she looked like the Dorothy I knew from school. I questioned whether she somehow had removed the Wrath from inside of her. Was Dorothy back? Was she once again on our side?

Walking swiftly toward the group of Architects firing upon us, Dorothy reached out and grazed the cheeks of several men standing closest to her. Instantly their heads slumped forward, and they crumpled to the ground at her feet.

She killed them!

The other Architects stopped firing and cowered away from her as Paulo finally steered the helicopter forward.

"What was that all about?" Trendon asked, his voice sounding in my headset. "Why did she do that?"

"You saw her too?" I kept my eyes on the ground as the helicopter accelerated, and Dorothy, Baeloc, and the other Architects faded in the distance. "Maybe she was trying to help us." But her actions felt wrong. Disturbing. Watching those men drop like lifeless dolls simply from her touch bothered me more than seeing Ashleigh getting shot by the Architects. What sort of power could do that?

"I think she didn't want those dummies to hit you," Trendon suggested. "She could care less about Pablo and me. She still needs you to carry out her plan."

Lowering my gaze, I stared at the floor. "Yeah, maybe you're right."

"So, can I call you Temel Junior?" Trendon peered over Paulo's shoulder at the myriad of gizmos and other dials on the helicopter's control panel.

"I'd rather you not," Paulo answered. "But thank you for saving my life back there. If you hadn't knocked me down when you did, I'd be burnt to a crisp."

"Don't mention it. Do we have enough fuel to make it back to the monastery?" he asked.

Paulo tilted his head to the side, checked the fuel gage, and flicked his thumb up in the affirmative. "Tank's full, and by my estimations, we're about two hundred fifty miles from St. Catherine."

"How long will that take?" I asked.

"Maybe two hours. That is, if we don't get blown out of the sky." Paulo adjusted his headset and turned a knob on the console.

"They can't hit us from all the way back at the hotel can they?" Trendon scoffed.

"I'm not talking about Baeloc. We're not authorized to fly in this airspace. Just pray we don't have company with missiles."

"Fantastic," Trendon said sarcastically. "Actually, you know what. I'd rather that happen. We might as well get blown out of the sky."

I swatted his chest with the back of my hand and immediately apologized. There I went again, resorting first to hitting him when I disagreed. "Why are you talking like that? You were the one who came up with the brilliant plan that helped us escape. Now you're giving up?"

"I'm not giving up. I'm just facing the facts. Even if we make it back to the monastery, it won't matter. There won't be enough time. Dorothy is coming for us. We're just prolonging the inevitable. She knows how to find us and they probably have a way of tracking this helicopter."

Paulo stared down at the console and nodded halfheartedly. "He's right. These vehicles come equipped with their own distinct signature. My guess would be they're already on their way."

It felt as though every step we took closer to ending the problem, Dorothy and Baeloc leapfrogged over us. We needed a way to throw them off our scent. To at least give us some time to find the answers we needed. "Paulo," I said, an idea striking me. "This helicopter has a tracking device, right?"

"Unfortunately, I believe so."

"No, that's good."

"How's that good?" Trendon asked. "That's definitely bad."

"Not if Paulo keeps flying until the fuel runs low." Trendon just blinked back at me confused. "After we hit the shore of the Gulf, how much fuel will you have left?"

Paulo tapped the gauge and bobbed his head side-to-side calculating. "Maybe half a tank."

"Could you keep flying in another direction? Somewhere remote with great places to hide?"

"Everything north of here is desert and rocky terrain. There would be plenty of places to lie low. Are you thinking we should try to lose them?"

"Not 'we,' " I said. "Just you."

Now Paulo looked at me, blinking in confusion.

"Set us down on the beach and then head north. If we're lucky, Dorothy and Baeloc won't notice we ever landed and they'll continue following you until your fuel runs out. You could keep them occupied searching for you for several hours." Paulo already proved his similarity to Temel, which meant he most likely had his father's same skill of vanishing.

"I . . . I don't think that's the best idea," Paulo stammered. "I would feel horrible if I left you alone and they didn't take the bait."

Trendon scratched his lower lip as he considered the plan. "It is way risky, but it would definitely give us a shot. How do you suggest we get to the monastery? Hitchhike?"

"You're not gonna like it at all, but I have an answer for that too." I pointed to his pocket. "Do you still have Joseph's number in your phone?"

21

A shade under two hours later, Paulo touched the helicopter down just off shore of the Gulf of Aqaba. Keeping our heads low, Trendon and I moved to a safe distance and Paulo immediately lifted the chopper back into the air. Waving good-bye, I inwardly wished him luck, but perhaps we would need it more if Dorothy didn't take the bait. Turning to face the Gulf, I checked for any signs of the Architects. No helicopter lights flickered in the sky and for the moment, we were alone.

"Come on!" Trendon squeezed my hand, and we dashed across the sandy ground toward a silver Jaguar parked on the road.

"You did the right thing by calling me," Joseph said as he stepped out of the passenger side of the flashy car. "My uncle is already alerting the authorities and securing the monastery. If anyone can buy you some time, it's my Uncle Jasher." Joseph looked at Trendon and offered the door. "Want to ride shotgun?"

Trendon bent forward, trying to look into the car. "Who's driving?"

"Your friend Darius."

Darius gripped the steering wheel, scowling as he watched the road ahead.

"Yeah . . ." Trendon flinched. "I think I'll pass."

"Amber?" Joseph held his hand out to me.

"We'll take the back."

Sinking into the leather, I fastened my seat belt, and laid my head against the headrest. The Jaguar provided an extremely comfortable ride, and I felt capable of drifting off to sleep at any moment.

"This seems like a stretch for a religious man," Trendon said, smirking. "How does Jasher justify driving a car like this to the rest of the monks?"

"He doesn't have to worry about justifying anything to the others. This is my car," Joseph explained, peering back. "Or at least it will be in three years when I turn eighteen."

"Good for you." Though he tried to say it subtly, I picked up on Trendon's sarcasm and suspected Joseph did as well since he immediately dropped into his chair and faced the front.

"How's your arm, Darius?" I asked.

The Egyptian acknowledged his heavily bandaged bicep and grunted. "Still works."

"That's good. I'm glad. And Jomo?"

"He's gone. The wound took on too much infection." Darius's voice rose with agitation.

"He's dead too?" Trendon threw his hands up in disbelief.

"Not dead!" Darius snapped.

"My uncle flew him to a better hospital in Amman. He'll be fine," Joseph said, watching Darius closely.

The car slowed as Darius eased on the brakes. "You said

'too.' Who else is dead?" He turned and looked at the both of us.

A sharp ache throbbed in my chest as I desperately fought back tears. "Cabarles was killed." Up until that point, I chose not to discuss my friend's death in fear of it crippling me. Simply saying those words aloud unleashed a wave of sadness. An image of Cabarles standing in the crowded Manila airport holding up an encrypted sign only I could decipher popped into my memory. From our first meeting, he instantly became my friend. How could he be gone? Not after all we had been through. All we had survived together. Only to die at the hand of a person he trusted. "Dorothy didn't mean to." My voice blubbered, trying to defend her actions. "She's not herself. She would've never hurt any of us on purpose."

Darius's eyes displayed no change in emotion. "Who else?"

"Ashleigh was shot by the Architects helping us escape," Trendon chimed in when I was unable to get my words out.

I knew Darius and Ashleigh were friends or at least they had a working relationship, and I feared how he would handle this knowledge.

Again, Darius showed no change in his expression, but turned and pressed on the accelerator. The red pointer on the speedometer increased until it surpassed one hundred miles an hour.

Greeting us in the monastery, Kendell Jasher directed us to a long table littered with several stacks of leather books and a desktop computer.

"You'll have full access to whatever you need to help your research. Part of my contribution was to further the cataloging of each sacred writ on the computer database. All the books have been logged—titles and authors—and we've recently begun including topical components into the database as well. Unfortunately, there is very little of that on the computer. Not even five percent of the data, I'm afraid. So unless you know the title of the book containing the information you need, you won't have much luck. I'll have some food brought out and I'll keep you posted of what I hear from outside. The moment the Architects appear on the grid, we'll know about it."

"Thank you," I said, still unable to hold his gaze.

"Come, Joseph, let's leave them to their work."

Surprised, Joseph glanced up from perusing one of the books. "I thought I would stay."

Jasher frowned. "I don't think that's the best idea, Joseph."

"But I could help them look."

Jasher held his hands out toward me. "I'll let you decide what's best for you."

"I'd say we're good without any more help," Trendon said, answering for the both of us. "We don't want to step on each other's toes. Joseph should go swim in his money vault or something."

Obviously embarrassed by Trendon's comment, Joseph closed the book and waited to see how I would react. Why did it have to be so difficult? I dreaded being the one to decide.

Leaning over, I whispered in Trendon's ear. "Why can't he stay?"

"Are you serious? You said in the helicopter we would just ask him for a ride. We don't need him for anything else."

"He came to our rescue. Plus, he could help us look. We don't have that much time to waste."

"Then why are we wasting it with this dumb conversation? Joseph can barely read."

Horrified by Trendon's lack of tact, I looked to see Joseph's reaction. Staring down at the floor, Joseph resembled a child being punished by his parents. I felt sorry for him. We couldn't just kick him out of the library. He lived there. We were guests of his uncle.

"Just give him a chance," I insisted.

Trendon rolled his eyes. "Whatever. It's your call."

Jasher's robes flowed as he briskly left the library, leaving the three of us in an awkward state of silence.

Musty pages crinkled quietly as Joseph and I sifted through book after book in search of clues. Trendon felt more comfortable on the computer, but since the monastery's database lacked sufficient information on the contents of their library, he spent the bulk of his time browsing the Internet. A handwritten list of keywords needed for our search leaned against an already-searched-through stack of books at the center of the table. By no means complete, the list continued to grow when one of us would blurt out a memory of something relevant to the past two years of our involvement with Dorothy.

Ornan, Araunah, Noah, Arayat, Ark, Staff, Elijah, Elisha, Axe, Moses, Babel, Philippines, Syria, Egypt, Tower, Architects, Despar, Syria, Moriah, the Weapons of Might, the Destroying Angel, David, the Source, the Tebah Stick, the Shomehr, Elijah's Fire, the Wrath, Finisher.

"How about this?" Joseph stuck his head out from behind a massive green book with golden letters, an image of an upside down pyramid, and the title, *A Side-by-Side Concordance of Doctrinal Insights on the Plagues of Pharaoh*, on the cover. "According to Maget Mubarak," he struggled to pronounce the name, "a world-renowned Egyptian Anthropologist, there have been several recorded accounts from various ancestral files passed through the ages since the time of Moses," he read, sliding his finger across the page to keep his place. "Each of these describe the Destroying Angel as being made of a wispy spectral material, faceless and silent, appearing to bear the semblance of goss . . . What's this word?" He pointed to the middle paragraph on page four hundred and sixty.

"'Gossamer strands of smoke,'" I read while leaning over his shoulder. A part of my hair tumbled in his face, and I apologized, tucking it back behind my ear.

"It's fine," he said teasingly.

"What did reading us that junk accomplish?" Trendon chided.

"It's not junk. It helps," I said. "Mark that page and put it with the others." So far, we had only dog-eared four pages in three of the books from the mountain pile of literature scattered on the floor.

"We're never going to find anything in this mess!" Trendon shoved the keyboard away from him on the table. "It's been over an hour and we've gotten nowhere."

"We have to keep looking. We'll bring out more books," I said. "Something in this library will give us the answer."

"The answer to what, I ask? Ah, we don't even know the question. Hmmm, that makes it tricky, don't you think?"

Trendon's sarcasm was beginning to wear on me. Of course this wouldn't be easy. I never said it would be. Why was he acting so obnoxious?

"Yeah, don't give up," Joseph agreed, siding with me. "You've done too much to just do that."

Trendon narrowed his eyes, but instead of commenting, he stuffed his mouth with cold chicken from the plate of food Jasher brought us. Wiggling his fingers, he went back to work searching the Internet.

"Have you found anything helpful online?" I asked.

"Same stuff as before. Everyone has an opinion, but none of the articles have anything to do with Araunah somehow ending up in Egypt or anything about the Weapons of Might. It's the world's biggest best-kept secret."

"But if anyone can find it online, it's you, buddy." Joseph grinned at Trendon.

"I'm not your buddy." Trendon chewed his food.

"He's trying to pay you a compliment! You don't have to insult him after everything he says!" I knew Trendon's hatred of Joseph would cause problems, but this was becoming ridiculous.

"I wasn't insulting him. He's not my buddy. He shouldn't be your buddy. I was just telling the truth. Remember what it's like to hear that from somebody? Or have you been sitting too long next to Joe Joe?"

I groaned. "Please stop."

"Yeah, Trendon," Joseph added, sounding a bit more aggressive. "Just because you have a crush on Amber doesn't mean she can't talk to somebody else. She's not your girlfriend."

His plate dropped and shattered on the ground as

Trendon lunged across the table and pounded his clenched fist into Joseph's chest. Joseph fell over backward with Trendon on top of him. The weight of the two crashing on the table broke the legs and the computer collapsed on the ground, shattering the monitor. I covered my mouth in shock as Trendon and Joseph rolled around knocking over the stacks of books we had yet to examine and mixing them with the ones we already looked through. Both of them exchanged punches, pulled hair, and grappled each other's arms. Joseph brought his knee up into Trendon's stomach and then countered with a punch to the side of Trendon's jaw. Grunting, but showing little effect from Joseph's blow, Trendon grabbed Joseph's shirt and ripped his sleeve clean off his arm. Joseph then punched Trendon in the mouth and I saw his eyes close from the pain.

"Stop it! Stop fighting!" I screamed, flinging myself onto Trendon's back and trying with all my strength to keep him from punching.

The door opened and several monks flooded in. They pulled me off Trendon and then, risking bodily injury, succeeded in breaking the two boys apart. Joseph shoved their arms away and scowled at Trendon, who kept his fingers balled into tight fists.

"Why did you do that?" I shouted in Trendon's face. "Why did you hit him?"

"Me?" Trendon looked appalled at my accusation as he rubbed his jaw from where Joseph struck him. "You heard what he said to me. Why are you taking his side?"

"He was just being a jerk."

"Hey!" Joseph exclaimed. "I was not."

"And I'm not taking anyone's side," I continued, ignoring Joseph. "We don't have time for fighting. I want this to be over."

After stopping the violence, the monks bowed respectfully and left the room. No one sat or went back to work. No one seemed to want to speak either. Gazing over the toppled books and destroyed computer, I felt defeated. How would we know where we left off?

I began shoveling books into a pile. "Please help me clean up."

"Clean up?" Joseph asked. "Are you finished with these?"

Puffing out my cheeks, I shook my head. "I'm finished with all of it. Trendon, aren't you going to help?"

Trendon still stood with his fists ready to strike. "So we're giving up now?" he asked. "Just because of one little fight?"

"Not just because of that," I said, smoothing out the pages of one of the books and neatly stacking it with the others. "Where are we going to look? Where could we possibly find answers?"

"This is a big library. We'll find something," Joseph said. "Here, why don't you go gather up some more books and leave the cleaning to us? It's our fault, after all. Right, Trendon?"

Trendon rubbed his jaw. "Yeah, I guess."

"You'll just start fighting again." We definitely didn't need another brawl. I still couldn't believe Trendon's reaction, how he dove across the table like someone possessed.

"We won't. We promise." Joseph held up his hand, solemnly swearing. "We'll get the books ready to go back and then we'll start again."

I looked at Trendon and sensed the will to fight in him wearing thin. Relieved for a moment on my own, I walked away from the table and slipped down a musty-smelling aisle of books.

22

On any other day, I could've easily spent hours upon hours lazily strolling through the aisles of the monastery library. I could plop down on the ground in one of the rows and read until they forced me to eat or sleep. I wouldn't even care what books I grabbed. They could be on geography or biology or any number of subjects and I would be just as content to turn the pages. But this wasn't one of those days. This was a day when the sheer volume of books and possibilities tied my stomach into knots.

We needed history books, but which ones were they? It was impossible to know just from their covers or titles and I didn't know what author to look for. I found myself grazing my fingers over the spines as I walked, but I didn't pick up any to take back to the table. I discovered the monks at the library had a unique way of organizing the books on the shelves. Some of them alphabetical by title, some by author, and others by subject. Some of them organized based on size, as many of the wooden bookshelves could only fit certain dimensions. We didn't have time to sift through old books, and we hadn't found anything of value yet. I began to doubt we ever would even if we had an endless amount of time to search through the library. These books contained plenty of interesting things, but scholars and authors wrote them. Not prophets. They weren't written by people who lived during the time of Moses or Elijah or who witnessed the miracles firsthand. These authors didn't know about the Weapons of Might. Only a few people in the world did. No one believed in powerful artifacts anymore, and they certainly never wrote helpful books about them.

The only words that mattered would come from four authors: Noah, Elijah, Moses, and now the mysterious Araunah. The original people who controlled the artifacts and went to great lengths to keep them hidden. But other than the Bible, where would we find any more writings by them?

Weaving through endless aisles until the book bindings blended together into a mesh of dusty, leather wallpaper with an occasional glint of gold leafing, my journey came to an abrupt end in front of the southern wall and a glass case atop a credenza.

The Codex Sinaiticus.

Beneath the box, Dorothy and the others discovered the key to the secret passage leading to the tomb under the mountain. I wondered if the key still remained. The glass felt heavy as I carefully lifted it off its pedestal and laid it next to the book. Running my hand across the waxy paper, I leaned closer to examine the strange characters. They didn't look Egyptian or Hebraic.

"It's written in Greek," Jasher announced from behind me, and I instinctively yelped in response. "They're called uncial characters. Very difficult to translate. And this is not the completed manuscript. There are four libraries around the world that carry a portion of the Codex. Here at St. Catherine we protect the smallest piece, but it is our most priceless treasure."

How could I think I could just stroll up to this valuable book and pull it out of its box? I had to control my impulses. The monks kept it safe for a reason, and there were consequences for vandalizing priceless antiques. "I'm so sorry. I . . . I . . . can't believe I did that," I stammered, grasping the glass case. "I should have asked first. I shouldn't be looking—"

Jasher held his hand out for me to be at ease. "Look, if it helps you." He held a magnifying glass close to the pages. "Do you know much about the Codex Sinaiticus?"

"No. Up until recently, I didn't even know it existed. Can you understand it?" I asked, unsure if Jasher possessed the skill for translation.

"I don't claim to be fluent, but I have spent a great a deal of time studying it. After all, I was the one who supplied the British Library with their portion of the Codex."

"*You* supplied?" Wincing, I realized how awful that sounded. "I'm sorry . . . again. That was rude." I never imagined Jasher as one who would willingly give up an archaeological find to a museum.

"I don't blame you for questioning my character and motives. And I have nothing to hide. I uncovered a part of the Codex with a team of researchers in Athens and though I kept it hidden for many years in a vault—yes, there's the Jasher you know and love." He winked. "I eventually turned it over to the British Library for a more thorough investigation. That was around the time I began associating with Baeloc, and I saw no need to venture after any other discovery. I can read most of the names and I recognize some of the stories from the Bible as I research. But the Codex is different than reading any other translation."

"Why is that?"

"The stories are different. Quite a few have alternate outcomes."

I blinked. "You mean according to this, Noah never built the Ark?"

Jasher laughed. "Now that one stayed the same, but others have changes. Some of them only slight, but others are quite noticeable. Take the story of Samson for instance. You know his tale. His hair gave him strength. He toppled the pillars of the Temple of Dagon."

I thought about the story of Samson I had heard multiple times growing up in Sunday school. "That one's different?"

"Distinctly. Samson has always been portrayed as being foolish and impulsive and even a tad sinister in his interactions with others. He killed so many for such trifle reasons."

A story about Samson surfaced in my mind when he tried to fool the Philistines with a riddle and it backfired. Because they guessed the answer, Samson owed them thirty changes of clothing. Out of anger, Samson killed thirty people and took their clothes as an offering to the Philistines. That definitely fell into the category of foolish and impulsive.

"According to the Codex, he was anything but a fool. He was a king, wise and just. He led his people into battle against the Philistines and performed many miracles, not just the ones involving his strength."

A book rarely touched by men and revered as something sacred and holy—I found the Codex Sinaiticus intriguing. If Jasher spoke the truth, this Bible could hold different stories than the ones I knew and grew up with.

Eyebrows rising inquisitively, I stared at Jasher. "Can you look something up for me?"

"I suppose."

"Could you look up the story of Araunah?"

Jasher appeared puzzled. "I'm not familiar with that story."

"It's in Second Samuel. Chapter twenty-four, I believe."

Jasher removed a pair of reading glasses from beneath his robe and began to leaf through the pages. "The Codex is organized differently than the standard Bible, but if the story exists, I should be able to find the general location." Within a few moments, he adjusted his glasses on his nose and pointed to a spot midway up one of the pages. "Here we are. Araunah the Jebusite. What exactly should I be looking for?"

Tapping my finger against my lips, I tried to think. What would be important? What would lead us to answers? "Does it talk about anything Araunah would've done before meeting David? Maybe a place he would've lived in."

Jasher muttered as he read, fretting whenever he stumbled upon the translation. "The land David purchased was in Moriah, which if I'm not mistaken, is present-day Jerusalem."

I already knew that and that didn't solve the mystery of how Araunah ended up in Egypt.

"Could it be in another book?" he asked.

"Chronicles!" My eyes widened. "Araunah was called

Ornan the Jebusite in the book of Chronicles, but it's the same story. Maybe that's where we'll find changes in the manuscript."

Jasher grimaced. "This portion of the Codex doesn't contain the book of Chronicles. It has the Pentateuch or the Law of Moses and the books up until Kings."

"There has to be something else," I griped as Jasher flipped the page going further along in the story. "Go back to the beginning. Before he sold his land to David."

Within a few scans of one of the columns, he snapped his finger triumphantly. "Maybe this is it. *And when the angel stretched out his hand upon Jerusalem to destroy it, the Lord repented him of the evil, and said to the angel that destroyed the people, It is enough: stay now thine hand.*"

I hoped he found something different, but he only succeeded in regurgitating the same elements of the previous story. Closing my eyes in frustration, I shook my head. "That's not it either. We need to look—"

Jasher held up his finger to silence me. "*And the angel of the Lord was by the threshingplace of Araunah the Jebusite,*" he continued to read. "*For the Destroying Angel was Araunah the Jebusite.*"

"What did you say?" My eyes jerked up at his reading of the last part, a new addition not included in the King James Version of the Bible.

Pointing to a spot on the page, he reread the passage. "Araunah was the Destroying Angel. I've never noticed this before. Is that different than from what you've read in the Bible?"

"How could Araunah be the Destroying Angel?" I whispered. In the story of Moses, the Lord sent the Angel to plague Pharaoh and the Egyptians. The movies always portrayed the angel as a faceless spirit. If this version of the Bible held the truest account of Araunah, then it changed things. Wasn't Araunah just a man?

"There's more," Jasher said. "Ornan was his original name, but he became Araunah upon the records after he went up into Egypt to be taxed."

I produced a chirping sound from shock. "Araunah went to Egypt?" Of course! Censuses were held every ten or so years for the populations to be counted and taxed. It would've been no different in Araunah's day and if all the great Pharaohs lived in Egypt, he would have had to travel there at least once or twice in his lifetime. Something happened to Araunah when he arrived there.

"Is there anything else," I probed. Jasher needed to read more. Unable to understand Greek, I stood at his mercy, hoping his translation was accurate.

"Nothing more about the Destroying Angel, but there's a part of Araunah being labeled as an unsanctified hand. A soul not fit to endure the Fury. I assume that has something do with—"

I made another chirping sound. *Unsanctified hand? The Fury?* I saw the piece of paper Dorothy handed me in the hospital when she first met us in Egypt and the words burned in my mind.

Thus allowing the final protector time to make certain no unsanctified hand unleashed the Fury of Har Megiddon.

Araunah was an unsanctified hand. Someone who didn't have the right to unleash the Wrath and the Destroying Angel. A man who no doubt caused terrible destruction until somebody stopped him. I then realized another critical bit of information. The Wrath no longer controlled Araunah, which meant there was a way to stop it—to stop Dorothy!

Staring at the ground, I let my mind return to the cave as I pieced together the memory of searching Araunah's tomb. Moses hid the artifact in the cave and it remained there for thousands of years before Araunah stumbled upon it on his journey through Egypt. How he found it and why he took it were questions I couldn't answer, but I didn't need to worry about that. Araunah went home to Moriah and, like Dorothy, somehow opened the Wrath, which took over his body. That was how he became the Destroying Angel. The Bible explained what happened next. As the Finisher, Araunah began destroying Jerusalem, but something stopped him. David came to him, paid him fifty shekels of silver for his threshingfloor, and thus ended the destruction. Leaving his home, Araunah returned to the cave and died inside the tomb. I remembered the placard above the skeleton's head.

Moriah, my place of refuge.

Perhaps a family member or a friend carved that statement into the stone, but the wording made me believe that Araunah himself did it before he died. It was a way to be remembered. A way to carry on his name, but leave his mystery intact just in case someone discovered his secret. Still, the question remained. How did David defeat Araunah? The story mentioned him being one able to convince the Destroying Angel to stop. Was that all it took? Someone of power, like a king, asking him nicely? In my experience, being asked by anyone could not simply stop these artifacts. Some other power was at work. Perhaps another item. Another artifact.

"Amber, this may be what you're looking for," Jasher muttered. "*And King David said unto Araunah, stay now thine hand and turn away thy wrath upon these people. And I will buy your peace at a price. And the king's offering of the fifty shekels of silver appeased the Finisher, and Araunah stayed his fury and departed.*

"The silver!" My voice startled Jasher. "Araunah had a bag of silver in his hand inside the tomb. It wasn't much. Maybe fifty pieces of silver." *Fifty shekels.* The payment David made to Araunah! Why else would it be all that remained in the tomb? "I think it's important we go down there. I think it can actually stop Dorothy!"

❧

Jasher rolled back the carpet and unveiled a wooden trapdoor with a tarnished brass keyhole in the center. Using the key from beneath the case, he unlocked the door and lifted it open. Cool air tingled on my skin as we descended a rickety ladder into the hole.

"What about Trendon and Joseph?" I asked. "Should they come with us?"

Jasher looked up the ladder and shook his head. "How much time do you think we still have? It's a long walk to the room."

"You're right. Let's just hurry."

Without flashlights or lanterns, Jasher and I hurriedly crept through the cavern, feeling our way along the walls with our hands. The trip took longer than before and we were fortunate there weren't alternate paths to take. Despite knowing this, my anxiety increased as each turn in the cavern took us deeper underground. Finally, after endlessly walking, the locator stone on my necklace released a pale blue glow and the opening to the room appeared in front of us.

"That's a remarkable piece of jewelry," Jasher said as we entered the room and the stone shone brighter. "Have you always owned a locator stone?"

"Dorothy gave it to me awhile ago, a few months before . . ." I hesitated to finish and watched Jasher's eyes closely.

"Before . . . she involved you in this race and I became your enemy?" he asked, smiling deviously.

"Yeah, that would be it."

Holding my necklace out as a lantern, I knelt beside the tomb and gazed inside. No longer repulsed by the skeleton, I felt along its ribs and fleshless arms for the silver. Grunting as I reached, I ran my fingers beneath its back, eagerly anticipating a graze of the leather pouch and sighing in frustration when I came up empty.

"It has to be here. Jackson and Ashleigh pulled it out of the skeleton's hand, but they put it back." My pulse quickened as I remembered Dorothy's alarm when she noticed Ashleigh holding the silver. Was that the artifact at work? Was it trying to keep the silver away from her even then in the early stages of her transformation?

Jasher and I shamelessly wedged our hands beneath the skeleton and hoisted it out of the tomb. Gagging, from the revolting texture of Araunah's bones, I helped Jasher lay the skeleton on the ground next to the opening. "There's nothing on his body," Jasher confirmed, after thoroughly searching it.

In the lower corner of the tomb, next to where

Araunah's feet had rested, I noticed a small object. Catching my breath, I closed my fingers around it.

"I think I found—" but I stopped before finishing the sentence. The object definitely wasn't a bag of silver. It was something else. Something light and spongy. Squeezing it in my hand, I recognized Ashleigh's stress-relieving ball—the object she had tossed into the tomb instead of the silver! Going against Dorothy's orders, Ashleigh kept it for herself and now lay in the parking lot of the hotel back in Saudi Arabia, hundreds of miles away.

"Oh no, no, no!" I repeated over and over, furiously compressing the ball into a tight wad.

"It's not it, is it?" Jasher asked, clicking his tongue in sympathy. "I take it I haven't been too helpful."

"You've been most helpful, old friend," Dorothy answered as she rose up behind him and grazed his cheek with her hand.

Kendell Jasher would not be able to fake his death again as he collapsed on the floor at my feet.

23

With Dorothy still stooping over Jasher's body in some sickening final good-bye, I slipped past her and raced through the corridor screaming my friends' names.

"Trendon! Joseph!"

"Don't run, Amber," Dorothy announced from somewhere behind me. Blinded in the extreme darkness of the cave, I clung to the wall for guidance, praying I wouldn't stumble. Heart pounding furiously in my chest, I didn't dare look back, knowing my former archaeology teacher could only be trailing me by a few yards. Something snagged my shirt, wrenching my body back against the wall and I screamed. But I had merely brushed too close to the cavern wall, a jagged stone edge the culprit.

"I promised I wouldn't hurt you. Don't you trust me?" Dorothy's voice sounded farther away than I first calculated. Hearing its distance, my waning confidence grew and I pumped my legs harder when I caught a glimpse of the ladder descending from the library door.

Scaling the ladder, I once again screamed for help. "She's here! Dorothy's here! We have to get out of here now!"

I darted past the Codex Sinaiticus, my footfalls echoing against the hollow-sounding floor. My shoulders uprooted several dust-covered books from their resting spots as I ran, sending them tumbling to the ground.

Rounding the corner, I felt the little bit of hope burn away when I saw Joseph and Trendon and at least two dozen monks lying on the ground, their hands and legs bound with cords. All of them struggled against their bindings, but Baeloc stood behind them. When he noticed me standing in the center of the library, the Architect held his hands out wide as if inviting me in for a warm hug from a friend.

No more tricks up my sleeve. No more escape routines. And no need to wonder how they covered the distance from Tabuk to the monastery so fast. Paulo's bait never tempted them to travel north.

"And here we are at the end of it all." Dorothy stepped behind me and squeezed her cold hands around my arms.

"No!" I whimpered as her fingers tightened and I waited for death to take hold. Would it be quick and painless? A thought of my parents finding my shriveled corpse flashed through my mind and I realized I would never get a chance to say good-bye.

Dorothy laughed in sympathy. "You thought I would kill you with just my fingers. Dear Amber, I can control whose life I take. Did you think I would do that to you? Finish you?" She pulled me into her arms and prevented me from struggling. "How could I do that to you? You need to think better of me. Am I not your friend? Was I not your teacher year after year at Roland & Tesh?" The voice belonged to Dorothy as did the memories, but the rest of it wasn't her anymore. I needed to keep telling myself that. Reminding myself what she was capable of doing.

"You're not Dorothy anymore!"

"Look at your friends," she purred. "They're still alive because they are my friends too."

"Oh really?" Trendon's muffled voice rose from the ground. "Well, how about you untie your friends so we don't have to keep licking the floor?"

"I can't protect you from yourself if I untie you," Dorothy explained. "You'll do something dangerous and force my hand. But don't you remember when you were flying here in the helicopter? I stopped those men from shooting you."

"You killed them!" I yelled.

"A necessity for ensuring your safety. I would do it a million times again." I cringed as Dorothy ran her fingers along the back of my hair, sliding her fingers through the tangles. "I've kept you safe, Amber."

"Dorothy, can't you hear how crazy you sound? Listen to yourself! This isn't you. We were in this together to stop Baeloc. To keep bad things from happening." I shook my head in disgust. "You killed Jasher!" Gasping for breath, I fought against her powerful hold.

"He was my enemy. He was our enemy!" She grew loud with excitement, and I noticed her voice change into something else. Deeper. Masculine. "Or have you forgotten what that man did to me? Held me prisoner. Tortured me. He did the same to you and Trendon. How can you so easily forgive him of his horrible crimes? Killing Jasher was a necessary deed and he deserved to die as punishment."

"What about Cabarles? Was he our enemy? Did he deserve to die too?"

Dorothy clucked her tongue next to my ear. "Accidents happen." Though she didn't hurt my arms, she held them tight, and I felt the will to fight against her dissolve. Where were the adults now? Where were the people who could make the decisions to save us? Temel and Jackson could still be sifting through the burning rubble of the hospital searching for us. Dorothy separated everyone in our group, knowing she would have me all to herself to persuade me in the end.

"Fight against it. You have to try!" I begged. "I know you can beat this."

"I'm going to let go of you now, but I encourage you not to run. I have not harmed Trendon or Joseph, but I will without hesitation if you try to escape."

"What does it matter?" I straightened in defiance of her threats. "You're going to kill us all anyway. Why should I do what you say?"

"As you wish." She released my arms, and I wobbled on my feet as she knelt beside Trendon and held her hand out to touch him.

"Uh, Amber. Do you want to rethink that?" Trendon asked, his face pressed against the floor.

"Stop! Don't!" I clamped my hands over my eyes but lowered them once Dorothy released an unnerving cackle.

"Am I teasing you too much? I'm not going to kill them like this. And I don't think you quite understand what I intend to do here. Baeloc had the same confusion. He was so intent on ending this world, he never realized what would really transpire. World destruction doesn't require everyone to die. I'm not destroying it all. We just need a clean slate to correct our mistakes."

What did she mean by that? Leaving a few of us alive to start over while wiping out the rest of the human population? The way she said everything in such a casual way sickened me.

"Please don't make me do this." I felt I could pass out at any moment and I actually welcomed the idea. With everything about to happen, I didn't want to be awake for it.

The blasting clatter of a machine gun ripped through the library and several Architects ducked as the bullets ricocheted off the wall. Dorothy heaved me to the ground and, as my eyes scanned the room, I saw Darius barricaded behind several overturned desks, aiming his gun over the edge. Shouting in Egyptian, Darius pulled the trigger once more, and one of Baeloc's men dropped from the shot. The Architects returned fire, splintering the wooden table, but Darius continued to poke his head out, taunting them.

Eyes widening with rage, Baeloc stretched out his fingers, igniting them, and directed a bolt at the table, which instantly exploded. But Darius had already moved to another spot behind his barricade.

Again Baeloc unleashed the fire, and again he only succeeded in sending another table up in flames. Darius's face surfaced and I almost laughed when the normally scowling Egyptian stuck out his tongue and dropped another Architect with a quick burst of gunfire from his machine gun. He was an incredible shot!

Dense gray smoke filled the air as the fire on the tables blazed brighter, spreading up the walls and across several heavy bookshelves. The tattered, ornate drapery along the windows vanished amid a swirling wall of red and orange. Books fell from their shelves as Baeloc's handiwork fed upon the feast of old, dry paper and expanded through the library.

Two more Architects met the painful end of Darius's bullets, then the Egyptian turned his gun toward Dorothy, and several rounds whizzed over our heads. The gunfire temporarily distracted her, and she released her grip on my arms. Abandoning me on the floor, she stood and slunk away down one of the aisles.

Wasting no time, I slid across the room next to Trendon and frantically worked with one of the knots in his bindings. "I can't do it! They've tied too many of them!"

"There's a knife on the belt of that dead Architect right there." Joseph pointed with his chin.

Other Architects stood close to the dead one on the ground, but with Darius occupying their attention, I easily slipped by unnoticed and collected the knife. After cutting them both free, Joseph immediately got to his feet.

"Where are you going?" I asked him, watching his eyes scanning the library.

"I'm going to go get my uncle," he said harshly.

"Your uncle? Joseph, he's dead."

"You don't know that!" Joseph glared at me, his eyes filling with tears. "You don't know for sure!"

"I do know for sure. I saw him die. If you go after him now, you'll run into Dorothy." I tried to pat his arm, but he slapped it away.

"Whoa, dude! That's uncalled for," Trendon said, squaring off with Joseph.

"I bet you're happy now, huh?" he spat. "My uncle's

dead. Just like I said before. Now you can't call me a liar. I guess you finally got what you wished for!"

Trendon narrowed his eyes. "Maybe."

I stepped between them. "Now's not the time to fight again."

"I'm going after him. You two do what you want." Ducking low, Joseph raced across the opening toward the bookshelves.

As the fire grew in intensity, Darius began to run out of places to hide. He also had to be running out of bullets. Shielding his eyes from the heat, he managed to fire off a few more shots. Then Dorothy stepped out from one of the blazing rows behind him and raked her finger down his arm. Three more bursts of gunfire erupted from his gun, but out of reflex only, as our last hope of escape fell over dead.

Trendon pulled his hair in shock. "Game over!"

"Follow me!" Leading him out of the library, we raced through the monastery and stepped out the main entry doors. Several black helicopters similar to the one Paulo flew earlier that evening sat on the lawn, their pilots no doubt inside with the others. Trendon took off in a sprint, and then stopped when he realized I still stood on the steps.

"We have to go!" Trendon demanded.

Eyes burning from the smoke and with tears of defeat, I sadly shook my head. "I'm not going with you. You have to try to contact Temel or Paulo. They can come and help the rest of the people here."

"What kind of stupid idea is that? You can't stay here!"

"Listen to me! Dorothy is going to take me somewhere to do this. I'm guessing somewhere high up. Probably the mountain. I'm going to try to reason with her. See if I can bring her back. There's still some of the old Dorothy in there somewhere, and I think I can reach her."

"You heard her just now. She wants to start the world all over again. That's psychotic! There's no reasoning with her," Trendon argued.

"I have to try. I just can't believe she'll carry through with this. But you need to go now. You won't get another chance to get help."

"Fine. I'll go with you." He looked over my shoulder, checking to see how much time we had before Dorothy appeared.

"I don't want you there."

"What?" Trendon recoiled. A mixture of surprise and sadness swirled in his eyes.

"If I'm going to try and talk some sense into her, I can't have you there. Dorothy will use you to make me do what she wants. I won't be able to be strong if she threatens your life. You have to leave now. Knowing you got out and are trying to save everyone will be enough to keep me focused."

Though he looked hesitant, Trendon moved backward down the steps, his shoulders slumping. "I guess I'll say good-bye then."

I knew at any moment, the door would burst open, but I couldn't let him leave like that. Reaching out and grabbing his hand, I pulled Trendon close and kissed him. It lasted only two seconds before I broke free and forced him away with my hand. "Hurry!"

I watched him run east toward the city as Dorothy and Baeloc stepped down from the monastery's entry doors.

24

A dangerous wind buffeted the helicopter, threatening to smash us against the jagged peaks of the mountain. There seemed to be no flat surface to land, but the pilot, following Dorothy's orders, continued to lift the aircraft. To the west, an expansive body of water glimmered, reflecting the moonlight from overhead. It was a part of the Red Sea and beyond it, mainland Egypt sat cloaked in early morning darkness.

More than a mile below and to the south, the fires of the St. Catherine Monastery flickered in silence. If Trendon had any sense, he would get as far away from Egypt as possible. Maybe there would be time. Maybe the destruction caused by the Weapons of Might wouldn't be immediate. More important, maybe I still had a chance of bringing the old Dorothy back.

A plateau of flat rock appeared on the western shelf of the mountain and Dorothy instructed the pilot to land. The man, also an Architect, shouted in his language, pointing to the ceiling and indicating the rotor. I couldn't understand his snarling words, but I knew he was warning

Dorothy about the danger of landing there. The helicopter blade needed clearance and if it struck any part of the rocks, the results could be disastrous.

"Do it!" Dorothy held her hand next to the pilot's throat.

Bracing myself, I gripped the seat until my knuckles whitened as the pilot attempted to set the helicopter down on the rock. A whirlwind of dirt whipped through the opening and the helicopter swayed as the landing skids touched down on no more than a foot or two of ground from the cliff's edge. The rotors cleared the rock, but I tensed as more wind pounded the side.

"Stay right next to me." Grabbing my arm, Dorothy led us from the helicopter and we moved clear of the rotors.

The pilot shouted something incoherent to Baeloc and jabbed his thumb in the air, begging to take off. A violent blast of wind rocked the helicopter to one side and the rotor blade struck the mountain. The piercing scrape of metal against rock rattled my ears as Dorothy shoved me down to the ground. Several grueling seconds slipped past with my face pinned against stone and dirt, unable to move, before the sound of an explosion carried up the mountainside. When Dorothy finally allowed me to stand, both the pilot and the helicopter were gone, and I realized what had made the explosion.

Dusting me off, Dorothy pointed to a trail heading farther up. "Baeloc will lead us. Be careful of the edge." Absent of any trace of emotion, her lack of concern for the pilot's welfare concluded how far the true Dorothy had changed.

Stepping over a small boulder, I pressed my back against the wall and tried not to think of the sheer drop-off beyond the narrow path. If I fell, would I survive? A fall from that height would flatten any normal person, but I contained the artifact inside of me. Perhaps it would keep me alive, but that didn't mean I wouldn't suffer painful injuries. Dorothy kept silent, her eyes watching Baeloc as he walked ahead of us. We hiked a short amount of time before he stopped in an area where the trail widened and a full view of the western horizon expanded before our eyes. Mount Catherine's peak still loomed above us, with more than one trail winding up from the clearing, but the spot met both Dorothy's and Baeloc's approval. The mouth of a cave opened in the rock wall, but I couldn't see how deep it stretched due to the darkness. Another cave? I had spent more than enough time in caves the past few years of my life.

The wind died, no longer whipping along the path, and the mountain seemed almost serene as though asleep beneath a cloudless silver sky.

"This will do," Dorothy muttered. Turning her back on the cave's opening, she stared at Baeloc, and the two of them shared a silent understanding.

"Can we talk about this?" I pressed. "Can you just think about what's going to happen? There's no coming back! You're meddling with powers not meant for you. The artifacts were hidden for a reason!"

Undoubtedly realizing the magnitude of the moment, Baeloc didn't speak. About to fulfill his ancestor Despar's destiny in combining the Weapons of Might, he looked solemn, ready to let loose his revenge on the world he hated.

"Be quiet now, Amber." Dorothy's voice once again changed into something else and the white surrounding her pupils filled with blackness. "I will now unite the artifacts within me."

Baeloc knelt to one side of Dorothy and closed his eyes, his hands folded at his waist. "You do the same," she instructed me, pointing at Baeloc.

"I won't do it. I'm not going to make this easy for you!" But then I felt the will drain out of me as a sharp, burning pain formed in my chest and my knees bent on their own.

"On the contrary. By defying me, you make it that much easier. I see no need to treat you with respect." Her blackened eyes glistened as the pain in my chest grew, and I could no longer resist the urge to stand.

"It . . . it . . . hurts!" I whimpered, wanting so desperately to clutch my chest, but unable to pull my hand away from my side. "S-stop! Please!"

Baeloc quivered as well. His eyes opened and shut rapidly, as though he too felt the unbearable pain.

"The Fire first and then the Source," Dorothy muttered as she knelt between us and placed a hand on both of our chests. She stared into Baeloc's eyes as a white light appeared at her fingertips. The light seemed to pour out of Baeloc's chest, swirling around her fingers like a sprouting vine made of smoke. Baeloc howled from the pain and foaming saliva poured from his mouth. His hands ignited and fire coiled around his forearms and up his shoulders. Bright yellow at first, the fire turned orange, then blood red, then black as it enveloped Baeloc's whole upper body to where I could no longer see his writhing face. Horrified, I watched his hands clenching and unclenching at his sides. Then the black flames dimmed and once again I saw the distinct veins bulging in his forehead. An image of Baeloc's head exploding from the pressure entered my mind, and I fought to force it out.

The fire on Baeloc disappeared with the sound of an extinguished candle, and he fell over backward, breaking the connection with Dorothy.

Dorothy gasped with delight, her eyes glowing red as a tiny bloom of fire formed in her upturned palm and flickered in a gentle breeze. Mesmerized by its appearance, she smiled as the flame seemed to dance with every subtle movement of her fingers.

"It's beautiful," she whispered. "Don't you think so, Amber?" She extended her hand toward me, the intense heat burning my cheek. I wanted to pull away, but the pain in my chest prevented me from moving. "Baeloc squandered this ability. You should've taken greater advantage of this gift," she scolded Baeloc.

Baeloc stood and took in deep breaths of air through his nostrils as though it was the most satisfying sensation he could experience. His hand clutching his chest, the Architect backed away from Dorothy, no longer interested in her fire-making ability. He seemed uncertain of where to go and moved beneath the overhanging rock of the cave's opening. Staring up at the ceiling, Baeloc realized his mistake and took a step back toward us as two bright eyes appeared behind him in the darkness, floating above his shoulder.

"Good-bye Baeloc," Dorothy said as powerful claws closed around Baeloc's throat. He managed to release a scream, which hung in the air as the Shomehr dragged him away into the cave. The creature had traveled an impossible distance from Tabuk to arrive there, crossing the Gulf of Aqaba and scaling the treacherous mountain. In that fleeting moment, our minds connected and I saw through its eyes as it greedily gazed upon its prey.

Baeloc stood with his back pressed against the wall, his mouth clamped shut, as the Shomehr moved in close. Though he appeared determined not to beg for his life and meet his death courageously, Baeloc saw something in the creature's face and unexpectedly released a wailing scream in agony. Being united with the Shomehr, I knew the hazy mist had dispensed, and as it drew close to Baeloc, I saw something reflecting in his eyes.

A white light covered the surface of the Shomehr's face.

It glowed bright but not blindingly, and I couldn't understand why the light caused Baeloc to suffer so immensely as he looked upon it. What little color the Architect possessed in his skin drained from him completely. Now a wraith of his formal self, Baeloc shrunk away from the Shomehr. He rambled in his language, undoubtedly pleading for mercy. Maybe the light appeared different to him. Maybe Baeloc could see its true form. Whatever the case, the Architect's will to resist vanished. My thoughts disconnected with the Shomehr as its final strike extinguished Baeloc's screams.

"Did you think Baeloc's life mattered to me?" I heard Dorothy ask once my mind cleared. The faint image of the unusual light still lingered in front of my eyes. "Did you think I would not know how to continue with him gone?"

Dorothy believed I summoned the Shomehr to kill Baeloc. Once again, I possessed no memory of directing the creature's actions.

"He served but one purpose. A carrier of the artifact I needed." Her hand on my chest began to brighten as I once again felt the pain intensify. "You serve the same purpose."

Clamping my eyes shut, unable to escape, the power of the artifact began to sap energy from my body. A mass of images swirled in my mind, memories not my own, but ones coming from some place else. I saw several Shomehr at my side bowing before a man holding the Tebah Stick, and I heard their voices moaning beneath the mountain. The unrelenting pain in my chest caused the images of the Philippines, Syria, and Egypt to muddle together to the point I no longer recognized which events happened first.

An image of Architects firing their weapons in the hotel parking lot turned into the Shomehr removing the lid of the tomb and staring down upon Araunah's skeleton. Trendon setting fire to a road flare in the caverns of Mount Arayat became one of Jasher's bodyguards, Malcolm, vanishing beneath a distorted blur of claws and fur. Baeloc screaming into the face of one of the Shomehr as his life hung by a thread, changed into an image of me sleeping in my dorm room in West Virginia. The memories flashed like photographs on a colossal screen and then winked out, one by one, as my mind returned to Mount Catherine.

The pain dulled then disappeared as my mind cleared and I felt the final tug of the artifact's power diminish. Immediately, I noticed the Shomehr's absence. Before, even when not trying to communicate with them, I could almost sense their presence. I attempted to call to the last creature in my mind, to see if I could still connect with it, but I no longer felt any link.

A rumble overhead drew my attention to the heavens and to a black ominous cloud forming above the mountain. At its center, a white circle, like the pupil of an enormous eye, appeared. The roiling cloud rapidly spread until it covered the sky, leaving the small circle of white directly overhead as the only break in the blackness, an unfortunate blot of white ink against the black canvas of starless sky beyond it. Dorothy had succeeded in uniting the Weapons of Might and judging by how wide the endless black cloud stretched in every direction, there would be no way to escape its fury.

"Can you still hear me?" I looked at my teacher, her eyes closed, her jaw rigid with determination, and I reached over to touch her arm. A jolt of electricity burned my hand, and I recoiled from the invisible field of energy surrounding her body. My arm tingled from the shock, but I tried again. This time, the jolt sent me rocketing back. My entire left side of my body shook and my fingers grew numb. If I tried to touch her or even pass my hand through to the other side, the electricity could kill me. Massaging my arm until the pain subsided, I cautiously approached Dorothy once more but kept my distance. Kneeling inside her protective bubble, she interlocked her fingers in her lap and stared up at the cloud.

"Please don't do this." With my final attempt to sway her decision, I saw no need to shout or scream or ball my fists and attack the force field. That would accomplish nothing. "Do you remember when you gave me this?" I held up the locator stone by the necklace chain and rotated it in my fingers. "You made me promise not to lose it. It was important to you that I have it. You knew you could trust me. You left me clues in your letter just before the final exam, and we found a way into your safe. Even Trendon helped." She made no sign of acknowledgment, and I didn't know if my questions and memories would resonate with her.

"We went to your apartment and Abraham Kilroy helped us unlock your safe." At the mention of her former intern who was poisoned by Jasher's men, Dorothy's lip twitched. "You never talk much about him anymore. I liked him, though. I know he messed up when he stole some of your stuff, but he did the right thing in the end by helping us."

Dorothy's eyes lowered for a moment, dropping from the target of the storm. She gazed off in the distance, her lips pressed together in a cold and unyielding expression, but her eyes told a different story. The real Dorothy had heard me. Abraham had meant something to her, and I knew she felt responsible for his death.

"You can understand me, can't you?" I whispered. "You hear my voice and know it's me. You can beat this. I know you can."

Then her eyes flitted as she glanced at me and I felt that ounce of hope almost instantly crushed. She was smiling, but not in a friendly way, and the black hollowness I saw in those eyes sent an icy chill up my spine.

"Stop this!" I reached once more for her arm, but remembered the shock and held back. I began to cry, but I wasn't just sad. I was angry. It wasn't supposed to end like this. Not with Dorothy causing the destruction. She was the one who got us involved, Trendon and me and Joseph. We were supposed to win, not lose. And after everything we went through, we were still there doing all that we could to stop the Wrath. Wiping my eyes with the back of my hand, I glared at Dorothy. Why couldn't she fight against it? Why was she just giving up?

No. She wasn't giving up. Not yet at least.

"Because of you, I met a lot of great people. They're my friends now, and I would've never known them if it wasn't for you." The tears started up once more as I struggled to say the next words. "Cabarles became one of my dear friends. If it weren't for him, Trendon and I would've never found the Tebah Stick. He was so nice and so caring. So was his wife. Did you ever meet Cabarles's wife? I don't think he ever told me her name."

Dorothy's head dropped as tears glistened in her eyes. I caught myself from gasping, but refused to stop talking. "I almost forgot about Abelish. He died in our arms trying to keep us safe, but you were there with me when we brought him back." I hesitated. "Cabarles died too trying to keep me safe. I know he didn't want to die, but I also know he doesn't blame you."

"What have I done?" Dorothy sobbed, her voice returning to normal as the dark color in her eyes dissolved. "Why did I do this?"

It was the real Dorothy! Not the one controlled by the Wrath. The memories of her past had brought her back.

"It's okay! It's all right! We can fix it. Tell me what I need to do. Just think!" Rising up on my knees, I wiped my hands on my jeans and inwardly prayed she would know what to do. We still had time, didn't we? Everything could be undone if we just knew the right way.

"I'm so sorry, Amber. Please know this was never my intention. I wanted to stop Baeloc. I never wanted to bring about the end."

"Stop apologizing. It's not your fault." I dabbed the sweat beading up on my forehead. "Can you control it at all? Can you make it slow down at least to give us time to figure something out?"

"I can't." Her exhaustion overwhelmed her. She looked so weak and miserable.

"Can you at least get rid of this force field?" I waved my hand, timidly trying to sense where the barrier began.

Dorothy stared in bewilderment at my hand. "I don't know what this is," she whimpered. "You see? It's too late. I don't know how I'm talking to you now."

"Because it can be stopped. Don't you understand? Somehow you broke away, which means you can still control it."

"Not this time, Amber."

"Don't say that! There has to be a way to—"

"Get away from me!" The harsh voice returned, breaking free from inside Dorothy, and I fell to the ground. "Your time is up. Run and find a place to try and hide, but it won't matter!"

In my peripheral vision, I noticed something lowering from the eye in the cloud.

A funnel. The base of which easily stretched over a mile wide. A deafening boom shook the mountain and the funnel's tip touched down upon the ground, shattering through the surface and dissolving solid rock. Watching it from the mountain, the blackness appeared to move slowly, but in reality it crawled a mile within several seconds, covering everything it touched with death. The edges widened, expanding toward the Red Sea as the funnel gained momentum.

In the distance, a small cluster of twinkling lights from a village several miles from the shore, stood in its path.

Within seconds the village, along with all its inhabitants, dissolved beneath the shadowy carpet. One by one, other cities and villages disappeared. So many deaths and the Fury had only just begun. It would reach the sea in a few minutes, and after that, mainland Egypt. The funnel would continue to destroy everything in its path until it circled the earth and returned to the mountain and I would witness the end at Dorothy's side.

Dropping my eyes, unwilling to watch it spread, I faced the mountain and detected movement behind the opening as the last Shomehr stepped out from the cave. We no longer shared a bond, and I had no way of communicating with it. Dorothy controlled the Tebah Stick now, which made her the creature's master. I assumed it approached me to end my life.

So be it, I thought to myself. I wouldn't fight. Dying at the hand of the monster or by a life-sucking cyclone made no difference.

As the Shomehr towered over my head, I gazed into its eyes, admitting defeat. "You saw this coming, huh?" I asked. The creature stared back, the mist obscuring its face. "You knew this would happen and now you're here to kill me. I know you've hated me from the moment I touched the Tebah Stick. Go ahead then. Get it over with."

Holding out its hand, the Shomehr opened its fingers and I noticed an unusual object lying in its palm. A few pieces of silver tumbled from the mouth of the leather pouch.

Shaking my head in disbelief, I reached for the silver, but the Shomehr held it back. "How? How do you have that?" The funnel continued to roar behind me, surging forward, ripping life from everything it touched, but in that moment, the sound seemed distant, as my mind connected with the Shomehr one final time. I saw the hotel parking lot through its eyes: the ground littered with dead Architects and the charred body of the other Shomehr lying near the entrance. I saw Ashleigh huddled next to a car and watched in shock as she sat up and pressed her hand against the gunshot wound in her shoulder. Somehow she had survived, but she was trembling, frightened of what stood in front of her. I then saw the Shomehr's claw reach down toward her. Not to cause harm, but instead, to pull the pouch of silver out of her pocket.

"If you brought the silver to me, then it must be able to stop Dorothy." Once more I stared at her, still kneeling by the edge, as the funnel tore a part the ground below. It was possible the Shomehr arrived too late, that irreversible actions were set in motion, but it was the only option left to try. I remembered the painful shock of touching the barrier and realized what would happen to me. "I don't know if I'll be able to make it through without passing out," I said, again reaching for the pouch in the Shomehr's hand. "But if I can't, will you finish it for me?"

The Shomehr's hand closed tightly around the leather pouch, and it moved forward, stepping past me toward Dorothy. Passing through the barrier, electricity crackled around its body, singing its fur, as it dropped the bag of silver in her lap. The creature then fell over on its side, and I watched its chest expand a final time before it became completely still.

Dorothy's eyes shot open in alarm, darting in every direction. She opened her mouth to speak, but no words came out as she stared at the pouch.

"What is this?" she hissed, closing her fingers around the pouch. She attempted to throw it aside, but something prevented her. The pouch remained within her hand as she began to tremble. The funnel continued moving toward the sea, but it began to slow as sunlight broke through the wall of black clouds overhead.

Dorothy glared at me and I reared back from what I saw. Her face had changed. I could see so much rage in her eyes.

"Take it!" She reached out, squeezing the pouch and demanding I take it from her. "You have to take it from me!"

"No." I shook my head, but I was so afraid of her. She looked even more evil than before.

"I won't hurt you. I'll let you live," Dorothy reasoned.

"I won't do it." Taking a risk, I turned my attention toward the cyclone. I could see through it now! The wind began to weaken and the funnel wasn't as strong anymore. The silver was working, but how long would it take before the destruction ended?

Dorothy gnashed her teeth together. "If you don't take this from me, I will kill you both."

Both? Clearly, that wasn't Dorothy speaking. I supposed I knew that was the case, but hearing her refer to my teacher as someone else, not a willing partner but a prisoner, gave me strength to stand against its threats.

"You are going to kill us anyway. Why should I care?" Still, I put more distance between us. She was dangerous, even within her invisible bubble of electricity.

Dorothy growled, but then she shook it away and when

she looked upon me next, I could see pain and sorrow in her eyes.

"Amber, please!" Her lips quivered. "It hurts so bad. Please."

I wanted to reach over to touch her, so she could feel me and know I understood, but I didn't dare. "I know, but you have to be strong."

She reached out once more, extending her hand, pleading with me. "Just take it, Amber. You don't understand. This pain is crushing me from the inside. Burning me. If you don't help, it will destroy me." She swallowed and closed her eyes. "We can beat this together, but we'll have to do it another way. Just take this silver from me now." Having said that, she began to sob and my heart broke. How could I let her suffer like this? She was a dear friend to me and I wanted so badly to help her. Maybe she was telling the truth. Maybe we could find another way to beat the Wrath. I didn't know what to do, but I couldn't just do nothing while she endured such terrible pain.

Stepping forward, I reached my hand toward her, and as if sensing my action, Dorothy's own hand, the one holding the silver, rose up to meet me. The hairs on my arm stood on end as I felt the electricity surrounding her body. I could smell it in the air, a sort of intense burning scent filling my nostrils. I would just take the pouch from her, but I would wait to see how she reacted. If she changed back into the Finisher, I could easily throw the pouch back onto her lap.

As I readied to pass my hand through the force field, my foot nudged something on the ground. Looking down, I saw the lifeless body of the final Shomehr lying perfectly still. Having exhaled its final breath, the creature no longer moved. Up until that moment, I had always considered the Shomehr as monsters, hideous beasts that would sooner rip me to shreds than listen to my commands. But now I no longer believed that to be the case. This creature gave its life to save me and everyone else, for that matter. It had no reason to. I couldn't control it or even speak to it after Dorothy broke my connection with the Tebah Stick. Why would it have done that? More important, if I took back the pouch of silver, would I undo everything? Would I waste the Shomehr's ultimate sacrifice?

"Come a little closer, Amber," Dorothy whispered, her voice raspy and strained. We were within inches of each other. One more step and my hand would pass through the force field. Instead of taking that final step though, I stopped and moved away.

"I'm sorry, Dorothy," I said meekly. "I can't do it." A lump formed in my throat as I cried.

"Come back here!" the sinister voice of the Finisher returned. "There's still time! Come back here!" She screamed over and over, and I could no longer face her. I knew if I didn't turn my back on her, and block the image of her begging for her life, I wouldn't be strong enough to resist.

Instead, I watched as the dark funnel began to disappear. It no longer moved forward and the sky overhead contained more sunlight than darkness. Dorothy's screams filled my ears, the horrible sound of her suffering, but the Finisher had to be stopped. This had to end.

Within a few moments, the funnel had all but vanished,

leaving behind a wispy shadow of what it once was. The sky cleared, the wind stopped, and from behind me I heard Dorothy release a deep, echoing breath.

Mount Catherine fell silent.

25

Holding her right arm in a sling, the bullet having shattered her collarbone, Ashleigh leaned over one of the caskets and said her good-byes. When she noticed me watching her offering condolences, she gave me a polite nod. I knew we would never really be friends, but our experience together made it possible for us to at least be cordial. Jackson stood next in line with Jomo behind him. The Kenyan looked perfectly healthy, as though never having suffered any injury at the hand of the Shomehr. Of course, he concealed it beneath his sports coat and I noticed him moving slowly as not to aggravate his wound. Jomo whispered something in Jackson's ear and the two of them shared a quiet laugh.

Three days had passed since my flight to the top of Mount Catherine, and the funeral in the southern Egyptian city of Ras Muhammad had drawn quite a crowd. Our unawareness of who to trust of the local authorities, combined with the surviving Architects slipping into hiding, made it necessary for us to find a safe location outside of St. Catherine. The rustic church overlooking the Gulf of

Suez provided a peaceful place to bid farewell. Including all the St. Catherine monks who made the four-hour trek to Ras Muhammad, and our gathering of friends, over one hundred people attended the services of Darius Chalthoum and Kendell Jasher.

"I hate funerals," Trendon grumbled.

"Me too," I whispered. "Joseph hasn't come back, has he?" I watched the door anxiously.

"I haven't seen him."

Jomo and Ashleigh saw Joseph say his good-byes to his uncle the night before, but neither one of us had spoken to him since he ran off to look for Jasher in the library. I knew the death of his uncle weighed on him heavily, and I felt horrible for his loss. I also knew things could never be the same between us. So much had changed over the past two years. I was a different person. So was he. Sliding my hand into Trendon's and squeezing his fingers, I knew it was for the best. I stared at Trendon and watched him squirm awkwardly from my gaze, but with a bashful grin, he squeezed my hand as well.

The door to the assembly room opened quietly and an old friend stepped in.

"Abelish!" I whispered, unable to choke back the tears.

"Hello, Amber." Abelish lifted me off the ground and enveloped me in a warm embrace. "So good to see you."

He held me for what felt like a long, wonderful amount of time, and I laughed as I held his face in my hands. "I can't believe it! You look amazing!"

Though almost fifty years old, Abelish could've easily passed as someone in his early thirties. I marveled at his perfect skin and remembered how lesions and vicious sores once marred nearly every inch of his face, arms, and chest. Before the miracle happened, Abelish suffered from the crippling disease of leprosy.

"I owe it to you, my brave warrior. Thanks to you, I live again."

I couldn't take all the credit. We owed that to the powers within a mysterious tomb. But it was my idea to lower Abelish into the prophet Elisha's grave, which ultimately saved his life and cured him of his leprosy.

"What are you doing here?" I asked. "I thought you lived with your niece in Sahab."

"I did. But I was born in Egypt. My parents are buried less than ten miles from this church. Of course, after my disease manifested at a young age, I left here and went into exile. Once you healed me, I felt the time had come for me to return home." He patted my cheek with his hand. "How's everyone holding up?"

"We're doing okay, all things considered. Did you work with Darius much?"

Abelish shrugged. "I met him once, but we weren't close." He eyed the procession of people filing past the open caskets and folded his arms. "As bad as this will sound, I'm not exactly mourning the loss of Jasher. Don't think me harsh for saying that, Amber. I am grateful for him assisting you in the end, but . . ."

"It's okay," I whispered, squeezing his arm. I understood the way he felt. Jasher spent the bulk of his life and resources causing Abelish and Dorothy grief and pain. One good act of kindness couldn't sway their opinions so easily.

"How's my friend Trendon doing?" Abelish cocked his head to the side and acknowledged Trendon.

"Starving. But I'm not allowed to talk about it until after the funeral," Trendon grumbled.

Abelish's eyes twinkled. "I brought some Mansaf with me out in my truck. I can share with you afterward, if you'd like."

Trendon scrunched his nose. "Goat salad?" He thought about it and then curled his lower lip. "All right. I'm cool with that."

"Seriously?" Abelish looked impressed. "Wow. You've grown up, haven't you?"

"Either that, or I'm so hungry I'm about to make dumb mistakes with food."

Abelish checked his watch. "I have a better idea. After this is over, I shall take you both to my favorite restaurant and we shall eat like kings one final time before you leave for home. When does your flight leave?"

"In like six hours," Trendon answered.

"I'll make the reservations then. Agreed?"

We both nodded.

"Wonderful!" Abelish clapped his hands. "But, first, I need to have Amber follow me outside for a while."

"Why?" Trendon asked, squeezing my hand tighter.

"There's one more reason why I'm here."

Following Abelish out of the building, I hesitated on the stairs when I saw Temel perched behind the steering wheel of an idling minivan. As usual, he wore his trademark sunglasses and lazily chewed on a toothpick. Sitting beside him in the passenger seat, his son, Paulo, mimicked his father's actions by also chewing on a toothpick. Had Temel been a few years younger, the two of them could have easily passed as twins. I then noticed the person sitting in the backseat of the van; her face buried in her hands.

"Dorothy didn't want to come in. Said she didn't want to bring confusion to those mourning their losses. I'm afraid she refuses to relinquish the blame for so much death." Abelish descended a few steps. "But she needed to speak to you before leaving."

"Where's she going?" My voice quavered.

"I shall let her tell you."

When the Shomehr dropped the bag of silver into her lap, Dorothy once more fell into a comatose state. I remained by her side on the mountain, afraid to move her, but unsure of whom would reach us first—the Architects or one of my friends. Fortunately, Trendon succeeded in contacting Temel, who was already in route to St. Catherine. The next three days passed by in a blur. Participating in secret meetings of the Society of the Seraphic Scroll to determine the next point of action. Staying in two different hotels while keeping a low profile as to not alert any remaining enemies of our hiding place. Not knowing Dorothy's whereabouts or the progress of her recovery.

Tapping on the window, I signaled Dorothy, who promptly opened her car door. "Hello, Amber. Would it be all right to hug you?"

I shrugged one shoulder. "Yeah, I guess."

Wrapping her arm around my neck, she pulled me into her chest. After a moment's hesitation, I returned her embrace. I honestly didn't know how to act around Dorothy, and a part of me wondered if some of the Wrath still lingered within her.

Leaning back, Dorothy looked at me, her eyes blurry behind her tears. "I made so many mistakes, and I feel terrible for so many reasons. However, there's one thing for which I deserve a smidgen of credit. I do believe I was the one who recruited you for this mission. For that, I am grateful."

Dorothy couldn't have known her choice to leave school two years ago in pursuit of deadly artifacts would nearly result in destroying the world. Her actions and choices almost killed me and brought about the tragic ending of several close friends. How could I stand there and lie to her when we both knew the truth? But this was still Dorothy Holcomb. My beloved teacher. My friend. Perhaps the person I idolized most and who I intended to pattern my career after, though with a few changes in my decisions.

"Mind if I ask you a question? How did you know the silver would reverse the effects?"

My eyes wandered to the front of the vehicle and settled on Paulo staring back at me. He smiled bashfully but kept silent as he listened to my explanation.

"The Codex Sinaiticus told a different version of Araunah's story; how David's payment of silver appeased the Destroying Angel," I answered.

Dorothy sniffled and a look of awe came over her. "You read the Codex Sinaiticus? I didn't know you could read Greek uncial characters."

"I can't. Jasher read it to me. He helped me figure everything out and then led me to Araunah's tomb to look for the bag of silver. If it weren't for him . . ." My voice almost cracked from the need to cry.

Dorothy expressed her understanding with a solemn nod. "Then he proved his value in the end. I only wish I could've been stronger, Amber. I wish I could've fought against it. I may have felt anger toward Jasher in the past, but I would've never wished to harm him in that way. You know that, right? You know it wasn't me who did that to him. To Darius or Cabarles."

"I know." I shifted my wait uneasily and battled the urge to break down in front of her. If I let myself go now, I would never be able to stop crying. "How did it work?" I asked, deciding to move the conversation in a different direction. "The silver. Fifty shekels wasn't worth much, was it? Why would that have the power to stop something as deadly as the Destroying Angel?"

Dorothy wiped her nose with her handkerchief. "Artifacts come in all shapes and sizes. You've seen them with your own eyes. They can be formed into weapons such as spears or axes, or you can find them in insignificant objects such as Canopic jars or small bags of silver. The question we should be asking is how King David came to have the artifact in his possession. Anything capable of turning away the wrath of a Destroying Angel is powerful indeed. But what do we know about David? He slew Goliath. Killed a bear and a lion while defending his flocks. Captained thirty of the mightiest soldiers the world has ever known. Such endeavors seem fit for a heavenly being, or at least by a seasoned warrior, and yet David accomplished so much while still a small boy. It is an intriguing mystery."

"Is that what you plan to do? Find out the truth about David?"

Dorothy looked away. "Not immediately. Right now, Temel and Paulo have agreed to accompany me as we take Cabarles back to his family."

My jaw tightened. Cabarles's wife and four

children—Marley, the youngest, was only nine years old—were waiting to bury his body in the Philippines.

"Maybe I should come too." A part of me wanted to be there when the plane landed. I didn't know his family well, but perhaps I might say something to comfort them during this difficult time.

"No. You've done enough. We'll take care of this for you. I think Cabarles would want you to go home with Trendon and return to your normal life."

A normal life? I hadn't experienced anything normal in quite some time. "And then what?"

"What do you mean?"

"What's going to happen next?"

Dorothy smiled meekly. "Life will go on. At least I hope it will."

"Boss?" Temel nodded toward the road and Dorothy sighed.

"Yes, we should be going. Good-bye, Amber. Thank you for everything."

"Wait!" It couldn't just be over. A good-bye and that was it? Dorothy looked at me thoughtfully, waiting for me to speak. "We're not finished are we?" I asked.

Dorothy raised one of her eyebrows. "Finished?"

"Yeah, I mean, you still have a job to do. The Weapons of Might may have been some of the most dangerous arti-facts and we managed to destroy them, but there are still others out there. And there are other enemies out there as well. People like Baeloc that need to be stopped."

"Of course, but that's not your concern anymore. I'm not going to ruin every one of your high school years."

Folding my arms, I fixed her with an unrelenting stare.

"That's not your decision anymore. I'm an official member of the Seraphic Scroll and I have just as much right to be involved as you." I said it so forcibly that for a moment I was worried my words would make her angry.

But Dorothy knew better. After drying her cheeks, she narrowed her eyes mischievously. "Hmmm. You may be an official member, but that doesn't mean you have access to all our secrets. Not yet at least. Ain't that right, boys?" She smacked the back of Temel's seat.

"Yeah, boss," Temel agreed. "We need at least two days head start before Amber catches up." He lowered his sunglasses and winked.

"I'm just playing with you," Dorothy said. "We don't have a heading just yet. But we will soon enough. Once Ashleigh completes the translation on the document."

I rolled my eyes. "You're still going to trust Ashleigh to translate for you? Even after everything that happened?" I kept my tone jovial, but not entirely. I may have forgiven Ashleigh for how she treated me, but that didn't convince me of her competence.

"She's all we have at the moment. Once you've finished another semester or two at Roland & Tesh, and if you're interested, I'll have a job opening waiting for you."

"Do you think you'll ever come back to teach?"

Dorothy stifled a laugh. "Oh no. I've worn out my welcome there. I don't believe I ever told you this, but I think they fired me when I never came back from Syria, although I've never officially had my end-of-term review with the school board to find out."

"We could still have our class off campus. There are probably school grants you could finagle to fund it." I didn't like the idea of Dorothy no longer popping up at the school. Sure, I hadn't sat through a class with her in quite some time, but I had always held onto the hope she would return.

"I'll definitely miss my students. Trendon sneaking in all sorts of snacks. Joseph dribbling his soccer ball while reciting the names of excavation equipment. Lisa with her compact mirrors and makeup. And especially my prized student, Amber Rawson." She once more wiped her nose with her handkerchief and stuck it in her pants pocket. "That was a different life. Good memories, but something in my past." Unzipping her backpack, Dorothy handed me a small envelope and fastened her seat belt. "This is for you. No, don't read it yet." She placed her hand on mine when I attempted to open it. "It's nothing. Just a thank you. That's all. And now we really need to be going." Throwing her arms around my neck one last time, Dorothy kissed my cheek and whispered in my ear. "You know I love you, Amber, and I hope you'll find it in your heart one day to truly forgive me. Until then, take care of that Trendon of mine. And try to keep him under control."

As the van pulled away and I waved good-bye to the three of them, I felt a warm hand resting on my shoulder.

"She'll be just fine, won't she?" Abelish asked as I peeled open the flap of the envelope and discovered a folded letter and a single piece of silver.

This was all that remained of the Weapons of Might, and I thought you should have it. Dorothy's handwriting explained in the letter. *Maybe it will bring you luck. Maybe not.* The rest of the letter consisted of the original note Dorothy showed me back at the hospital more than a week ago. The message

Ashleigh translated from the scroll they discovered in the cave north of Jerusalem.

And Moses hid up the final device in the mountain wherein he first found the Lord. Thus allowing the final protector time to make certain no unsanctified hand unleashed the Fury of Har Megiddo.

Dorothy circled the final sentence in red ink and scribbled five words beside it.

Amber Rawson, the final protector.

Acknowledgments

My wife, Heidi, has been my greatest support through all the ups and downs of book writing. She's been there to celebrate with me during my triumphs, feed me plenty of comfort food during my defeats, and she didn't head for the hills directly following one of my psychotic night-terror episodes, which were almost always related to my writing. Without her, none of this would be worth it.

My family and friends have done so much to place me where I currently am, and hopefully that's on the verge of something great.

It's taken me seven different acknowledgments to finally realize someone I should've thanked from the beginning. I'm pretty sure that if it weren't for Lee Nelson's grandson, my first book, *The Adventures of Hashbrown Winters*, would've never made it to print. Thank you for laughing.

I have to thank those who I've been blessed to have as beta-readers of my books. B. K. Bostick, Tyler Whitesides, Susan LaDuke, Taylor Fleming, Christen Reid, and I'm sure there are others I'm missing as well. Having you find the holes in my stories has helped me in so many ways and I really do appreciate your time.

The wonderful staff at Cedar Fort has allowed me to publish seven books in four years. All I can say is "Wow!" I truly am grateful for the opportunity to work with you and it still humbles me each time I reread my first acceptance letter.

Last, I'm grateful for Amber and Trencon. Yes, they're imaginary characters I created, but they're real on so many levels and I'm sad to see their story come to an end. Whenever I've had the privilege of autographing one of my books, I've usually written something along the lines of "Keep Reading." Well, to my readers who have filled their valuable reading time with my work, my goal is to continue to give you great stories that make you want to keep on reading. I hope the Guardians series did just that.